Home is Where the Heart is

FREDA
Lightfoot

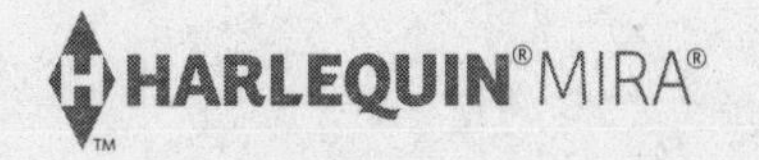

First Published in Great Britain 2015
By Harlequin Mira, an imprint of HarperCollins*Publishers*
1 London Bridge Street, London, SE1 9GF

ISBN 978-1-848-45414-9

58-1115

Our policy is to use papers that are natural, renewable and recyclable products and made from wood grown in sustainable forests. The logging and manufacturing processes conform to the legal environmental regulations of the country of origin.

Printed and bound by
CPI Group (UK) Ltd, Croydon, CR0 4YY

Also by Freda Lightfoot:

Historical Sagas

LAKELAND LILY
THE BOBBIN GIRLS
THE FAVOURITE CHILD
KITTY LITTLE
FOR ALL OUR TOMORROWS
GRACIE'S SIN
DAISY'S SECRET
RUBY MCBRIDE
DANCING ON DEANSGATE
WATCH FOR THE TALLEYMAN
POLLY'S PRIDE
POLLY'S WAR
HOUSE OF ANGELS
ANGELS AT WAR
THE PROMISE
MY LADY DECEIVER

The Luckpenny Series

LUCKYPENNY LAND
WISHING WATER
LARKRIGG FELL

Poorhouse Lane Series

THE GIRL FROM POORHOUSE LANE
THE WOMAN FROM HEARTBREAK HOUSE

Champion Street Market Series

PUTTING ON THE STYLE
FOOLS FALL IN LOVE
THAT'LL BE THE DAY
CANDY KISSES
WHO'S SORRY NOW
LONELY TEARDROPS

Women's Contemporary Fiction

TRAPPED

Historical Romances

MADEIRAN LEGACY
WHISPERING SHADOWS
RHAPSODY CREEK
PROUD ALLIANCE
OUTRAGEOUS FORTUNE

Biographical Historical

HOSTAGE QUEEN
RELUCTANT QUEEN
THE QUEEN AND THE COURTESAN
THE DUCHESS OF DRURY LANE
LADY OF PASSION

Chapter One

1945

Cathie gave a squeal of joy as she read the letter that had arrived that morning. 'Alex is coming home!' she cried. She'd waited so long for this news she couldn't quite believe it. It must be nearly two years since she'd last seen her fiancé and now the war was over he'd be home for good, at last. She quickly scanned the letter again to make sure she'd read it correctly. 'He says he hopes to be home by Christmas.'

There was no one to hear her exciting news except for the baby, bouncing up and down on her chubby little legs in her cot, holding fast to the rail and giving a happy gurgle as if to echo Cathie's delight.

Gathering the child in her arms, Cathie screwed up her nose and chuckled. 'I think you need changing, sweetie.' But even as she smiled into the baby's soft blue eyes, her own filled with tears. 'Oh, I do wish your mummy was here, and your daddy, of course. It's so desperately sad that you'll never get to know or love them. I shall tell you all about them as you grow, of course. Particularly Sally, my dear sister, who loved you so much, and was very much a part of my life.'

At least a baby did not experience the pain of grief that she had suffered, Cathie thought, as she laid the infant on a towel-covered table to strip off the wet nappy and set about cleaning her plump little bottom.

What a dreadful war it had been. First her sister had lost her beloved husband, who'd gone down with his ship in August 1944 when it had been sunk by a U-boat. Tony had never even learned his wife was pregnant, let alone seen his child. As if that wasn't bad enough, her mind flew back to that dreadful day, barely a month after the birth of her beautiful daughter, when Sal had gone with her friend Rose to the Gaumont Cinema on Oxford Road to see Judy Garland in *Meet Me in St Louis*. Cathie might well have accompanied them, but somebody needed to stay home and look after the baby. She'd happily volunteered for the task as she hoped the film might lift her sister's depression. Still enveloped in grief, Sal had been in desperate need of an afternoon out.

Cathie had been happily sitting feeding little Heather with her bottle when the door had burst open. She'd glanced up with a smile, fully expecting to see her sister now that dusk was falling. Instead, she saw their mother standing rigid, her face as white as a ghost.

'She's gone.'

Cathie recalled how something inside her had jolted as she'd stared in shock at Rona. 'Who has?'

'Our Sal.'

Her memory became a blur after that, as a cold numbness came over her. Cathie had felt strangely detached. Everything went silent, even the sound of children playing in the street, and the odd passing car or motorcycle. It was as if she was standing outside of herself, watching as she gently set down the baby's bottle and patted little Heather's back to settle her tummy while the horror of what Rona was saying slowly penetrated.

It seemed that on their way home the driver had lost control on the icy roads and the bus had tipped into an old bomb crater, killing many on board, including her beloved sister.

Now the pain of her loss resonated afresh as, staring out of the window, Cathie watched two young women walking arm-in-arm past the bomb-damaged houses opposite, laughing and chattering. The pair reminded her so much of how she and Sal used to step out together, whether as young girls trotting off to school, or grown women going shopping or to a dance together. So many treasured memories.

The sad irony was that they'd come close to death many times during this last six years with constant air raids on the nearby railway, warehouses, wharfs and canals, and once when their own house had been bombed. A terrifying incident that Cathie still fiercely blocked from her mind.

The effects of war could be devastating and so long lasting.

Cathie stopped this train of thought in mid-track. To lose

her beloved sister was bad enough, but for it to happen just as the war was coming to an end was even more heartbreaking. Sal's death had left a huge hole in her life that nothing and no one could ever fill. It felt as if a part of her too had died as well as their family having been decimated.

Blinking back tears as she smoothed talcum powder over the baby's soft skin and began to pin on a fresh nappy, Cathie's heart was swamped with love and pity for her niece. With scarcely any family left, what kind of future could this little one be facing?

Not that they'd had much of a family to begin with, their father having left home while both girls were very young. And their mother, Rona, was not an easy woman. Cathie felt she'd endured a dreadful childhood: a selfish mother with a string of lovers and an absentee father whom she hadn't seen in years. Sal had been the one person to give her the love she'd so badly needed. Cathie certainly had no wish for little Heather to suffer a similar fate. And who else was there to care for the poor child but herself? A responsibility she'd accepted without question.

Were it not for having to care for the baby, she might never have found the will to carry on, or even get up in a morning. She'd needed to locate a nursery, of course, to look after the child during the day, as Cathie couldn't afford to give up her job at the tyre factory down by the docks. She'd also queued at the Citizens Advice Bureau for hours, to ask them if she was entitled to extra clothing coupons for the baby. They'd agreed that she was, and had told her to ask for form CRSC/1. All such a fuss, but money was tight and Cathie had very little in the way of savings in the post office.

There was a tidy sum stashed away in an account left by dear Sally and her husband, but that was for their precious daughter when she grew up, not to be wasted on trivial bits and bobs now.

Breathing in the sweet scent of her as she cuddled the baby in her arms and kissed her soft cheek, Cathie murmured, 'You were so loved by your mummy, and if Sal were still with us, she'd be celebrating Alex's return along with me, despite having lost your lovely father. I promise that you will never feel unwanted, sweetie, even if there are only a few of us left. The war is over and it's time for a fresh start.'

But how would her fiancé react to taking on someone else's child? Did she even know Alex well enough to be certain? Of course he would, as he was such a kind, sweet man. As Cathie warmed some milk for the baby's morning porridge, she kept glancing across at his letter, her heart radiating with hope and pride. She'd loved Alex Ryman from the moment she'd met him over three years ago, back in 1942.

One Saturday, as Sal's husband Tony had been home on leave, they'd treated themselves to a night at the Palais. It wasn't cheap, being ninepence a ticket, but it proved to be worth the expense when this gorgeous man had approached her to ask for a dance.

'I couldn't take my eyes off you. You are so lovely with your long curly red hair, that smattering of freckles on your cute little nose, and the sweetest smile,' he'd said.

Cathie remembered how she'd flushed with pleasure at the compliment, never for a moment having thought of herself in such terms. 'Not strictly red, more a strawberry blonde,' she corrected him, with a smile more shy than sweet, or so she thought.

'Still beautiful, however you describe it, as are your hazel eyes. I'm not the greatest dancer in the world, but please would you do me the honour?'

'I'd be delighted,' and, taking his hand, she'd allowed him to lead her out on to the dance floor. She felt entranced by the fact that this tall handsome man, with his crop of short brown hair, chestnut brown eyes and square jutting chin, could be at all interested in her. His quiet conservative manner, and the respect he showed her, also proved him to be the perfect gentleman.

They danced almost every dance, the feel of his arms wrapped about her slender body, as if she were too precious to let go, filling her with joy. Was this how it felt to fall in love? Something she'd never experienced before. By the end of the evening, Cathie happily accepted an offer of a date, all too aware of a dazed longing in her eyes as she cast him a shy sideways glance from beneath her lashes. Could this be the man of her dreams? It most certainly felt like love at first sight for both of them.

After he returned to base, they'd exchanged letters

almost daily. At that time he was stationed at Squires Gate, Blackpool, which before the war had been a holiday camp but was now used for army training. Barely able to put him from her mind, she'd gone out with him at every opportunity. Most wonderful of all, when he was granted a week's leave before being sent overseas early in 1943 following weeks of training in Silloth, he'd presented her with a ring.

'I wish I could afford to buy you something more splendid, but the thought of not seeing you again is devastating. I need to be sure that you'll be here, waiting for me, when I return.'

'Oh, I most certainly will,' she'd assured him with love and pity in her heart, utterly thrilled and excited by his proposal.

Sadly, she hadn't seen him since, or received quite as many letters as she would have liked, but then he'd been stationed in Egypt, and goodness knows where else. Now he was coming home at last, and she could hardly wait to become his wife.

Cathie's new-found happiness was very slightly curtailed as she considered what his reaction might be to the fact that this little one now occupied a large place in her heart too. She certainly had every intention of keeping her, not least because she understood how it felt to be deprived of parental love. And she owed it to her sister. For little Heather's sake, and to celebrate Alex's homecoming, Cathie fully intended to push these concerns from her mind and make this the best Christmas ever.

'It may only be October but Christmas will be here before you know it, which means I must start shopping and preparing right away, as rationing makes everything so difficult,' she told her giggling niece, as she popped her safely back in her cot.

Oh, she really couldn't wait to welcome Alex home, and to be in his arms again. He too had no doubt lost friends and loved ones, maybe suffered injuries in battles and campaigns he'd been involved in. So surely he would appreciate how necessary it was to move on and live with the consequences of whatever this dreadful war had thrown at them. Cathie was quite certain he would come to love her little niece as much as she did.

* * *

'Never in a million years,' said her mother later that day when Cathie showed Rona the letter and spoke of her intention to ask Alex to agree they adopt little Heather. 'No man is willing to take on another chap's child. Why would he agree to do such a thing?'

'Because Alex is a lovely kind man. Why would he not?' As so often when dealing with her mother, Cathie felt instantly irritated by Rona's sarcasm and negative attitude. She had always been a dogmatic, stubborn person, obsessed with her own needs and busy social life, with little thought or care for those she was supposed to love. Even her show of grief had been entirely self-centred, worrying more about how she would cope without Sal's help in the house, rather than any genuine sense of loss.

'Who'll do the washing and ironing now?' she'd moaned. 'Who will clean the house, mop the floors, make the beds, and keep the fire going? You're not half as good at house-work as our Sal was.'

'Who cares about such things?' Cathie had sobbed in her distress. 'It's losing my lovely sister that hurts, like a knife in my heart, not the loss of the work she used to do around the house.' Sal had been like a mother to her, as well as an elder sister, something Rona never could be.

'Well, someone has to do it, and I'm certainly not up to all that hard work any more,' had been her mother's sharp response, and still was to this day as she made herself comfy now in her chair by the fire. She began filing her already per-fect nails as she patiently waited for Cathie to tell her when tea was ready. She was an attractive woman, despite being well into her forties, with her smoothly styled blonde hair and blue eyes, lovely oval face completely wrinkle-free, pencilled brows and red lipstick. She would even rub some of the lipstick on to her powdered cheeks. Not for a moment did it enter her lazy head that perhaps she should help, if only to lay the table, let alone peel the potatoes.

'You could brew the tea,' Cathie politely suggested, striving to keep her temper.

'You're the one standing by the stove, so why don't you do it? And you're the one with energy, being young, so be quick about it as I'm meeting Tommy at seven o'clock at the Pack Horse.'

Cathie stifled a weary sigh, all too aware it was a complete waste of time and energy to argue with Rona. She had no real objection to dealing with household chores, but a little assistance now and then would help. Unfortunately, nothing would persuade Rona to take the slightest risk of breaking a nail, or spoiling whatever pretty dress she happened to be wearing. Nor had she ever lifted a finger to help care for little Heather, or shown the slightest interest in the child, despite being her only grandchild.

It was Cathie who fed the baby, changed and washed her nappies, and got up with her in the night when she was hungry or teething. Fortunately, she was a good baby, but the work was exhausting nonetheless. It was Cathie who wheeled the pram to the nursery on her way to the factory each morning, and collected the baby on the way home at the end of her long working day. If Rona was on the early shift at the local cotton mill, it never brought forth an offer to pick up her grandchild, or to make a contribution towards the cost of her care.

As for offering to babysit, that hadn't happened in the entire seven months since Sal's death. Not that this troubled Cathie one bit, as she'd been far too sunk in grief to be interested in going anywhere. But things would need to change in the future, and she had every faith that Alex would support her, as well as provide her with the love she'd always longed for.

'You haven't even agreed to meet him yet, so how can you possibly judge?' Cathie said, returning to their original difference of opinion as she placed two plates of corned beef hash on the table.

'Men are men and not interested in babies. You are such an innocent. It's long past time you grew up and entered the real world.'

'I think the war ensured I did that, Mam,' Cathie sharply responded. 'I'm twenty-two, if you recall, no longer a child.'

'So you are, and with a face on you like a line of wet washing. Stop sulking, girl.'

'Actually, I'm feeling much better, really quite happy now that Alex is on his way home.'

'Aye, well don't be too naïve, or expect too much from that fella of yours. He'll have his own plans for the future, whether you like it or not.'

'I'm sure he will, but I'm entitled to my wishes too.'

'Ooh, what an independent little madam you've turned into.'

'That could be the result of the war too,' Cathie said, thinking that she really hadn't been given much choice in the matter with a young baby to care for, a useless mother and a living to earn.

After lifting Heather into her high chair and tucking a bib about the baby's neck, she began to feed her the soft hash from her own little dish and let her mind drift away from her mother's nagging. Despite her ignorance so far as baby care was concerned, the nine-month-old was doing well. She'd sat up at six months, and was now showing every sign of wanting to walk. Precious little Heather had been successfully weaned and was doing well with her eating, though she did have a tendency to fling her dish on to the floor if she didn't care for whatever was on offer, or grew bored with the process. Today, she seemed to approve of the mush she was eating, which was a great relief. Feeding spoonfuls to the baby as she ate her own food, Cathie focused her thoughts upon her happy news.

The biggest worry she and Alex faced was where they would live when they did marry. The idea of moving in with her mother as newly-weds was too dreadful to contemplate, even supposing Rona would agree to such an idea. Cathie had already made a few enquiries about finding a house to rent, so far with no luck. So many homes had been destroyed by the bombing that they were in very short supply. 'Homes for Heroes' they'd been promised by the government, but there was little sign of any so far, apart from a few prefabs. She could but hope something would turn up soon.

Everything would work out just fine, she was sure of it. Father Christmas was about to deliver the best present possible by sending Alex home to her. Now she would give her fiancé the best present she had to offer, her love forever, and a beautiful ready-made family to start their wonderful life together.

Chapter Two

The next day being a Saturday, Cathie set off early to Campfield Market, intent upon making a start on her preparations for Christmas. Most of their food was purchased from the local Co-op where she could benefit from an annual dividend and other special offers. At Christmas they would allow customers a little extra sugar, butter and a tin of condensed milk. But she still loved to visit the market for bargains.

Cathie had carefully written out a list, which included little gifts to put in crackers and some sticky strips to make paper chains. She already had a box of Christmas tree baubles and ornaments that she and Sal had collected over the years, many of them home-made. Later, Cathie meant to buy a small tree, which she would decorate. Right now she must find the right ingredients to start cooking. Dried fruit for mincemeat and a Christmas cake, dried egg, prunes or dried apricots, spices and vanilla essence to make everything taste good, and ground rice for some mock marzipan. Hopefully there'd be an end to rationing soon, but while it continued, this would not be an easy task; so the sooner she started searching, the better.

The food shops and stalls were mainly in the top section between Tonman Street and Liverpool Road, and that was where she headed first. A brisk wind made her tighten the scarf about her neck, sending scraps of grubby paper bags and rotting cabbage leaves flying everywhere. But the baby was tucked up safe and warm in her pram with the hood up and the apron clipped in place over the blankets.

Cathie decided she would try ordering a goose from one of the butchers, although sometimes it was better to come to the market late, just before it closed as prices were cheaper then. The problem with that was there might not be anything left, and Cathie really had no wish to make do with another mock goose comprised mainly of lentils and onions. If this was to be the best Christmas ever, to celebrate Alex's homecoming, genuine poultry was essential.

Cathie loved exploring the market, with its huge iron girders arching across the roof beneath a range of dusty windows, the supporting pillars beautifully decorated with red roses in patriotic honour of Lancashire. She would lovingly stroke a hand over one as she passed by, as if to bring herself luck, something she still felt in need of despite the war being over. Outdoor stalls jostled for space from here on Tonman Street right across to Deansgate, many of them piled high with second-hand goods, as anything new and cheap was quite rare with rationing still in place.

As always the market was heaving with people: harassed

mothers scolding their children for wandering off, old men in flat caps and mufflers huddled together by the hot baked potato cart, no doubt busily putting the world to rights. Perhaps discussing how the General Election in July had brought a Labour landslide with Clement Attlee now Prime Minister in place of Churchill. The terrible bombs that had been dropped since on Hiroshima and Nagasaki, and the fact Britain was pretty well stony broke.

Nevertheless, morale remained high, despite the threat of austerity and restrictions growing ever tighter as young men returned from the war. It was true that ex-servicemen were not always in one piece, or a happy state of mind, often damaged either physically or mentally. But families were delighted to see their loved ones safely home.

Cathie could barely wait to see Alex again.

She studied various grocery, vegetable and biscuit stalls, happily pausing to watch a man in a bowler hat cleverly juggling pots, pans and plates, appearing to let one fall then easily catching it in order to gain people's attention. 'I'm not asking five shillings. I'm not asking one shilling. I'm not even asking sixpence. A threepenny bit and this beautiful plate is yours,' he shouted to the large crowd gathered about his stall.

Smiling at his showmanship, Cathie queued at her favourite butcher's stall, where she was a regular customer, and bought a few sausages for tea. He gladly took her order for a goose, offering to give it priority once he heard that her fiancé was returning from the war.

'Can't promise it'll be big, mind, but I'll do my best, and let you know if I don't find one.'

Thanking him, Cathie moved on to the Maypole Dairy, which sold margarine, butter, cheese and bacon, also nuts and dried fruit. Checking her purse, she made a mental note to choose with care, as she certainly couldn't afford to buy everything at once. But after careful browsing, and a very helpful shop assistant, Cathie purchased the necessary ingredients to at least bake a Christmas cake. She'd worry about the mock almond paste, icing sugar and mince tarts later.

Having finished her shopping and carefully negotiating the pram between the crowds of shoppers, Cathie went to meet up with her two best friends for a snack at the market café, as they loved to do on a Saturday. After greeting each other with hugs and a few moans about the cold weather, the three of them gave their orders then sat drinking tea together while Cathie told her good news.

'Oh, that's wonderful,' Brenda said, instantly sharing her friend's excitement.

'When does he arrive?' Davina politely enquired.

Davina Gibson, who worked on a second-hand clothes stall, was new to the area, having moved into Castlefield just a couple of months ago. Cathie had met her while buying some clothes for baby Heather. She'd been sympathetic of her loss, and so helpful in allowing Cathie to negotiate a low price on everything she needed, they'd become firm friends ever since. Brenda Stuart, on the other hand, was a best friend of some years' standing, as she and Cathie had been in the same class at school all those years ago, and worked together at the rubber factory producing tyres for motor cars, army vehicles and trucks.

Both these women had been left widowed by the war, as had so many others. Davina was something of a beauty with her voluptuous figure, long dark hair, green eyes beneath winged brows, and full lips. While dear Brenda claimed to be a plain country girl with scraggy brown hair, plump figure and puffy cheeks. But her round face nearly always wore a smile, and there'd generally be a twinkle in her downward-sloping dark eyes.

'I'm not sure, but in time for Christmas, or so he hopes. It's so exciting. I can hardly wait to see him again.'

'Have you set a date for the wedding?' Davina asked, the corner of her mouth twisting into what might pass for a smile. She wasn't the most exuberant or lively friend Cathie might have hoped for, being slightly cool and distant. Whatever she'd suffered during the war had clearly badly affected her.

'Not yet, but I know Alex is keen for us to marry as soon as possible.'

'I do hope I receive an invitation,' Brenda said, eyes sparkling at the prospect.

'If and when it happens,' Davina added.

'Of course it will happen, fairly soon, I hope. How would you both feel about being bridesmaids? I have some lengths of parachute silk, which Mam managed to buy cheap from the mill. It has one or two flaws in it, which is disastrous for a parachute, but will scarcely show in a dress. We could sew them together.'

Brenda whooped with joy. 'That would be wonderful, so long as you teach me how. Never was much good at sewing but I'm willing to learn.'

Looking slightly stunned by this request, Davina murmured, 'Oh, that is so kind of you to ask me, Cathie, but I'm not sure I could cope with attending a wedding so soon after losing my own husband.'

'Oh, I'm sorry. I didn't think of that. I've no wish to upset you.'

'When and how did you lose him, darling?' Brenda asked. 'You never did tell us.'

Davina's lips tightened. 'I don't care to speak of it.'

'Ah, I can fully sympathise with that feeling,' Brenda agreed. 'Painful things have happened in my life that I cannot bear to remember either. I've locked them in a box in my mind, never to open them again. However, sometimes it helps to talk.' When no response came, Brenda leaned over the pram to tickle the baby's nose, making her giggle. 'So what about this little one, Cathie? Have you told Alex that you now think of her as your own?'

'No, not yet,' Cathie admitted with some reluctance. 'I told him of Sal's death and that we were safe, of course, but didn't go into any details about her child.'

'Why ever not?'

Taking a bite of the cheese rarebit the waitress had

just brought her, Cathie took her time to chew on it for a moment before answering. Her old friend knew her better than most, how she tended to be far too cautious and wary of making a mistake in life. She'd been this way ever since watching her parents' marriage collapse after years of rows. Having Sal to cuddle her close in bed as they listened to them yelling and screaming at each other had been the only way to deal with her misery. The sisters had made a pact never to involve themselves in these arguments, and never to discuss what they'd heard.

Giving a pragmatic shrug, she said, 'Letters to the Front need to be upbeat and cheerful. Mine to Alex were generally asking how he was coping, and chatting a little about myself, which was what he wanted to hear. I put in no bad news that might depress him. Besides, like Davina, I'd no wish to talk about Sal's death.'

Davina said, 'Keeping silent about painful subjects may be commonplace in these difficult times, but being open and honest with Alex about what you hope to do for the baby is surely very necessary.'

'I'm afraid she has a point there,' Brenda agreed. 'Did he never ask about the child?'

Cathie frowned, struggling to remember. It had indeed been painful, a time of complete anguish. The weeks following Sal's death had passed in something of a blur, almost as if she were locked behind a pane of frosted glass and not part of the real world at all. 'I don't think he did. But then I'm not certain I ever mentioned that she'd given birth to a daughter, as Heather was barely a month old when her mummy died. My memory of that time is very hazy. Then Mam kept putting me off, insisting it wasn't right to dump this problem upon him when he had enough to deal with fighting a war.'

'I'm sure he did have enough on his plate,' Davina agreed. 'Still, he does need to know, so the sooner you tell him the better.'

'I'm ashamed to say that the longer I left it, the harder it became to broach the subject. I could never quite find the courage, and finally decided it would be better to wait and tell him in person, once he is home and can see for himself how adorable she is.'

Smiling down at the baby, Brenda gave her cheek a gentle stroke. 'You might be right. She certainly is adorable, how could anyone resist her?'

'Mam is not convinced Alex ever will accept her, which is absolute nonsense. He's a real gentleman, so why wouldn't he?'

'Men can be a bit sniffy about such matters, certainly where children are concerned,' Davina pointed out, rubbing a hand over her face, which Cathie noticed was suddenly looking rather pale and strained. What other problems did she have? she wondered. Her new friend's past life was something of a mystery as she was reluctant to speak of the war, not unusual these days. Even so, Cathie had made several attempts to ask Davina about her past, where she'd lived before, what job she'd done, and what had happened to her. But for some reason she always avoided answering such questions. And, as she was still grieving for the loss of her husband, Cathie had decided not to pursue the matter for fear of upsetting her further. Their shared grief was what had cemented their friendship in the first place. Just as her own reluctance not to keep going over Sal's death was perhaps the main reason why she had neglected to tell Alex the whole story.

Brenda, however, was the absolute opposite. Despite having lived in France during the German occupation, and becoming one of many British women arrested and confined, apparently for no other reason than her nationality, she firmly believed that talking about problems helped you to cope better. Even so, Cathie was aware of occasions when Brenda too would clam shut and find it impossible to speak of past pain, as she herself had just admitted.

'I do agree that Alex must be told soon. Once he's settled in, I'll explain everything,' Cathie said, with a smile that appeared more confident than she actually felt.

'I think you should write and tell him now,' Davina suggested. 'If he's going to be this child's father, you'll surely need his agreement and support in order to achieve that wish, or it won't ever happen.'

These words had a disconcerting effect upon Cathie. It was kind of Davina to be so concerned for her, although echoing her mother's negative comments was not exactly what she'd wished to hear. Poor Davina's expression was looking even more pinched and doleful, perhaps because she was facing the prospect of life with no hope of a child of her own, as her husband had not survived the war. So many atrocities, so much grief. Cathie had to confess that the timing of Sal's death couldn't have been worse, not only because the war had been in the process of coming to an end, but as she herself was about to be married.

Brenda gently patted her hand. 'I can understand that you might feel a little nervous about telling Alex of your wish to keep Sal's child, but be brave, darling. He loves you, so not for a moment do I imagine he'll refuse to accept her.'

'Oh, you are so right, he does.' Her worries and sadness dissolved as joy ricocheted within once again. With no one ever expressing any love for her but Sally, Cathie could hardly believe her good fortune. 'And he is such a kind man.'

'There you are then, no problem,' Brenda said, kissing a cheek damp with the odd stray tear.

Davina put her arms around Cathie to give her a hug that felt just a little stiff and awkward. 'Please know that I'm here to offer support too, should this Alex give you any problems.'

'Thank you so much! You are both such good friends to me. Not that I think I will need your help, as I have every faith in him.' The baby began to whimper and squirm, and Cathie got quickly to her feet. 'Now, I really must go and see to some food for this little madam.'

Brenda jumped up too. 'I'll walk back with you, darling, at least as far as my gloomy little bedsit.' And, saying their goodbyes, the pair walked off, Cathie oddly aware of Davina standing watching for some time as she wheeled the pram away. Something was troubling the girl, but she couldn't make out quite what it could be.

Chapter Three

Over the coming days and weeks, Cathie continued to work hard at the factory as well as take care of the baby. She also busied herself with cleaning and tidying the house from top to bottom, much to her mother's irritation as she was moved from room to room, not offering to even lift a duster to help. Buying a pot of brown paint from the ironmonger, Cathie gave all the doors a quick coat, hoping the landlord would not object. But, as they'd been bombed out of their own home, and were now renting in a ramshackle street in a rather poor area of Castlefield, Cathie was anxious for the house to look as respectable as possible when Alex arrived home. She felt rather pleased with the result, and proud of herself for having picked up quite a few skills over these last years.

'It costs very little to at least be clean,' said her Aunt Evie, not for the first time when Cathie popped in to fill her in on what was happening, and ask her advice. Her aunt too had suffered a horrible war, not least by the fact her children had been evacuated.

'Your Uncle Donald hasn't been demobbed yet, although

no longer a POW. He's undergoing some help, or so I'm told, by the Resettlement Service or whatever they call themselves. But my little ones will be home soon too,' she said, cuddling baby Heather on her lap. 'Not that they'll be little any more, and goodness knows what they'll think when they see me again. I've turned into a real old crow.'

'Don't be silly, they adore you,' Cathie said with a smile. Evie, her father's younger sister, was very maternal, the kind of mother Cathie would have loved to have. 'So when do you think I should tell Alex about little Heather?'

Her aunt considered the question with a frown. 'Not easy to answer. Judge your moment when it feels right. Believe in yourself, sweetie.'

It felt like good advice, and surely her courage and sense of independence had increased throughout this long war. Or had it all vanished again with the loss of dear Sal? Uncertainty and panic swelled in her, which yet again had to be quelled as Cathie resolutely devoted the entire afternoon to baking a Christmas cake, and thinking positive thoughts about the future. It was admittedly rather plain but at least it had real fruit in it and not just prunes, as was the case last year. Wrapping it in greaseproof paper and storing it in a cake tin, she hid it safely away on a top shelf in the larder where Rona wouldn't find it. Next, she set about making paper chains and tiny Chinese-type lanterns, which she strung up around the front parlour.

'We need the house to look good as Father Christmas will be here soon,' Cathie explained to the baby, as the pair of them sat together on the rug. Heather's soft little lips pursed in concentration as she tried to help by flicking bits of paper about, some of them sticking to her little fingers, which made Cathie laugh. She'd also bought a tree, which she now decorated with home-made Christmas crackers, a few baubles and pipe-cleaner dolls dressed in scraps of wool and cotton that she and Sal had made when they were small.

Stepping back to admire her efforts with a glow of satisfaction, in her mind's eye she could see Sal standing on a stool as she fixed a fairy to the top of the tree. As the elder of the two, her sister had always insisted on this being her job, carried out when the tree had been fully decorated. The thought that this would be the first Christmas without Sal, filled Cathie with fresh pain. Brushing away her tears, she strived not to dwell on past memories.

'What do you think?' she asked her mother, keeping her voice deliberately bright and with a cheerful smile on her face.

Rona gave a careless shrug. 'The tree's a bit small but I expect it will do. But all them decorations seem like a lot of effort for just the two of us.'

'The war is over, and there won't be just the two of us. Alex is coming home, remember, and it's Heather's first Christmas. I mean to make it very special.' Cathie fully intended to honour Sal's memory by giving her precious child a wonderful time. Even if Heather was only a baby and had never even heard of Father Christmas, Cathie had already found her a stocking to hang up, and bought a few small toys to put in it, together with a few jelly babies and chocolate creams.

'Don't expect me to look after the nipper over Christmas, even if your boyfriend does get home in time. I have my own plans, and it doesn't include going back to child-minding and washing nappies. I had my fill of all that with you two.'

'I wouldn't dream of expecting you to,' Cathie caustically replied, feeling this comment proved what a neglectful mother Rona had been. 'I did wonder though, if you would be willing to babysit for *one* evening at least, so that we could go out for a meal together to celebrate his homecoming. I haven't seen Alex in nearly two years.'

'I'd need to meet him first, to give my approval. Why don't you ask him to join us for tea one day, or Sunday dinner perhaps?'

Whenever he'd walked her home after they'd been out on a date, he'd never actually stepped inside, claiming a reluctance to intrude upon her life. In reality it may well have been the lack of welcome from her mother. Now, despite them living in a much shabbier property, Cathie smiled with relief. 'That would be lovely. I'll do that. I'm quite certain that you'll like him.' She made to give her mother a kiss in gratitude, but Rona moved quickly away, as ever resisting any show of affection from her daughter, although she rarely refused a kiss from a man.

Fortunately, Cathie reminded herself, she no longer depended upon her mother for love, not now she had Alex, and the baby. She ached with longing to see him again, but everything was ready: the goose ordered, mince tarts made, and having failed to find any icing sugar she'd coated the Christmas cake with a mock butter cream. Cathie had even treated herself to a new dress in Christmas rose red, and Davina had trimmed and styled her corkscrew curls for her. Half her personal savings were gone, but Cathie was delighted with all the preparations she'd made.

When later that day the postman delivered a second letter from Alex asking her to meet him at Victoria railway station at eleven o'clock the Sunday before Christmas, her heart turned over with happiness. She rushed to tell her friends at the very first opportunity.

'So pleased for you,' Brenda said, giving her a delighted hug.

'How exciting. When does he arrive exactly?' Davina coolly enquired.

Cathie read out the necessary details from her precious letter, without revealing his private comments to her. 'I can hardly wait.'

Now her life would truly change for the better.

* * *

At the end of the week, as she clocked in as usual at the tyre factory to start her morning shift sharp at eight, she found a note from her boss. Answering his call to enter, she breezed into his office with a happy smile on her face, her heart feeling as if it was bouncing with happiness. 'You wanted to see me?'

Glancing up from the account sheet upon which he was working, he removed his spectacles and gave a brief nod. 'I wish to thank all you ladies personally for the sterling work you've done throughout the war, and can now release you from those labours as the men are returning.'

Cathie stared at him in disbelief. 'I beg your pardon?'

'The war is over, if you haven't noticed. The soldiers, sailors and airmen are all coming home and need their jobs back. So while you women have done splendid work, you are now free to return to your domestic duties.'

Her mind in a whirl at this unexpected announcement, the last thing she'd wanted to hear right now with a baby to feed, Cathie couldn't think of a polite way to protest, however much she might feel the need to defend her own rights. Women who had refused to take a war job back in 1941 had been threatened with prison. She'd been happy to do her bit, young as she'd been at the time. She'd loved her work, the independence it had brought her, as well as the companionship of other women. 'I do appreciate what you say, boss. Of course fighting men have the right to get their jobs back, but do women need to be dismissed entirely in order to achieve that? How are we supposed to survive without a wage coming in?' she asked, attempting to sound reasonable.

He gave her a wry smile. 'I hear you'll be married soon,

Cathie, so what's the problem? A woman's role is to produce babies and support her husband.'

'And no doubt clean fire grates, knit baby clothes and mend socks,' she said, with a sharp edge to her tone. 'But what if I have no wish to be confined to the kitchen sink?'

He seemed to find this remark so amusing he laughed out loud. 'That is something you must discuss with your dearly beloved. I'm sure hubby will take you out from time to time. And, as it's Friday, the job ends today, so don't forget to collect your final wages and card on your way out.' Having said his piece, he put his spectacles back on and returned to the task of adding up company profits, which might well drop now they'd be paying higher men's wages.

Walking back to her bench in a complete daze, Cathie felt tears prick her eyes. How on earth would she cope without any money coming in? It felt as if a whole different world was opening up before her, one where she would have very little say over her own future. But once she'd listened to the woes of the other women, many of them war widows with children of their own to feed, she swallowed her own worries and said very little. She, at least, would have a loving husband to depend upon, one who would be home in just over a week.

'How on earth can I continue to pay the rent without a wage coming in?' Brenda snapped, also complaining bitterly about being sacked. 'I certainly have no wish to return to my late husband's family home out on the Pennines.'

Judging by the expression on her friend's face, Cathie

thought it wise not to ask for an explanation on that point, and instead gave her a consoling hug. 'I'm sure if we look hard enough, we'll find other work, even if it's only part-time. We do have considerable experience at our fingertips, after all. Surely all these years of hard work we've done must count for something?'

'I do hope so. We should have seen this coming, of course. Those brave soldiers do deserve their jobs back. I'd just never got around to thinking how that might affect me. Nor did I expect it to happen so suddenly.'

'Me neither. A little warning might have helped, or better still an alternative offer of a job here in the factory, one that involved us in work we know so well.'

According to the general conservation buzzing around them, other factories were likewise laying off women workers, so a new job might not be easy to find. And thinking of the busy week ahead in preparation for Christmas, helping with a charity event at the local Co-operative Society, and with a goose to pay for, Cathie attempted to mentally calculate how much money she had left to live on.

As for Alex's homecoming, her feelings were becoming increasingly muddled. Much as she longed to see him, she really had no wish to be dependent on her fiancé from the outset. In any case, war might have badly affected him too, and she had no wish to add to his distress by expecting him to be entirely responsible for earning all the money they would inevitably need. It was necessary to be practical as well as supportive and loving.

The rest of the day passed largely in gloomy silence and, as the factory clock chimed six strokes, the women packed their bags, collected their wages and walked out grim-faced, into what they'd believed would be a brave new peaceful world, and now wasn't looking quite as good as they'd hoped.

* * *

'Have you considered asking for a job here at the Co-op?' This question came from Steve Allenby, an old friend who had returned from the war some time ago with serious injuries. Cathie was helping him to organise a Christmas concert in the Co-operative Society rooms above the shop, and had casually mentioned the fact that she'd lost her job, although she felt she really had no right to complain too much. A V1 rocket had exploded close to an airfield where Steve was working in Holland. It had so badly damaged his leg an amputation had been necessary. He now had an artificial limb on his right leg from the knee down, and walked with a slight limp. He was making a good recovery, if still suffering from pain and post-war traumas, looking even thinner and more raw-boned than when he was a scraggy kid. But then losing a leg was far more serious than being dismissed from a job, however worrying that might be for her.

In between blowing up balloons that were piling up all around them, she turned the idea over in her head, a little hope lighting up within. Could that be a possibility? She wondered. Cathie knew that in the past the Co-operative movement had supported workers during strikes, as well as throughout the war, keeping tally sheets for folk who couldn't settle their household bill till their next wage was paid. Whether they would be willing to offer her a job was another matter entirely.

'I'm not intending to work here for ever,' Steve was saying. 'I do have other plans. But Cyril Leeson, the manager, generously kept my job open and I'm proud to be employed by a business that has been in operation since the mid-nineteenth century and an important part of the community. They are expert at juggling prices to suit customers' needs, give dividends, and run holiday clubs in which money can be saved for Wakes Week. Generally a week in Blackpool, as we know.' He laughed.

'I do approve of their Christmas club, which has helped me to finance this expensive season by saving up in it week after week,' she said, thinking of her dream to make this the best Christmas ever for Alex. 'Unfortunately, my skills are more concerned with checking tyres.' She gave a dry little laugh. 'Can't see that being of any use slicing bacon, butter and cheese, let alone keeping track of people's accounts. I'd be hopeless.'

'Probably you would at first, but with a bit of effort you might at last learn to count, and even add up.'

'Cheeky!' she snapped, playfully punching him on the shoulder.

He laughed as he ducked, in case she tried again. 'I

trained as a junior instructor in the army and eventually became a trainer myself, doing a lot of work with small arms. What has that got to do with cheese? You'd soon get the hang of it, Cathie. It's plain to see that you've grown much more confident and capable as a result of this war.'

Was that true? Cathie rather hoped it may well be. She had changed quite a lot over the years, gaining considerably more courage and faith in herself. Had Steve noticed that in her, or was he playing her for a fool yet again? They'd been friends from childhood, as he came from the same rough area as herself. But although he was fun to work with at these charity events, she still had her reservations about him.

She recalled how once he'd built them a tree house down by the River Irwell, and persuaded her to climb up and sit in it. Then he'd dashed off to play with his mates, leaving her stuck up the tree, too afraid to climb down without assistance. Hours later, soaked to the skin from a downpour of rain, she was rescued by Sal who came looking for her. Steve claimed he'd meant to return but forgot. Knowing how he loved to play endless practical jokes and tricks upon her, she'd never entirely forgiven him, refusing to speak to him for months afterwards. They'd fallen out countless times over the years due to her innate caution, while Steve, on the other hand, had always been a bit reckless and impulsive, lively and ruddy-cheeked.

Now his face was drawn and pale with a bleakness to his blue-grey eyes. Out of pity for the pain he was suffering, their friendship was slowly improving. But not for a moment could she ever feel the same way about him as she did for Alex, who was much more handsome, smart and sweetly polite. Steve would never be anything more to her than an old friend, but at least he was trying to be helpful now.

'Maybe I should make a polite enquiry, just in case.'

'Good. I'm sure you'll find another job, Cathie, assuming you decide you need one.'

She looked at him in surprise. 'Why would I not?'

'I heard that Alex will be home soon. You must be looking forward to seeing him again, and may soon be busy raising a family instead.' He glanced across at little Heather, contentedly asleep in her pram with her thumb in her mouth.

They both fell silent as Cathie considered this point. Was she eager to have children of her own? She hadn't thought that far ahead, obsessed only with seeing Alex again, as well as caring for Sally's little one. But a job could well prove to be unnecessary if they married quickly and she fell pregnant. Did she want that to happen? 'It's certainly true that I can't wait see him. It's been two years or more.'

'Let's hope he soon settles into Civvy Street. I found it difficult at first,' Steve admitted, as he gathered the balloons into a net. 'Once everyone has welcomed you home by buying you a pint, they tend to forget all about you. Life can feel a bit flat after that, and rather lonely to suddenly find yourself without all the mates you've lived and worked with for years, let alone shared untold horrors.' He drew in a deep sigh, a frown marking his too thin face. 'And some of them I'll never see again.'

Cathie was filled with sympathy as she waited for him to reveal more of his war story, but as always his mouth clammed shut. Could it be that grief overwhelmed him, the pain of remembering being too much to bear, or was he holding back some secret he wished to keep to himself? 'It must have been very difficult for you, Steve. But I'll be there for Alex, as I'm sure his family will too.' Not that she knew anything about his family, never having met them.

'He's a lucky man to have you. I was not so fortunate.'

'Maybe you will be one day.' Tucking the blanket over the baby's sprawled chubby body, Cathie decided it was time to change the subject. 'Will Father Christmas be coming to this charity concert?'

'I've written to invite him,' Steve replied in all seriousness. 'It wouldn't be Christmas without him, would it? He's promised to call in towards the end, with presents for all the children. There's a special group coming from Styal, St Patrick's and other local orphanages.'

Glancing again at Heather, thankful that her niece hadn't ended up in such a place, she smiled. 'That's wonderful. I always feel so sorry for all the poor orphans created by this dratted war.'

Steve gave a grim little nod. 'Yes indeed. At least we can provide them with a good Christmas party, thanks to the generosity of the Co-op. And a fun concert.'

Before leaving, Cathie called at the office downstairs to ask if by any chance they did have any vacancies, and was politely informed that sadly that was not the case.

'Hope you didn't mind my asking, Mr Leeson. Admittedly, I don't have any experience as a shop assistant, but I'm willing to learn. Should there ever be one, do please let me know.'

'Of course,' the manager, said. 'Keep your eye on our window, Cathie, which is generally where we post vacancies. Although people tend to hang on to their jobs rather a long time these days.'

Over the next few days, having had the idea of being a shop assistant planted in her head, Cathie enquired about work at several other shops too, only to receive the same response. She called in at warehouses and factories, explaining her skills and experience during the war, forced to walk away as heads were shaken. She chose not to apply at the cotton mill, as working with her mother did not appeal.

Only a short time ago they'd been celebrating the end of the war with ticker tape and dancing, street parties, funny hats and flags. Now everyone seemed to have sunk back into a gloomy depression. Except that in two days time she'd be welcoming Alex home, which lifted her heart afresh. Their future together was surely all that truly mattered now?

Chapter Four

A cold north-east wind was buffeting her as Cathie stood anxiously waiting on Victoria station platform, pacing back and forth, and constantly glancing up at the big clock high on the wall. The train must be running late as she seemed to have been standing here for an awful long time, yet she felt more concerned about the coming reunion with Alex than worrying about the cold. Did she properly remember him? How well had she got to know him in the excitement of their love match? Cathie recalled a kind, gentle, handsome man, very polite and caring. Would he still be the same, or might he have suffered some injury that he'd chosen not to mention in the few letters that had managed to get through? More importantly, would he still love her?

Cathie had tried to look her best, dressed in a tailored navy jacket and skirt with a neat pleat down the front, over which she wore a beige raincoat to protect her against the weather. A wide-brimmed red wool hat decorated with a navy hatband sat carefully tilted to one side over her neatly styled hair, a matching handbag dangling on one arm, and warm red gloves. But what if he remembered her as being far more glamorous and beautiful, instead of homely and ordinary, which was how she saw herself now? If only the weather had been better, then she could have worn a pretty dress.

Just as she'd almost given up hope, a whistle sounded, making her heart bump as if in unison. Then the air was filled with choking steam as the train came puffing slowly along the track. She could barely see the passengers as they hastily disembarked, thanks to the smoke and the crowds filling the platform. Cathie could hear the cries of joy, and the clatter of heels as women ran to fling themselves in the arms of their returning heroes.

Then like a ghost emerging from the mists of the past, she saw a vaguely familiar figure walking smartly towards her. At first sight, Cathie didn't recognise him as she was accustomed to seeing Alex in uniform, not this dreadful demob suit with trousers that didn't quite reach his ankles, trilby hat and a greatcoat stripped of its usual army buttons and braid. Seconds later, he was enfolding her tight against his chest, smothering her with kisses. Her heart felt as if it might explode with happiness.

'Let me look at you.' Releasing her, Alex stepped back a pace so that his gaze could roam over her, taking in her rosebud mouth, flushed cheeks and sparkling hazel eyes before sliding downwards over her slender figure. 'Even more beautiful than I remember.'

Glowing with joy, she gave her most bewitching smile.

'Oh, it's so good to see you too, Alex, I can't quite believe you're here at last.' She whipped off her gloves and stroked his face as if to prove to herself that he was.

'I've missed you too, darling,' he said, quickly responding with yet more kisses, his stubbled chin scraping against hers.

'I've got so much to tell you.'

He looked down at her, his chestnut brown eyes darkening with desire. 'We have a great deal of catching up to do, not simply involving talk,' he said, chuckling as he slid an exploring hand over her breast. 'How soon can we be married? I can't wait too long. I could eat you all up here and now.'

Cathie felt her cheeks grow hot as she gave a little giggle. 'We can fix a date for the wedding any time you like. But I haven't even met your parents yet, nor have you met my mother, which you are now about to do. Mam suggested I invite you for Sunday dinner, I do hope you can come?'

'Not today,' he said, looking surprised by the suggestion. 'My mother and father are anxious to have me home. We'll need to arrange that for some other time.'

'Oh, of course!' Even as Cathie agreed, disappointment bit deep in her. But then perhaps she hadn't been thinking clearly. Naturally, his parents were keen to see their only son again, after all this time away fighting in a war. It was easy to forget that other families were close when her own was not. She also thought with some regret of the expense of the half shoulder of lamb she'd left roasting in the oven. 'Can we at least walk some of the way together?'

'It will be my pleasure.' Linking her arm in his, he hitched his kitbag on to his other shoulder and they set off to walk along Deansgate.

* * *

Cathie felt a little downhearted that, even though she was his fiancée, she had not been included in his plans for his first day home. Surely on such a special occasion she should have been allowed to share it? In all the time they'd been going out together, not once had he thought to invite her to meet his family. Alex lived on St John Street, as his father was a doctor who worked at the local hospital. Unlike where she lived, close to the Potato Wharf district, it was quite a smart area even if it was still in Castlefield. Cathie couldn't help but wonder if that was the reason.

For now though, she should be simply relieved to see how fit Alex looked, marching as if on parade, straight-backed with his head held high, if unshaven and his expression somewhat stern. All her anxiety and worries had evaporated in seconds on seeing him as, unlike Steve, Alex seemed perfectly normal with no sign of any injuries. After six years of war, being only nineteen when he'd been called up in 1939, he was now a grown man of vast experience. And if there was a slight sense of distance between them, surely that was to be expected after these long years apart.

But it was wonderful that they were together at last. Her future secure.

'I look forward to you coming some other time, at your convenience. I should warn you in advance that my mother, Rona, is not an easy person, being rather selfish, and very full of herself. She doesn't believe in sitting still for five minutes. She has ever been obsessed with giving herself a good time, always going off somewhere: to dances, band concerts, pubs or horse racing. Having a bit of fun is how she terms it.'

'There's nothing wrong with that,' Alex said. 'I dreamed of doing very much the same when I was stuck out in the desert in Egypt.'

'I'm sure you did,' Cathie said, filled with remorse for having implied that living a full life was somehow wrong, even if she had only been attempting to explain her self-obsessed mother. 'And we all had fun when peace was declared. Did you get to celebrate VE Day?'

'No, I was still overseas,' he responded grimly.

'Oh, you poor thing. We went to Albert Square, everywhere ablaze with lights and hordes of people all dancing and singing 'Roll Out the Barrel', 'White Cliffs of Dover', 'Bless 'Em All', and loads of other popular songs. It was fantastic fun. Manchester was so jam-packed with folk there was no room for traffic, not even the buses could get through. There were flags everywhere, posters saluting the Allies, fireworks going off. There were thanksgiving services at various churches, and the King spoke to us on the wireless. Oh, it was a wonderful celebration with dozens of street parties held over the next few days. Mam and I attended several, and treated ourselves by opening a tin of peaches.' Cathie chuckled at the memory, preferring not to mention that they'd both also wept over the fact Sal was not present to share the celebrations with them.

Alex groaned. 'We missed all of that, but I see us going out quite a bit over the next few months, to the theatre, dancing, concerts, all manner of stuff. Can't wait to start enjoying life again.'

'Of course, you deserve to after all you've been through,' she said, feeling a little guilty that they'd been privileged to enjoy the bonfires and parties, and cheer as the blackout curtains were taken down.

Turning right along Quay Street, they walked in silence, Cathie's mind racing as she wondered whom she could call upon to babysit whenever they did go out. Rona had made her position on the issue very clear. Would Brenda mind the baby for her? Maybe, on the odd occasion, as she was doing today, but Alex sounded as if he wished to go out almost nightly.

And when should she bring up the subject of little Heather?

Remembering what her Aunt Evie had said, Cathie decided the moment wasn't quite right, as he looked so grim and rather tired. Which was to be expected as he'd only just arrived, and it would take a little time for them to re-establish the closeness they'd once enjoyed.

When they reached the corner of St John Street, he paused. 'How would you feel about a night out at the Palais, or maybe the Ritz? Going to a dance is how we met, so let's revisit old times.'

'Oh, that would be wonderful,' Cathie agreed, heart racing.

Then, putting his arm about her waist, he gave her a rather chaste little kiss as he smiled down at her. 'More of this later, eh?' And after agreeing to meet at the bus stop on Wednesday evening, he turned smartly on his heel and strode away, whistling happily.

Walking home alone, feeling just a little flat as this was not at all how she'd expected their first day together to be, Cathie deliberately turned her mind to what she would wear for the dance. It was, after all, something to look forward to.

* * *

'How did it go?' Brenda asked, when Cathie called to collect Heather following a Sunday dinner with her mother that had been even more dull and boring than usual. 'Did Alex look as you remembered?'

'Not quite, I almost didn't recognise him as he's no longer a smart soldier, a bit unshaven and shabby-looking, although he still marches like one. But he seems fit and well, which is all that really matters, and he still likes kissing me,' Cathie added with a shy giggle.

'Wonderful, and how did he react to the news about this little one?'

Cathie ruefully explained how she hadn't found the courage to tell him, and how his plans for the day had not included her. She was struggling to keep her emotions in check, feeling a slight sense of rejection. 'He didn't seem too keen to spend his first day home with me. It was as if we'd just met and were strangers, not engaged at all. A really weird feeling.'

'That's not so unusual, darling. It must feel a bit odd to be back in Civvy Street. Another friend of mine said her husband went to the pub first, and was pretty drunk by the time he arrived home, somewhat later than expected. She was not pleased, but he claimed he needed to celebrate peace at last, as he'd missed all the street parties.'

'I dare say you're right, Brenda. Alex too is upset at missing out on the celebrations, and his parents haven't seen him for a long time either, so his family should come first.'

'Parents can be very controlling,' Brenda sadly remarked as she slipped Heather's chubby arms into her matinee jacket. 'And his father, Doctor Ryman, does have a reputation for being rather grand. Some men tend to be that way. You should see how my brother-in-law behaves, as if he has the right to own the world. He goes on and on at me, constantly nagging and insisting I do whatever stuff he demands.'

'What sort of stuff?'

'Oh, legal stuff in the main. He's so arrogant, but then

my late husband did inherit the family estate, now in his brother's hands. Anyway, enough of my stupid problems. I'm sure Alex will make it up to you soon,' she said, giving Cathie a warm hug.

'Oh, I'm sure he will,' Cathie agreed, instantly brightening as she explained about the Ritz. 'Can't wait for Wednesday to come. Now what on earth can I wear?'

CHAPTER FIVE

The Ritz was every bit as beautiful as Cathie remembered, luxuriously appointed in red and gold, with its arched ceiling, two tier bandstand, tables and chairs set around the dance floor, and with a gallery above where you could watch the dancing. The band was playing Doris Day's 'Sentimental Journey' as they walked in, which quite touched her heart. To her great surprise, in spite of the war having been over for some months, there were still many men in uniform, happily smooching with their partners to the music. Others were standing around eyeing up the girls and women who stood chatting and giggling at the opposite side of the ballroom.

'I'm amazed there are still servicemen around,' she said.

'Maybe they are men returning home, looking to find themselves a wife.'

'Or husbands who have left their poor wives stuck by the fireside minding the kids,' she said, giving a small sigh of disapproval.

'Which would be perfectly reasonable.'

She looked up at him, startled by this remark, but

decided he must be joking. The next instant she was in his arms, moving slowly around the ballroom, and it felt so wonderful, her insides lighting up as brilliantly as that highlighting the band.

There were very few American GIs around, she noticed, or Yankee-Doodle Dandies as they used to be called. 'This ballroom was once so popular with the Yanks, they called it the forty-ninth state,' Cathie told him with a laugh. 'Whitworth Street always seemed to be full of American jeeps, and MPs with red armbands and batons, whose task it was to keep the boys of Uncle Sam in line.'

Staring grimly down at her, he asked, 'Did you used to come here and dance with them?'

'Heavens, no! I was too busy working for one thing, and waiting for you, of course.'

'Sorry, of course you were,' he said with a smile that warmed her heart.

Cathie caught a glimpse of them dancing together in one of the many mirrors set around the walls. Was she dancing close enough in his arms, or a little more distant than that first time when they'd met at the Palais? Perhaps it would take a little while for them to relax together, as her friend Brenda had suggested. Still, she was here at the Ritz, in his arms, a dream come true. Cathie was relieved to see that she looked quite respectable in a pink flowered dress with a matching flower in her hair. Almost pretty. Stuck for something to talk about, she continued chatting about the way things used to be during the war years.

'British servicemen outnumbered the Yanks, of course, but only just. I believe the ballroom did used to be packed with scores of excited girls throughout the war, all seeking their dream hero.'

'That's all women want from a man, someone to bring in the money each week.'

'Goodness, what a thing to say.'

'Are you implying that you want more from me than that?' he asked.

'Of course I do. I love you, darling.'

It was then, as the lights dimmed and the music changed to 'If I Loved You', that he kissed her, quite thoroughly this time.

* * *

'We should come here more often,' Alex said, when later he walked her home. 'I love dancing with you. We could try the Palais again, and Belle Vue.'

Thinking of how fortunate she'd been to persuade Brenda to babysit for her, Cathie cleared her throat, then in a light, philosophical voice, not wishing to sound bitter, she hesitantly pointed out the poor state of her finances as a consequence of losing her job. 'We women have been disposed of now that the men are coming home. Fair enough, I suppose, but money is a bit tight right now. I'm out and about every day searching for a new job. I dare say you will be too, once you've settled in.'

'I'll certainly be on the lookout for one eventually,' he

agreed. 'Although I have my demob money to tide me over, and shall insist upon it being the right job in the right place. For now, I'm in desperate need of a rest, as well as a bit of fun. It's easier for you as a woman as you won't even need a job, once we're wed. You can simply relax and return to your cosy domestic duties.'

Cathie chose to make no response to this, much as the remark slightly irritated her, as it had done when Steve suggested this might happen. It was true that some women were glad to be free of work at last, and more than happy to return to the comfort of their own hearth. But she was missing hers already after only a week of being unemployed. Sadly, Alex hadn't even expressed any sympathy over her losing her job, and she really had no wish to spoil their first evening out together by pressing for her independence.

They walked on down Lower Byrom Street that had suffered badly from incendiary bombs, many of the houses now without fronts or roofs, as in Duke Street, where they used to live, and many other streets they passed. It was then that he suddenly pulled her into the shadows of a broken building and began to kiss her most urgently. 'God, I've missed you,' he sighed, when some moments later he finally released her.

'And I you.' Desire burned within her, tempered a little by nervous caution. This didn't seem quite the place to be engaging in lovemaking.

'You are so sweet I could lick every part of you.'

Cathie giggled. 'I'm not a lollipop.'

'Really? That's a shame, because I'd love to eat you all up.' He was kissing her again, this time her ear and eyelids, and then exploring her mouth with his tongue. As he bent to kiss her throat, she felt her senses skitter with longing, remembering how she used to spend wakeful nights dreaming of moments like this. Now, as his hand slid over her bottom, then down her thighs and began to inch up her skirts, she was filled with a flash of panic, and quickly put out a hand to stop him.

'Sorry, but it's been so long since we last kissed like this, I don't want to rush things.'

His eyes were glazed, as if in some dream world of his own. He carried on touching and kissing her, not really listening to a word she said. Cathie could hear him panting for breath, feel the hardness of him pressed against her. Suddenly overwhelmed by shyness, and feeling slightly taken advantage of, she gave him a shove and eased herself from his arms. 'That's enough, Alex. We aren't married yet, remember.'

He took out his handkerchief and dabbed at his sweaty brow. 'Sorry, I can hardly wait until we are. But you're quite right, I should remember that you're not some tart I picked up.'

She gasped. 'Is that what you used to do?'

He burst out laughing, making a joke of it. 'Of course not. Don't fret, sweetie, I'm just impatient to enjoy life following the misery of war, but I need to remind myself how to behave.' He offered her his arm. 'Allow me to be the perfect gentleman and escort you home.'

Smiling, Cathie hooked her arm into his and they set off again.

When they reached the grimy old River Medlock littered with broken bricks and rubber tyres as it slid darkly into the culvert that took it under the city, Cathie felt a sting of shame for the shabby state of the district in which she lived. It wasn't helped by the stink of coal dust in the air, and noise from the railways, which were ever present. Having lived in this part of Manchester all her life, she had become largely oblivious to such things, perceiving this as a fascinating historic and industrial region. But Castlefield, like many other parts of the city, had suffered a severe battering during the war. Now, seeing the area through her fiancé's eyes, Cathie couldn't imagine him ever settling for living here. This would not be the right place for Alex Ryman at all.

'I'm sorry everywhere looks such a mess,' she remarked quietly, as his gaze roamed over the depressing scenes: black pits marking the ground, heaps of rubble and broken buildings roped off. 'But it's been a difficult war. We've all suffered greatly.'

He gave a snort of disbelief. 'Not as much as those of us who were at the Front and suffered from constant air-attacks, shelling and fear.'

'I'm sure that's true, but it was pretty terrifying on the Home Front too. You can see from the damaged houses that there have been regular hits on Manchester, Salford and neighbouring areas.'

'Not in recent years,' he coldly remarked. 'You've been most fortunate.'

Cathie glanced at him in astonishment. 'I do appreciate that you and your comrades must have suffered worse traumas, but we haven't been as lucky as you might think. One night we rushed to the air raid shelter when the sirens went off, believing we'd be safe. Instead, it suffered a direct hit. Brave Sal saved both our lives by pushing us out of the bunk we were sharing just before the concrete roof collapsed.'

Cathie had suffered an even worse incident, but, like Brenda, preferred not to dwell upon such things, certainly not right now, as Alex didn't seem to be taking any of this in.

'At least you survived,' he said, a slightly scathing note in his tone of voice. 'So what was the problem?'

'The terror of it. We did escape largely unhurt on that occasion, if almost suffocated and blinded by the stink of gas,' Cathie said, feeling slightly let down by his lack of sympathy. Not least by the dreadful fact that in the end her lovely sister had not survived, of which he was fully aware.

A memory she preferred to keep blocked out suddenly resounded in her head with startling clarity, as if it had taken place only yesterday. It was during the Christmas Blitz in 1940 that their home in Duke Street had been bombed. The three of them had been rushing to the nearest air raid shelter when her foolish mother had suddenly ordered Cathie to go back and collect some warm blankets.

'What? Are you mad? There are bombs falling all around.'

'Then don't just stand there arguing, get on with it afore it's too late. It's that cold we'll all freeze to death if you don't look sharp.'

Cathie ran as fast as her legs could carry her down the street, her boots clattering on the cobbles. Fear pounded against her ribs, as she felt desperately anxious to carry out the task as quickly as possible and escape back to the shelter. But speed proved to be counter-productive. Had she walked at a sensible pace, all might have been well. Instead, the moment she raced in through the front door, the house was hit.

She found herself suspended in mid-air for several long moments before walls and ceilings began to fall in upon her from all directions. It felt as if the world itself was collapsing. Cathie had never known such terror in her entire life. The dust and stink of smoke was suffocating, as she lay buried beneath the debris for what felt like days, but was probably only a few hours. She fought to move her limbs and crawl out of the mire but failed completely, a strange heat escalating through her. Was she about to be burned alive?

She could hear crying, yelling, screaming, not realising it was her own voice. After that she must have passed out, as a darkness overwhelmed her. She finally woke to hear someone calling, 'Can anybody hear me? Is there anyone there?'

'*Yes!*' Cathie screamed. '*I am. Please help me.*'

She was badly cut and bruised, her dress scorched by the explosion, but at least alive. Others had been less fortunate. The sight that met Cathie's eyes when she was lifted out and carried to a nearby ambulance would live with her for ever: faces burned, limbs missing, dreadful injuries among the walking wounded, and dismembered body parts scattered everywhere. It was an experience she would never forget. To this day, if she heard a crash of thunder, let alone a bomb going off, she would go running for cover into the pantry or wardrobe, but then suffer terribly from claustrophobia. She'd be riveted with fear just by the sound of the siren.

Blinking away the nightmare flash of memory, she offered a cautionary smile. 'Now that the war is over we can at last look forward to a bright future.'

'Whatever that might be,' Alex growled. 'And so long as it doesn't take too much effort to achieve.'

He sounded somewhat dismissive and scathing, not at all the calm, well-mannered young man he used to be. Perhaps the war had badly affected him, after all. Perhaps physically he was reasonably well, but not mentally. Returning to Civvy Street and the shambles all around them couldn't be easy, as Steve had tried to explain to her.

Cathie was filled with sympathy for his anguish. She too had grown increasingly devastated by the losses all around her, of bomb craters and fires leaping up everywhere, shops she'd once loved reduced to ashes, friends fleeing to the country to escape the city, and wounded men walking the streets. Anything even vaguely disturbing upset her greatly. Speaking of these experiences was quite beyond her, although she prayed that one day she might find the courage to share her pain with Alex. And he might share his with her. That way, they might both begin to recover.

Feeling a reluctance to make life even more difficult for him right now, since he'd been home for such a short time and this was their first evening out together, Cathie decided this was certainly not the moment to mention baby Heather.

* * *

'So you're this Alexander Ryman I've heard so much about,' Rona said, casting her shimmering blue-eyed gaze over him with open curiosity. 'Never expected my daughter to find someone so tall or half so good-looking.'

Cathie winced, filled yet again with that far too familiar sense of rejection. 'Actually, Alex found me,' she said, trying to laugh the cutting remark away.

'And what a treat that was,' he agreed. 'Which is why we went dancing tonight, to relive that wonderful moment. It's a delight to meet you too, Mrs Morgan, as you are as beautiful as your daughter.'

'If not more so,' Rona said with a little swivel of her shapely hips as she stood before him in her too-tight, too-short skirt and flimsy blouse through which her cleavage was clearly visible.

He seemed to find this amusing and, reaching out, gave her hand a lingering shake of apology. 'I'm sorry I wasn't able to accept your invitation for lunch the other day. I'm sure I would have enjoyed your cooking enormously. Perhaps another time?'

'We call it dinner, not lunch. But you're very welcome to come whenever you like, chuck,' Rona said, making no mention of the fact that she did not actually do any of the cooking.

'Thank you, I shall be delighted to accept, hopefully one day soon. Now if you'll excuse me, I will say goodnight.' Putting his arms about Cathie, he gave her a quick hug. 'You will meet my parents soon, sweetie, when you come to spend Christmas with us.'

'Oh, but…'

'No buts. It's long past time you did meet them, and I can think of no better occasion. After that, we can start planning the wedding.'

Stunned into silence, Cathie simply nodded and hugged him back.

Rona flickered her neatly trimmed eyebrows and gave him a teasing wink as he smiled at her from over her daughter's shoulder. Maybe for once the girl had brought home someone of interest.

Chapter Six

'How I wish I'd followed your advice, Davina, and written to Alex before he arrived. It was a bad mistake to leave it so long, as it's now more difficult than ever. Delighted as I am to receive the invitation to spend Christmas with him and his family, how can I possibly accept because of baby Heather?' Cathie said, sharing the problem she now faced with her friends. 'Yet if I refuse, it will look as if I've no wish to spend the day with his family, and it's long past time I met them.'

They were enjoying one of their customary snacks together, this time midweek as neither she nor Brenda had any job to go to. The sound of carol singing by the Salvation Army filled the frosty air, as Cathie slowly sipped her bowl of hot vegetable soup. She was taking her time over it, knowing it might be the most food she would get to eat that day. How she would manage to keep the pantry stocked in the coming weeks really didn't bear thinking about. She would be entirely dependent upon her mother's wages to feed them, a dismaying prospect. Rona hadn't a clue about the cost of anything, the difficulties of shortages, or even how rationing worked, as she'd always left all of such domestic matters to her daughters.

Now even Christmas, which she'd been so looking forward to, was turning into a nightmare. It meant that all her efforts to prepare the best Christmas ever for Alex had been entirely in vain.

'I'd offer to help only I've agreed to spend the holiday season with my late husband's family,' Brenda said, pulling her face as if this gave her little pleasure.

'I could mind baby Heather for you, if you like,' Davina offered, taking her entirely by surprise.

Cathie blinked. 'Really? Are you sure?'

'Perfectly. I'm not an expert on baby care, but this is a time of goodwill, after all, so why shouldn't I help?' she said with a smile that seemed much warmer than usual.

How could she decline such an offer? It was too good to refuse, even though this was not at all what Cathie had planned. 'I don't suppose you'd be willing to have a practice this evening as I need to attend the concert Steve and I have helped to organise? The Co-operative Society is very much involved with local charities, holding dances, whist drives, sports events and children's parties, with which I'm always happy to help. I was going to tuck Heather into a back room, but it would be much better if you came and sat with her at home. My mother will be out on the razzle, of course, as usual. Never thinks to offer any assistance at all.'

'No problem, I'd love to. Then if you're happy with

my services, I shall be equally happy to babysit for you on Christmas Day.'

'That's very generous of you,' Brenda said with a frown, almost as if she didn't quite believe what she was hearing either. 'Have you no other plans? You aren't going home to spend time with your own family?'

'Not just now, no.' When she said no more, Cathie rushed in with her thanks.

'That would be great! So kind of you, thank you, Davina.' She could hardly believe her good luck on both counts.

They agreed a time for Davina to arrive that evening, early enough for her to be shown how to change a nappy, and feed baby Heather her bottle before putting her to bed.

In fact she very kindly came early and carefully went through the routine of baby care, which worked wonderfully. Satisfied that all was well, and with little Heather tucked up in her cot and her friend reading a magazine by the fire, Cathie put on her hat and coat and went off to meet Steve, arriving in good time to help him get everything ready before starting to collect tickets at the door.

* * *

It was just as well she hadn't brought baby Heather with her as it proved to be an incredibly busy evening. Cathie was rushing about all over the place, helping people backstage with their dresses and make-up, checking that props were in the right place, and controlling the children as they waited for their turn to perform in the school choir. She also sold programmes, helped the ladies of the Women's Institute to serve the tea during the interval, and generally scurried about doing all manner of tasks. She even found herself helping the lighting technician resolve a problem with the sound system when for some reason it failed.

'You've improved your talents considerably,' Steve said in surprise, not sounding half as mocking as he might once have done when they were young kids.

'I'm certainly not the useless lump you used to accuse me of being,' she retorted. 'Thanks to my war efforts.'

'Well, you couldn't be any worse,' he said with a laugh, and she scowled at him. Perhaps at heart Steve wasn't quite as kind and caring as he appeared at first sight, and still a bit thoughtless at times, although his charity work deserved considerable admiration.

The Christmas concert was a great success, with various locals volunteering to do a turn. These included a butcher who performed some magic tricks, much to everyone's astonishment and delight; a group of acrobats who usually worked at Belle Vue, and two young women shop assistants who sang 'I've Got My Love to Keep Me Warm' and most appropriately 'I'll Be Home for Christmas', which brought forth cheers all round. They finished their performance by singing 'Have Yourself a Merry Little Christmas', with which everyone in the audience joined in, save for Cathie. Cathie was in tears, as she knew it had been sung by Judy Garland in *Meet Me in St Louis*, the film Sal had gone to see on the day of her fatal accident. How unfair life was.

Recognising her distress, Steve gave her shoulder a little squeeze. Brushing the tears from her eyes Cathie took a deep breath to calm herself. She really must be brave, for little Heather's sake, she reminded herself, however difficult that might be.

As a prelude to Christmas a choir from the local chapel sang the 'Hallelujah Chorus' from Handle's *Messiah*. There wasn't a textile town in all of Lancashire and Yorkshire that didn't revel in the glorious sound of this old favourite. After which, the concert concluded with the pianist playing a medley of carols, from 'Hark the Herald Angels Sing' to 'O Come All Ye Faithful', accompanied by both the school and chapel choir singing in perfect harmony. This brought forth a rousing applause and a merry singalong from the audience.

'What a wonderful concert that was,' she told Steve as they said goodnight at the door, having quickly stacked chairs, swept the floor and generally tidied up, with stalwart help from the WI ladies.

'I couldn't have managed half so well without you,' he said with a grateful grin. 'Particularly keeping those kids happy and stopping their fights and arguments.' They chuckled together as they recalled some of the disputes she'd resolved, and the songs and poems the school children had performed individually.

'Some of them were so talented they put me to shame.'

'What little stars they were. Anyway, thanks for helping to organise the concert. It's been great fun.'

'Happy to do so. I enjoyed myself enormously. Any time you have an event on, just let me know,' she said, pecking his cheek with a quick kiss before turning to leave.

It was then that she saw Alex, standing to attention before them, his brow puckered into a grim frown. 'Alex, goodness, I'd no idea you intended to come tonight.' His sudden appearance was startling, and he looked so stern and regimented that Cathie thought for a moment Steve might be about to click his heels together and salute.

'I can see you weren't expecting me,' he remarked icily.

Noting the scowl of jealousy on his face, Cathie hurried to give him a kiss. 'It's lovely to see you, darling. You should have told me you were coming. This is Steve Allenby, by the way, who works at the Co-op and organised this event. It has raised a large sum of money for our returning heroes.'

'Cathie worked hard too, bless her,' Steve said with a smile, as he stretched out a hand for Alex to shake.

He didn't take it. Instead, he turned to address his fiancée in a firm tone of voice. 'I've come to see you safely home, not watch this children's concert.'

'Oh, of course, how kind of you. Well, goodnight Steve.' Hooking her arm into his, she allowed Alex to lead her out into the cold dark night.

The incident brought rather a sad feel to the end of what had been a joyous evening. But when they reached the corner of her street Alex pulled her into his arms and proceeded to kiss her with such vigour, any feeling of resentment quickly dissolved as she responded with equal passion. It was almost a compliment that a perfectly boring friendship with Steve had sparked jealousy in him. Alex's increasing fervour did cause her some alarm when he slid his hand down her thigh to lift her skirt and began to fondle her private parts. She almost slapped his hand away, feeling a sudden urge to protest that he was going too far, but then lost the courage as desire flowered within her. Hadn't he made it very clear that he wished to enjoy life again? Who was she to deny him a little pleasure, and after all these years apart?

Besides, didn't his need for her prove how very much he loved her?

* * *

On Christmas Eve, Cathie went through the ritual of hanging up the baby's Christmas stocking, and setting out a plate of mince tarts and a small glass of sherry for Santa Claus, even though little Heather hadn't the first idea what was going on. When Christmas Day finally dawned, the little girl instantly fell in love with the soft little teddy bear she found poking out of the stocking. What a joy the child was, so happy and giggly, and so easy to love. She stood holding tight to a chair as she dangled the bear with one hand. Then pulling it to her chest, gave it a hug as she took her first step, wobbled madly for a moment and then plonked down on her bottom. Cathie laughed and clapped with delight. She'd be walking soon.

'This was your mummy's teddy when she was a little girl. He's called Billy. I'm so glad you like him too,' she said to the bright-eyed child, who instantly planted a kiss on the stuffed bear's nose, then said, '*B-b-b*,' as if making an effort to start practising his name.

They had a fun time playing with her new toys – some wooden bricks and a little postbox with plastic letters to fit in. Later in the morning Cathie reluctantly handed Heather over to Davina. She hated the idea of them spending Christmas apart. Oh, how she wished she'd mentioned the baby before now, then she wouldn't have needed to leave her. But everything had seemed much more complicated than she'd expected, or else she was still very much the coward Steve remembered. Cathie was quite certain everything would have been different had she found the courage to do the right thing. Then Alex would have invited Heather. Now it was too late. It certainly wouldn't be appropriate to mention the subject today, but once Christmas was over Cathie fully intended to explain everything.

'So your mother didn't rise to the occasion then?' Davina asked, with a wry smile. She rocked the pram a little and then smiled down at the baby, who was sitting up straight and proud, cuddling the bear in her arms.

'I'm afraid not.'

Rona had already gone off to The Donkey, her favourite pub on Water Street, to celebrate Christmas Day with her friends. Having witnessed Alex's invitation at first hand, she'd quickly made it very clear that the baby was not her responsibility. 'The child needs a proper mother, not a young girl like yourself who can't even offer her a father.'

'I'm about to be married so I will be able to offer her one soon. I realise I should have told Alex about Heather long before now. You were wrong to advise me against doing that, Mam. But couldn't you just for once stand in for me, if only for a few hours. It is the season of goodwill.'

Rona had been sitting at her dressing table applying rouge and lipstick with her usual diligence, then fluffed up her victory roll hairstyle, scarcely listening to a word Cathie said, as her next remark proved. 'Tommy has invited me to his house for dinner. I gave him the goose we bought, and a few of the trimmings so as not to waste them.'

'You did *what*? You'd no right to do that, Mam. *You* didn't even buy that food, *I* did, and could have cooked it for dinner tomorrow, on Boxing Day.'

Rona shrugged. 'You never said you intended to do that. Anyway, it's too late, it's gone. No doubt the goose is already in Tommy's oven. He's quite a good cook, actually.'

Now, as Cathie met Davina's sympathetic gaze with anguish in her own, Cathie let out a heavy sigh. 'I've even lost the food I bought for Christmas, but there's really no arguing with Rona. She does exactly as she pleases, with no thought for anyone but herself.'

'Maybe you should tell Alex today about the child. It is, as you rightly pointed out to your mother, the season of goodwill, so this could be your best opportunity.'

'I don't think it would be quite appropriate on the day I meet his parents for the first time.'

'They need to know some time, so why not now?'

Cathie thought about this piece of advice as she made her way past St John's Church. Once she had met his parents and done the polite thing by chatting to them and enjoying the Christmas meal they offered, she hoped there might come a moment during the course of the afternoon when she and Alex would be alone. That would hopefully give her the opportunity she needed to explain her plan for adoption. What should she say? How could she put it? Are you willing to accept my late sister's child as your own? Perhaps that was a bit too blunt. And how could she begin to explain why she had kept silent for so long on the subject? Was it really just because she had no wish to speak of Sal's death, or more from a fear of losing him?

Whatever the reason, she must remind Alex how many orphaned children there were now, that too many were growing up without fathers. She had no wish for little Heather to feel abandoned when she had a loving aunt to care for her. Perhaps she should have brought the baby with her, after all. Surely once he met Heather all these worries would be resolved. Although how Alex's parents would react was much more of an unknown factor.

At least little Heather was safe and happily playing with Davina, so she'd hopefully enjoy Christmas Day, even without her aunt. Cathie had agreed to collect her later in the afternoon, around four o'clock. Tomorrow she'd make it up to the child by devoting the entire day to her.

Arriving at the door of a fine Georgian, three-storeyed terraced house bearing the name Doctor Victor Ryman written on a plaque fixed to the wall, Cathie was suddenly beset with the urge to turn on her heels and run back home. Instead, she took a deep breath to gather her courage and lifted the brass knocker. It looked so bright and shiny the maid had no doubt polished it that very morning. Cathie smiled to herself as it crossed her mind that she would probably have more success applying for such a job rather than the role of wife to a doctor's son. Giving the knocker a gentle bang, she almost hoped that no one would hear it.

Chapter Seven

If Cathie had been hoping to see jolly faces in funny hats, hear the sound of carols being sung or played on a piano, or even laughter resonating through the house as this was Christmas Day, she was instantly disappointed. There wasn't even any sign of Christmas decorations, save for a stately tree set in a corner of the large, spacious hall, sparingly bedecked with baubles. Nor was Alex waiting there to welcome her. The door was opened by an elderly manservant, who took her coat and hat before leading her upstairs to the drawing room. Cathie trembled with nerves. This was not at all how she'd hoped to spend Christmas, nor had she imagined that Alex's home would be so grand. How naïve of her to assume he would be happy to spend it at her own humble abode.

As she entered, the entire family, seated on leather armchairs set around a stunningly beautiful panelled room, all turned to gaze upon her in silence. No one spoke, or offered the compliments of the season. Was her Christmas rose dress too garish? Did it not suit her strawberry blonde curls, which suddenly seemed to be falling over her flushed cheeks in a scraggy mess, making Cathie feel even more uncomfortable? A crystal chandelier hung from the high ceiling, seeming to freeze the scene in its bright light, which even the flames from the coal fire burning in the stately fireplace failed to warm. Then, springing from his chair by the window, Alex strode over to put an arm about her shoulders and give her a quick kiss on the cheek. Cathie smiled up at him, sighing with relief.

'Merry Christmas,' she murmured.

'And to you, sweetheart. Come and meet my folks.'

Leading her by the hand around the room rather like a dog on a lead, he introduced her, one by one, to his family, a process she found totally confusing. There were so many of them that she instantly forgot every name and relationship the instant it was given. She had no difficulty, however, remembering his stern-faced father. Doctor Victor Ryman appeared quite old, stockily built, and really rather grand, as Brenda had told her he was. The very arrogance of his stance filled her with a sense of foreboding. He offered no compliments of the season either, or even a welcoming smile, merely muttered good day through clenched teeth, giving her a brief nod.

Alex's mother, Dorothy, a tall elegant lady, smiled somewhat coldly as she offered Cathie a slender hand sparkling with jewelled rings and bracelets. And his sister, Thelma, a perfect beauty with a sheath of glossy black hair that fell upon her bare shoulders, was wearing the kind of long stylish gown one would only expect to see worn by Rita Hayworth in such films as *Cover Girl*.

'It looks as if your family have lived here for generations,' Cathie politely remarked, admiring the range of portraits depicting Alex's ancestors that were hung upon the silk-covered walls. She felt utterly overwhelmed and intimidated by the apparent high status of his family. What kind of home had she stepped into?

'Not really, we've moved about quite a lot, and the portraits come with us wherever we go, don't they, Pa?' his sister said, glancing with a shrug and a smile at her father.

'Indeed, even to India,' he agreed. 'They are our heritage, which confirm who we are.'

Did she have such a thing as heritage, whatever that might mean exactly? Cathie wondered. It seemed highly unlikely as her mother rarely spoke of her own family, and they tended to get through life by taking one day at a time.

'I believe you live close to Potato Wharf, Miss Morgan?'

'Cathie, please.' How formal everyone sounded. 'We live near the River Medlock actually, but in that general area, yes,' she agreed, not wishing to be too specific considering the sad state of their street right now.

'Poor you, so glad I wasn't born round here.'

Her brother gave a hollow laugh, which to Cathie's ears sounded faintly embarrassed. 'It's not a bad thing to be Manchester-born.'

'How can you say that when you were born in Jaipur, as were the rest of us while Pa was working for the Rajah out there? Of all the wonderful places we've lived, I ask myself daily how on earth we ended up living in this dreadful city.'

'Manchester is a wonderful city,' Cathie bravely stated. 'Or was before the war destroyed so much of it. As is Castlefield.'

'What a silly name,' Thelma retorted. 'I don't see any sign of a castle.'

'I think it had something to do with the Romans who once occupied this area, so maybe they had a castle or a fort of some sort. It used to be called Castle-in-the-Field back in medieval times when even then Manchester was a famous trading port, or so my father told me. But over time the name of this district was shortened to Castlefield. I'm quite proud to be a Mancunian, actually.'

'Brave of you to take such a stand, dear, although you didn't have any choice on where you were born, so you have my sympathy.' Thelma flicked her winged brows in caustic amusement before graciously moving back to her seat, leaving a cloud of Chanel perfume in her wake.

Cathie almost wished she'd kept her mouth shut.

* * *

The atmosphere over lunch was equally chilly and fraught with tension, almost as bad as the cold sleet now slapping against the stained glass windows. There were various aunts, uncles and cousins seated around the large table. Cathie smiled vaguely at everyone, but no one smiled back, or even bothered to speak to her save for his Aunt

Mary, a wizened old woman with grey hair who prattled on at length about a book, *For Whom the Bell Tolls* by Ernest Hemingway, which she happened to be reading. Even Alex seemed sunk in some private world.

Cathie attempted to fill the frozen silence by mentioning the success of the charity concert the other night.

'Thanks to the Co-op we managed to raise a great deal of money for our returning heroes,' she told Doctor Ryman, who was seated opposite her, his wife by his side. Neither responded, offering not a word of congratulations.

Throughout the meal his mother, Dorothy, frequently cast curious glances in Cathie's direction while conversing quietly with her husband. Were they discussing her? They certainly seemed to be examining her in excruciating detail. Cathie felt as if she were on show in a shop window, the entire family watching the way she lifted her glass, held her knife and fork, and chewed upon her food. At one point, she slid a hand beneath the table to clasp Alex's knee, needing the reassurance of his presence beside her. Even that brought little response beyond a small sideways twist of a smile.

Striving not to appear offended at being so ignored, Cathie concentrated on eating the Christmas turkey. 'This is so tender,' she said at last, unable to bear the awkward silence any longer. 'We were going to have goose, unfortunately...' She stopped in her tracks, not wishing to explain how her selfish mother had given it away, despite the curious glances directed her way.

'What? You didn't know how to cook it?' Thelma asked with a laugh.

Cathie's cheeks flushed bright red. 'Well, yes, actually, I did, although my cooking is nowhere near as good as yours, Mrs Ryman.'

'Then perhaps you should take lessons from the WVS,' Dorothy remarked coolly. 'Particularly if you are soon to be married.'

'Oh, I'd never thought of that. Not that I could afford to, nor have I the time.'

His mother gave a wintry sort of smile that did not reach her cloudy grey eyes. 'Such classes are free. Besides, you have all the time in the world to make your husband happy. That will be your job from now on, so long as you feel up to the task, that is.'

Cathie felt a strong urge to dispute this remark, but fortunately her sense of caution won out and she kept silent. The conversation around the table again reverted to personal matters, which she allowed to drift over her head, making no attempt to listen, let alone join in. Alex was likewise ignoring her, exchanging a few words with his father. Perhaps, she thought, when lunch was over, there would be the opportunity for them to be alone at last and have time to talk. Till then, she'd button her lip and say nothing more.

But his mother's next question, directed specifically at her, changed everything. 'I perfectly understand why a young girl such as yourself would be eager to quickly tie the knot, but you need to remember that my son has only just returned from the war, so must be allowed some time to recover before you rush him down the aisle.'

Cathie let out a little gasp. 'I wasn't planning on doing any such thing.' The joy she'd felt in anticipation of Alex's homecoming, and their wedding, had now quite deserted her. 'We haven't even fixed a date yet, have we, Alex?' she said, turning to him for confirmation.

'It's none of your business, Ma. We'll marry when we choose,' he announced firmly.

'Don't speak to your mother in that manner,' ordered his father. 'She is only showing concern for you.'

'I don't need her concern. I'm perfectly well. No injuries, no loss of limb, not blind or deaf. Nor am I any longer the young boy I was when I joined the army back in '39, but a grown man who makes his own decisions in life.'

'You are most certainly not the man you were, darling boy,' she insisted. 'You don't even seem happy to be home, behaving ridiculously tetchy and bad-tempered one minute, and sunk into silent gloom the next.'

'You won't even tell us where you've been stationed, or what you've been up to these last years,' his father growled. 'Nothing about your role or rank in the army, let alone what you hope to do in the future.'

'We were shelled, bombed, friends killed, intimidated and attacked by our enemies. Why would I wish to speak of any of that?' Alex snapped.

'You could share some of your agony with us. It might help.'

'I have friends who don't care to remember painful times either,' Cathie hastily put in, anxious to offer Alex her support.

'Quite!' he grumbled, slapping down his knife and fork and pushing aside his half-eaten meal, his tone harsh with anger.

Dorothy cast Cathie a furious glare, as if the fault were hers that he'd abandoned his dinner, before turning with a gentle smile back to her son. 'Then it's even more important for you to take time to rest and recuperate. Landing yourself with the hassle of organising a wedding and finding a home as well as a new job is not a good idea right now. It's not as if this girl is in the family way, which would be the only reason to rush headlong into marriage. At least I assume that to be the case?' she caustically remarked.

Shocked by the question, and feeling the food clog her throat, Cathie took a quick sip of water to stop herself from choking, an attack of nerves making her shake. Was this the moment to reveal all? She was struggling to find the rights words to explain her position when the butler, who had quietly entered the dining room, whispered something in Mrs Ryman's ear. The woman seemed to freeze as her narrowed eyes glowered at Cathie with a flint-eyed glare.

'There's someone at the door asking for you. She has apparently brought *your baby* in a pram, and the child is crying for her *mummy*!'

All around the table knives and forks dropped, conversation halted and every pair of eyes fell upon her like daggers.

'Good God,' Alex said. 'You have a *child*? So who's the damned father? It certainly isn't me?'

* * *

They were seated in the conservatory, Cathie quietly sobbing into her handkerchief. 'I know I should have told you before now, Alex. I truly meant to. I tried on numerous occasions to summon up the courage to mention it in a letter, but was always put off by my mother. She insisted you had enough to contend with fighting a war. Also, I was still grieving, and couldn't bear to keep going over Sal's death.'

'Your reasons for keeping it a secret are much more basic than that,' he snarled. 'You were obviously reluctant to admit that you'd had a baby.'

Alex was striding back and forth, fists clenched, fury etched upon his handsome face. Cathie felt as if he were a commanding officer and she was one of his men, whom he was reprimanding for some alleged misconduct. Brushing the tears from her eyes, she whispered, 'You aren't listening to me, Alex. I've just explained that the child is my *niece*.'

His glance was scathing. 'Do you have proof of that fact?'

'Such as?'

'A birth certificate.'

Cathie shook her head. 'I'm afraid not. Sal hadn't got around to registering the birth before she was killed.'

'How very convenient.'

'Heather is most *definitely* the daughter of my sister Sally and her husband Tony, who, as you know, were both tragically killed. The poor child is an orphan and I'm the only relative she has left in the world, save for her useless grandmother. I love her, and rather hoped you would come to adore her too. Look at what a sweetie she is.'

Watching her aunt weep had earlier brought a rather sad expression to the baby's round face. Now Heather was smiling as she sat happily on Cathie's lap, rubbing her little head into her neck, obviously feeling the need for a loving cuddle. How Cathie longed for Alex to take her into his arms and offer the same sort of comfort, to somehow overcome this distance growing between them.

'That child's behaviour is appalling. I've never seen such a fusspot. She seems to be a right little madam.'

'Heather was upset, that's all.' It was true the baby had been screaming and kicking quite hysterically, in something of a tantrum when Cathie had dashed to the door. Davina had looked equally distressed. Holding the teddy bear in her hand, her friend had explained how the baby had refused to eat a thing, and wouldn't stop crying.

'I swear that I would not have brought her to you otherwise. I know you didn't want Alex to know about the child yet,' she said, adopting a woeful expression.

Only too aware that he stood hovering close behind her, a shocked expression on his face, and must surely have heard this remark, Cathie had hastily gathered the child in her arms and offered reassurance to Davina. 'Don't worry, it's my fault. I shouldn't have left her.' She paid little attention to the smile of satisfaction on her friend's face as she'd cuddled and kissed the baby's hot head. But she was deeply aware of the tension bristling within Alex, and still was as her efforts to explain the situation to him did not seem to be working.

Determined to do right by her late sister and the baby she already loved as if she really were her own, Cathie tried again. 'You need to understand, Alex, that because of the neglect I suffered as a child myself I wish to do my best for little Heather by adopting her. I did hope that you would agree.'

'You think I'm some sort of idiot that I'd believe such tripe? How many times have women pretended to adopt a long lost cousin or niece? The child might call them aunt in public, but everyone knows she's really the mother. Or else she gets her own mother to take the child on and makes out the child is her sister. Why don't you ask Rona to do that?'

Cathie almost laughed out loud. 'Absolutely not!' she spluttered. 'Not all women are natural mothers, and mine most certainly isn't. Besides, I've just explained who Heather is. Why won't you believe me?'

He glared at her, lips curling with disgust. 'Because I know when I'm being lied to. Were this child really your niece then someone else could easily adopt her. Someone who can offer the child a proper home and a father. Why should it be you, unless the child really is yours?'

Cathie let out a heavy sigh. 'I've already told you that Sal and I were very close, so I feel that I owe it to my late sister's memory to take good care of her baby.'

'Stuff and nonsense! I assure you that I've no intention of taking on another man's child. Why would I? It's that Steve fellow, isn't it?' he shouted, wagging a furious finger in her face. 'I saw you with him the other night, giving him a kiss. You could have told me all about this child then.'

Devastation hit her that Alex should imagine for one moment that she could love anyone but him, let alone engage in an affair. 'That's not true, Alex! Steve and I are just old friends, nothing more and never have been. We don't even get on terribly well, constantly falling out. And that was simply a thank you peck on the cheek for all the work he'd done. I'd been helping him run that charity event, as you know full well.'

'Don't take me for a damn fool,' he shouted, in the kind of dismissively stern voice that denied argument. 'Who else would it be, if not him? Some Yank perhaps? You did say when we were at the Ritz that there were plenty stationed near Manchester, and who attended the dances, so that's a definite possibility.'

'I also made it very plain that I was not involved with them in any way.'

He shrugged. 'Whoever the father is, like many other young women parted from their man by this dratted war, you've behaved like an absolute slut and betrayed me. Not even bothering to send me a "Dear John" letter. My mother was right. This is the reason you wished to rush me into marriage, to find a father for *your child*.'

Cathie felt herself start to shake, with anger now rather than nerves. Why wouldn't he believe her, or even listen to a word she said? 'I'm no *slut*! And it was *you* who said you were in a hurry to marry, the moment we met at the station. I didn't at all mind waiting a little while, as it's a job I'm most urgently in need of. You weren't very sympathetic about that either, saying I wouldn't even need one now we were about to marry.'

'Well, I was wrong there. We aren't going to be married, so it will indeed be necessary for you to find yourself employment fairly quickly, so that you can afford to feed this bastard child of yours.'

At which point Cathie stormed out of the house.

Chapter Eight

Cathie felt utterly devastated as she poured her heart out to Brenda as they strolled around the market a week later, Davina absent for once. She'd thought of Alex as the love of her life, and believed that he felt the same way about her. Yet he was convinced she'd betrayed and lied to him. 'All these years of waiting and praying for his safe return, and now he's tossed me aside as if I were some sort of harlot. Why won't he believe that little Heather is my *niece*? Nor has he offered sympathy for the loss of Sal, not even in any of his letters let alone in person.'

'It sounds very much as if he's turning his back on reality,' her friend quietly remarked.

'I can fully understand why Alex would have no wish to speak of his own traumas, whatever they might be, but why is he so dismissive of my own?'

Had he been a touch more sympathetic she might have shared her own horror story with him.

'Sometimes, the only way of coping is to "forget",' Brenda was saying. 'To shut the horrors from your mind, just as everyone else who has suffered in this war does.'

'I appreciate what you're saying, and you know that I have first hand experience of grief as a result of this war, and other traumas too. I agree that locking away painful memories does often feel like the best way of dealing with the problem. But, as you've told me many times in the past, Brenda, sometimes talking about these issues can help, so why won't he do that? Or properly listen to mine?'

'He's rather like Davina in that respect. Who knows what happened to that husband of hers? She won't even tell us his name. I can talk endlessly about my beloved Jack to anyone willing to listen, if not about the manner of his death. Isn't that how it should be?'

'Oh yes, I'm happy to speak of Sal's love of Christmas, of movies and singing, but not her accident. I prefer to remember her in life, not the manner of her death. With all the hardships I've had to face, and being forced to accept the wartime attitude of "we can take it", it was the prospect of Alex's homecoming that has kept me going.'

Brenda nodded, her round face filled with compassion. 'The problem is that despite the war being over, things seem to be getting worse, not better, which is hard for ex-servicemen, for all of us. Peace is not bringing the end to the misery that everyone hoped it would. There's a feeling of anticlimax, as if the bright blue, sun-filled sky has clouded over again, leaving a feeling of uncertainty about the future. A grey chill seems to hang over everything.'

'Oh, you're so right,' Cathie said, pausing to haggle over the price of a rather poor selection of fruit and vegetables on one of the stalls. She finally added two tomatoes, a small turnip and a few potatoes to her bag. 'There are still too many shortages, queues are even longer as rationing continues and austerity beckons. We barely have enough money to buy coal to keep a paltry little fire burning in the grate, assuming we can find any to buy. We've burned all sorts of stuff over the years, including stools and old chairs in order to keep warm.'

Brenda chuckled. 'I burned the clothes prop once, feeding it in an inch or two at a time.'

'But no longer can anyone say: "Don't you know there's a war on?"'

Both girls were laughing now as they recalled the number of times this mantra had been repeated over the years. 'Making ends meet is not easy, and bartering still very evident, if you have something to barter with,' Brenda agreed. 'I reckon only black marketeers are making any money.'

'So what happens now? How can I convince Alex that I'm innocent of this charge of having an affair?' Cathie asked, bleakness descending upon her once more. She valued Brenda's friendship greatly, but when suffering traumas in the past Sal had been the one she'd turned to for comfort. Sadly, having lost her lovely sister, to now lose Alex made Cathie feel more alone than ever, and everything so much harder to deal with. Tears welled in her eyes. 'How do I face life without him?'

'With courage, darling, a skill you've never been short

of, so have faith in yourself and the future you can create for this little one.'

Cathie smiled through her tears as she watched little Heather happily bobbing up and down in her pram, gazing about her with bright-eyed interest. 'Thanks, but being a little jealous is one thing, accusing me of sleeping with another man, quite another.'

'He is fond of you though. Steve, I mean. He always has been.'

'Don't talk daft. The pair of us were for ever at odds, and the number of tricks he's played on me over the years doesn't bear thinking of. He'd hide my favourite doll, set off bangers and crackers to scare me on bonfire night, and make me run round and round a gravestone then put my ear to it to listen to the dead talking. Which was no doubt his own voice speaking to me, which I didn't realise, idiot that I was. There's nothing Steve Allenby likes more than to stir up trouble, but we've done nothing wrong. I simply gave him a peck on the cheek to thank him for his charity work. Nothing more than that, I swear it. But yes, I should have come clean from the start about wanting to keep Sal's baby.'

'That would have been difficult while Alex was away fighting, and whenever you chose to tell him could easily have brought forth this same reaction. But you need to consider if he'll also take his anger out on Steve.'

'Oh, my goodness, I never thought of that. Alex is a bit reckless and unstable in his thinking at the moment, probably because of this dratted war, and poor Steve has enough problems to deal with.' She'd done her best, as a friend, despite their constant disputes, to help him to deal with his traumas. Cathie really had no wish for her old friend to suffer even more as a result of some stupid assumption on Alex's part. 'Sorry, but I must go and warn him, right away.'

Quickly saying her goodbyes, Cathie dashed off, intending to call in upon Steve at the Co-op.

* * *

'You've done the right thing, in dropping that silly girl,' Alex's mother assured her son, patting his cheek as if he were a five-year-old. 'She was clearly taking advantage of your offer to get herself out of a hole of her own making. How dare she cheat on you! The chit obviously had no idea how fortunate she was to find such a fine young man as yourself. Who is this other fellow, anyway?'

'An old friend of many years, apparently,' Alex growled, making no mention of the fact that he'd lost count of the number of times he too had cheated on Cathie over these last few years. Leave wasn't easy to come by out in the desert, but whenever he was granted any he would go to Cairo and spend his money on booze and brothels to offset his boredom.

He'd become so accustomed to that way of life, he'd done the same thing when he first returned home and was stationed near Salisbury. That was where he met a certain young lady. She was so beautiful that he soon become entirely besotted with her. The fact she was a 'good-time girl', or in reality probably a prostitute, didn't trouble him in the slightest. Keeping servicemen happy was her role in life, and it was perfectly acceptable for them to befriend girls when on leave. However, complete fidelity was naturally expected from wives and sweethearts. Ordinary women should be loyal to their man. That was their job, so Cathie had no right to betray him. But perhaps all women were whores at heart. 'May he rot in hell for stealing my girl,' he growled.

'I should think you are better off without her, darling. Having an illegitimate child is almost as bad as prostitution. Quite shameful and immoral, and would bring disgrace to our family.'

'So what are your plans for the future?' his father put in, in that authoritative tone of voice that always set Alex's teeth on edge. 'You must have acquired some skills while serving abroad, what were they exactly? Hopefully they will help you to find a new job, as you never stayed in one longer than five minutes when you were a lad.'

Alex had always felt unappreciated by his parents, in particular his father. If they ever found out what he really got up to during the war, their attitude would be even worse. Providing the proof that he'd suffered a taxing war was virtually impossible. His work at the front line had been very much that of a back-room lad. A part of him resented the fact the army had adopted such a low opinion of him that he was placed in the mess tent. Yet in the end he came to believe himself fortunate to have enjoyed an easy war, despite being sent overseas.

But if his imposing father ever discovered that he'd been trained as a cook and worked in the Army Catering Corps, Alex thought it unlikely he would ever speak to him again. The suitably named Victor constantly threatened to disinherit his only son if he didn't achieve his required standards. As a consequence, Alex kept these facts to himself, not wishing it to be known that he'd held such a lowly job, which would be viewed with contempt.

Even now, Victor was addressing him with contempt. 'It's quite clear to me from your tan that you did very little, other than spending too much time sunbathing.'

'I was living in sunny climes, and I'm afraid mum's the word, as they say,' Alex replied with a scathing smile, having no wish to admit he'd sweated out the war in a tented kitchen. Fortunately, keeping quiet about war work was perfectly acceptable, even rather liberating. 'As for the future, I'm making the necessary enquiries, and keeping an eye out for a job. I hope to have found one by the time my demobilisation leave is over.'

'There are training courses available in various skills,' Victor reminded his son, 'although they do tend to have more applications than places available, so you need to look sharp about it.'

Alex realised that new skills might indeed need to be developed in order to find employment. He certainly had no wish to continue working as a cook. But after a childhood ruled by a controlling, arrogant father who thought nothing of caning him if he disobeyed an order, followed by years of fierce army regime, being one's own boss carried considerable appeal. It really was time that he took control of his own life, as well as anyone who attempted to block that plan. Alex resolved to find some way of earning a living that would not put him under anyone else's command, or require too much effort on his part.

As for Cathie, it was rather a pity she'd behaved so badly as she was a lovely girl. But he'd find himself another obedient wife to look after him and do her duty, so long as he chose with care. In the meantime, at least he still had other choices available to offer him solace.

* * *

Cathie sat waiting for Steve in the corner café, a place where they would sometimes meet up for a cup of tea and a chat, although generally on a Sunday afternoon, not during the week. As he came out for his dinner break, Steve looked surprised and slightly concerned to find her sitting there with an expression of utter misery on her face. 'Are you all right, Cathie? You look a bit distressed.'

'Sorry to bother you when you're busy working, but we need to talk.'

Over a sandwich and a cup of tea, with little Heather happily sitting on her lap nibbling a chocolate biscuit,

Cathie told him what had happened and saw his face go pale with shock.

'How dare he accuse you of such a dreadful thing? The man's an idiot if he doesn't appreciate how fortunate he is to have you.'

'I'm afraid Alex immediately jumped to the wrong conclusion that the child was mine and refused to listen to common sense. I felt I should warn you, just in case he comes looking to put the blame on you.'

'Thanks, but don't worry, if he does I'll make it very clear that our relationship has always been a bit gladiatorial, and strictly platonic.'

There was something in the cloudy softness of his blue-grey eyes that looked almost sad. Was he feeling pity for her, or something else entirely? A shiver ran down her spine as Cathie recalled what Brenda had said about Steve having always been fond of her. That couldn't be right, could it? It was true that he'd helped her to cope with her grief, just as she had been there for him through his pain. But his description of their relationship was entirely correct. There'd been many instances in the past when they were at loggerheads, almost like sworn enemies at times. Dismissing Brenda's views as nonsense, she blocked out the rush of emotion that threatened to unhinge her, as was her way.

'I'd call it more cut-throat,' she said with a smile.

He laughed. 'Mebbe you're right. Do you remember when we were kids how we'd go fishing with a net in the

River Medlock, competing for who could catch the most fish, or build the biggest dam?'

'I do, and how you managed to trip me up once so that I fell in that black mucky water, in grave danger of getting myself caught up in all the rubbish.'

'I swam in it often and never came to any harm.'

'That's because you were always prepared to take more risks than me. And at least you could swim.' Memories of their long-standing friendship came flooding back. 'Do you remember chasing the Salford kids on Irwell Street Bridge?'

'Oh aye, I thought of Salford as enemy territory and if a rival gang came looking for trouble, battle would commence. I also remember you and I racing each other on bogies made from planks of wood with pram wheels at each end.'

'I loved dancing round the maypole on May Day, the Whit Walks, and a trip to Peel Park was always a real treat. Sal and I would take a bottle of lemonade, and a jam butty to eat. I have such happy memories of my childhood with her.' She paused to cast him a sideways glance. 'And a few with you.'

'Me too,' he said with a grin. 'Riding bicycles on St John Street was a favourite of mine, because it had a smooth, tarmacked surface instead of stone setts.'

Mention of St John Street instantly wiped these happy childhood reminiscences from her mind, bringing Cathie back to the moment she'd sat in Alex's posh conservatory listening to him make his accusation.

As if reading her mind, Steve said, 'Why on earth did Davina bring the child, when she knew you still needed to explain everything to him?'

'I don't know. Little Heather is a sweetie, not usually any trouble at all,' Cathie said, kissing the baby's head and laughing as she kicked her little legs with joy. 'Nevertheless, babies can be a bit difficult to deal with, I suppose, if you aren't used to them, and Davina isn't.'

'Not sure who was the most stupid though, her or him,' Steve growled.

Cathie shook her head, feeling unwilling to blame her new friend, or Alex either for that matter, as she still hoped he might relent and take her back. 'As he won't speak of his problems I can't be certain, but I suspect he suffered traumas of his own during the war for him to be so angry. I do understand, having had issues of my own to deal with.'

He nodded with sympathy as Cathie topped up their cups with tea. 'Me too, which is the reason I've involved myself in charity work as I feel the need to do something in return for the help I received. In fact, I'm planning to hold a little talent contest soon, in a bid to raise money for orphans.'

'Oh, do let me help.'

He smiled softly at her. 'I rather hoped you might offer. You are so kind, Cathie. I feel I can talk to you.'

Silence fell at these words as they regarded each other quite seriously, their constantly fractured friendship resonating with a new understanding. Cathie felt her heart lift a little, as if by talking to Steve she'd slightly eased her sense of loss and abandonment. An unexpected closeness seemed to have sprung up between them. Or was that some fantasy on her part? Bringing herself back to reality, Cathie glanced up at the clock on the wall. 'Goodness, your dinner hour is over, and I must take this little one home for her own lunch.'

As they came out of the café, chatting and laughing, Cathie was shocked to find Alex standing waiting at the door, arms folded and cold fury etched on his face.

'So I was right, you are the father of her child!' he yelled, and punched Steve in the jaw.

Chapter Nine

Cathie flew to Steve's side as he lay sprawled on the pavement, desperate to help him to his feet, which was not easy with his artificial leg. She shouted at Alex as she did so. 'You are absolutely wrong! I've explained everything about the baby, so stop this nonsense right now.'

Recovering his balance, Steve took a step back, holding up both his hands in defence. 'I've never touched Cathie in that way, and I've done enough fighting to last a lifetime, so let's not take this any further.'

Alex's upper lip curled into a scornful sneer as he half turned away, before suddenly whirling about and throwing yet another ferocious punch. This time Steve managed to duck, missing it by a whisker, then, flinging himself at Alex, he grappled him to the ground.

Crowds gathered to watch as the two men battered and thumped, punched and kicked each other, rolling about on the dusty pavement. Some were cheering, others shouting out instructions to one or other of them on how to retaliate. Several times, Cathie tried to put a stop to the fight, only to be pulled back by someone attempting to keep her safe.

'Your baby's crying,' a woman told her, pointing to little Heather who was sitting in her pram screaming with distress. Cathie wanted to shout that this wasn't her baby, that Alex had no right to accuse Steve of being the father of her niece, but, gathering the child in her arms, she just sobbed.

The fight might have got even more nasty had not Mr Leeson, the manager of the Co-op, heard the commotion and come running out. Even then it took the assistance of several of the more sensible onlookers before he managed to drag the two men apart.

'So help me, I'll pummel your brains out if you ever sleep with her again,' Alex roared.

'I've already told you, I never touched her!'

Alex brought up his fist in a left uppercut and knocked Steve out cold.

* * *

Dear Aunt Evie was so sympathetic when Cathie called round to fill her in on this latest bad news, even though she was still busily battling for the return of her own children, which was taking far longer than she'd hoped. Cathie explained about the fight, and how Alex had accused Steve of being the father of little Heather. 'It was dreadful. I thought for a moment he might kill Steve. We had to call a doctor to make sure he was all right. Even so, Alex obviously doesn't love me enough to be prepared to accept the baby,' Cathie sobbed. 'And I love little Heather far too much to let someone else have her. What on earth can I do?'

'Dry your eyes for a start, as you're upsetting this little one by crying.'

'Oh, she's seen too much pain lately. Poor little love.' After grabbing the handkerchief her aunt offered, Cathie quickly dabbed her eyes and managed to give a smile at Heather who was sitting on the rug with a sad expression on her plump little face. 'Sorry, Auntie, you're right, no more tears, I promise. I really must get a grip on myself.' Taking a breath, she asked again, 'So how do I deal with this problem?'

'You could ask the authorities if you could adopt the baby yourself.'

'Without a father? Why would they allow that?'

'We've suffered a war, and men are in short supply. Besides, they surely can't expect to put all these poor lost kids into orphanages, not when a family member is willing to adopt. Anyroad, it's worth asking.'

* * *

Cathie did so the moment all the New Year celebrations were over, hurrying round to Children's Services only to be coolly informed that it was not possible for her to adopt a child, not unless she was married. 'Although you can foster your niece,' the woman added with a more kindly smile when she'd heard the full story. 'Then, one day, when you find the man of your dreams, you could adopt her.'

'Oh, that would be wonderful!' Cathie said, relieved to at least be made legally responsible for her darling niece. It put her in a much brighter state of mind. This might not be the future she'd planned or hoped for, but if she was forced to choose between the baby and Alex, then there could be no question about where her responsibility lay, or a large part of her heart. Giving Heather up for someone else to adopt, or dumping her in an orphanage, was most definitely not on her agenda. Although, she might still secretly hope and pray that she could persuade Alex to change his mind.

It would take some weeks to deal with all the necessary paperwork, but having resolved the problem of her lovely niece, Cathie went next to see Davina. She readily accepted her friend's apology and offered forgiveness for revealing the truth to Alex. 'I'm sure you did your best for the baby. I really don't blame you for coming,' Cathie told her, managing a smile.

'The little girl was so upset, she simply wouldn't stop crying. I felt I had to bring her to you, and could only hope you'd got around to telling him by then.'

'I'm afraid I hadn't, as we'd had no time alone to talk. But Alex is certainly aware of the facts now, and Brenda thinks he might always have reacted in this way. Sadly, he is clearly not interested in children, is convinced she is *my* child, and has accused me of sleeping with another man.'

Davina raised her beautifully pencilled brows in surprise. 'So the marriage is off then?'

'It would seem so.'

'Well, I'd say if that's his attitude, you're better off without him. Forget him.'

How could she forget him when she loved him so, Cathie thought, misery closing in on her yet again. But, making no response to this remark, she buried her hurt feelings by changing the subject and asking Davina about her own family. 'Did you get to see them over New Year, if not Christmas?' she asked.

'It wasn't possible for me to find the money to pay the fare for such a long journey. Besides, I left home years ago so it's not as if we're close any more.'

'I'm sorry to hear that. How old were you when you left home, Davina? Was there some sort of problem?'

'Aren't there always with families?' her friend said, and quickly changed the subject to talk about how busy they'd been on the market stall over Christmas, and how she felt in need of a good rest.

Her answers were as vague as ever, but Cathie was at least thankful that their friendship remained intact.

* * *

Watching her so-called new friend wheel the baby away, Davina smiled to herself with satisfaction. What a naïve idiot Cathie was. Davina had never understood why Alex had been so obsessed with returning to the girl after nearly two years apart, particularly considering the many nights he'd spent in her own bed since they got together many months ago. She'd believed in her heart that he loved *her*, not this one-time fiancée of his, and that one day soon they would marry. Davina saw herself as the innocent victim in this ridiculous love-triangle, not Cathie Morgan.

He hadn't even written to the girl much in recent years, let alone gone to see her, although whenever he spoke of Cathie, he said what a wonderful person she was. True, she was a pretty young woman, if somewhat shy and innocent, irresistible qualities to a man like Alex Ryman. No doubt she'd attempted to make a strong case for him to accept little Heather, but thankfully failed.

Davina was delighted her plan seemed to have worked and she'd won the battle to convince Alex that adopting this unknown child would be a bad mistake, which should put paid to any hopes Cathie had of a marriage between them. Nevertheless, she was already playing with further ideas, just in case he got it into his head to take the girl back.

Brenda might share her old friend's faith in Alex, but Cathie's mother clearly nursed serious doubts, which should help. Whatever steps Davina decided to take in order to permanently shatter this foolish girl's dreams, though, she must tread carefully. It certainly helped that he could never find it in himself to resist what she had to offer.

Lighting a cigarette, Davina recalled with pleasure the moment he discovered she'd moved to Castlefield, which surely proved that her love for him was greater. She'd deliberately travelled to Crewe, carefully checked the time of his train, due to arrive at Manchester Victoria on the dot of eleven, so that she could meet him before Cathie did. Progressing slowly along the corridor of the rocking train, she'd carefully searched every compartment for the one man she was desperate to find. Packed with soldiers returning home, it had not been an easy task. Yet she knew Alex was in one of those carriages.

Davina had walked the entire length of the train, chatting and laughing with scores of servicemen when suddenly she'd heard his voice. She would have known the sound of his rumbling laughter anywhere. Smoothing down her hair, she tapped on the compartment door and, when his startled gaze met hers, gave him a seductive little smile.

Seconds later, he was by her side. 'What in tarnation are you doing here?'

'I've come to welcome you home, darling,' she said and, wrapping her arms about his neck, gave him a long deep kiss, which brought forth a chorus of cheers and a huge applause from his buddies. Putting his arm about her waist, he drew her further along the corridor, out of sight of his comrades. Then, pulling her into an area between carriages, he lifted her into his arms and began to almost devour her with the urgency of his kisses, her breasts crushed against his hard chest. Triumph soared in her as she helped him fumble aside her coat and skirts and hitch her a little higher. Within minutes he was inside her, bumping hard against her hips as she cried out in ecstasy.

'Lord, that was good,' he sighed, when finally he released

her to catch his breath. 'I can't quite believe you actually came, or that we're doing this here on a public train.'

Chuckling softly, she stroked his jaw, noticing how it bristled with the start of an unshaved beard. Poor man, he seemed to forget such obvious routines these days. 'Why wouldn't I? We love each other, Alex, and I need you. You do still want me, don't you?'

'Of course I do. The time we've spent together has saved my sanity these last months. But you know that I'm promised to a sweet young girl.'

'I think you mean to a naïve idiot. Forget her. Why would you need Cathie Morgan when you now have me?'

'Our relationship is a bit different. Besides, promises must be kept.'

'Why should they be? I'm the one you truly love. I want you to choose *me*, not *her*.'

Laughing, he pulled her back into his arms to fondle her breasts. 'Maybe I don't have to choose, since I love both of you, if in slightly different ways. What's wrong with that?' And as he started to kiss her some more, Davina elected not to dispute his argument, much as she might wish to. Her need was far too great to take the risk of him choosing this so-called sweet young thing he hadn't seen for years, and who was now a beautiful young woman.

Later, as she got off the train at Salford, before it reached Victoria where Cathie was waiting for him, he slipped a few coins and a packet of cigarettes into her pocket, making her laugh with delight. Smiling at these memories of their lovemaking, she thought what a generous man he was. She'd walked away revelling in the scent of him upon her skin, the burn of his kisses on her lips and the delicious ache in certain parts of her anatomy, which proved how very much he needed her. Always thrilling.

Now she simply had to convince him that not all promises needed to be kept, and she was the one he couldn't live without. With luck, and a bit more effort on her part, this time she fully intended to win more from him than the odd night in his bed.

* * *

Exactly as he'd planned, Alex took to going out every evening. He would go to the cinema or theatre, to a club, football match or a pub to meet friends and drink. Sometimes he'd go alone, although Davina would often accompany him. He'd been seeing her regularly ever since she'd come to meet him on the train just before Christmas, and they'd joke and have fun together. Living life to the full was what he so loved to do, and he fully intended to continue doing so. There'd been nothing much in the way of entertainment out in the desert, save for those far too short leaves he'd spent in Cairo, so he felt that he deserved to live the life he'd been deprived of for years.

He did miss his army mates as he'd quite enjoyed army life: if not the discipline, at least the routine, the good meals, uniform and regular pay that arrived in his bank account through little effort on his part, and with no great danger involved. The camp was once bombarded, but he'd managed to evade injury by fleeing.

And he certainly had no wish to return to a boring desk job or dull domestic routine, or to be cooped up in a world of wrecked houses with dreadful food. A part of him almost regretted that the war had ended, or that he'd ever left the army. The life that he'd once known here in Manchester had gone, the city, like the country, had completely changed and become much more bureaucratic. Alex felt he'd suffered enough of rules and regulations, and disliked having too many decisions to make.

Even Cathie was no longer the pretty, adoring girl she'd once been, but a firm young woman with a mind of her own. She was still quite lovely, but not exactly glamorous, as she tended to favour easy-to-wear, more practical clothes. Very boring of her. As for this tale about that child being her niece, it was such a common excuse he really had no patience with it. Even if it were true, Cathie should have told him long since, and asked his permission to keep the baby, not made the decision on her own without his consent. He really was sick to death of his opinion being ignored.

Tonight Alex was in the Pack Horse, one of his favourite pubs in Castlefield, having a good old moan about the issues he was facing with a bloke he'd just met. He'd introduced himself as Eddie, and was quite flashily dressed in a wide-lapelled suit and brightly coloured tie, sporting a trilby hat tilted rakishly over his forehead. They were sharing a grumble about regulations, which seemed to be dominating everything.

'I went to the butcher's the other day to buy some sausages for my mother,' Alex told him, 'and having queued for the better part of an hour the bloke refused to sell me any, even though he had plenty left, because I wasn't one of his registered customers. I nearly throttled him there and then, only an elderly woman poked me in the backside with her umbrella and told me to buzz off. What a world!'

'That's the way things are nowadays,' Eddie said, slurping on his beer. 'But folk have learned to tip shop assistants in order to get special service. Stuff will then be kept under the counter for 'em.'

'Is that legal?'

'It's not *illegal*. The line between the two has become a lot less well defined. Folk are weary of regulations, particularly now the war is over, and happy to turn a blind eye. Besides, it's a good way for shopkeepers to hang on to their well-off customers. Salmon and peaches are generally supplied that way. Just because you can't see what you want on display doesn't mean summat isn't available.'

'There seems to be a great deal I need to learn after so long overseas. The country is in such a dreadful mess that I'm beginning to ask myself, was the war worth it?' Alex grimly remarked.

Eddie laughed. 'It is if you can make good money out of it.'

'How can you possibly make money out of a war?' Alex enquired sarcastically.

The man tapped his long nose. 'That'd be telling, but I certainly know how to get hold of as many sausages as I fancy, and at a decent price.'

Alex frowned, puzzling over this remark. 'Is that so? And how would you manage that with rationing tighter than ever, to the extent that the government is threatening to ration bread and potatoes too, or so I'm told?'

'It's all about knowing the right people,' Eddie explained. 'Whether you're looking for spare parts for your car, petrol, nylons, perfume, cigarettes, alcohol, owt that takes yer fancy, I usually know a chap who can supply it.'

'At a price, I presume?'

Eddie chuckled. 'Well, I have to make a profit. That's how I earn my living.'

'Is it indeed?' Alex looked him over, then his mouth twisted in an interested little smile. 'And it looks as if it's a good one.'

'It certainly is.'

The man was a wide-boy, a wheeler and dealer, or 'spiv' as they were often called, but judging by the cigar he was smoking and the classiness of his clothes, he clearly did have money. 'As an ex-servicemen with no job to go to, I'm looking for a decent income myself, and am equally pissed off with bureaucracy. Can I get you another pint of beer? I'd like to know more.'

Chapter Ten

Cathie lived in hope of Alex calling in to say how much he was missing her and that he wanted her back. But, as each day passed without any sign of him, she became increasingly despondent that he never would. She felt lost without either a job or her fiancé, spent the mornings looking for work, and the afternoons walking the baby, thinking it would be good for both of them to be out in the fresh air. The cold days of January were passing, if achingly slow and endlessly boring.

This afternoon she passed Potato Wharf with its maze of iron and brick railway arches, the Bridgewater and Rochdale canals sliding darkly beneath. Rails and posts circled the giant basin, and even little Heather, sitting up in her baby harness, seemed fascinated to watch the swirl of water below.

Why couldn't Alex be as spirited and brave as Steve? Had he led too pampered a life? Perhaps his family – his imperious father, arrogant mother and snobby sister – were all secretly pleased that he'd called an end to his engagement with a girl from the rougher, more industrial part of

Castlefield. Thelma had made her opinion of Manchester all too clear, making no allowances for the aftermath of war. But why did being born in Jaipur in India make her a better person?

Courage, and the ability to face life's problems, surely came from within yourself and the strength of your beliefs, not the place you were born, or even where you happen to live.

War, however, could have a devastating impact.

Cathie felt weary to the bone. Not simply from being entirely responsible for the care of a child, as well as waiting hand, foot and finger on a useless mother, but also from six years of hard work, sleepless nights in a damp air raid shelter, fear and anxiety that yet another bomb might drop at any minute, and constant worry over her one-time fiancé. Losing Alex completely had only deepened that sense of dejection.

Instead of the warmth of a new future together to look forward to, she felt as if she'd been discarded into an icy heap of debris all over again.

Carefully guiding the pram around the fenced barriers set to guard the bomb-ruined houses, Cathie walked slowly on. Finally, she reached the section of the River Medlock where trees grew upon the sloping grassy banks. Even if most of them were still bare of leaves at this time of year, buds were beginning to form, and a few snowdrops and wild daffodils were already springing into flower.

Cathie revelled in the fresh scents of country air and the

glory of open spaces. It felt wonderful to be out and about. She hated being confined indoors day after day with no job to go to. As hard as she struggled to find one, she'd had no luck so far. But with spring coming, perhaps things would improve. She could but hope so. Yet again she felt filled with sympathy and admiration for Steve's strength when finding himself trapped in a wheelchair. Cathie told herself that she could perhaps learn a lesson from her old friend. She needed to hold on to the confidence that had built up in her over the war years, and never allow it to be destroyed.

Think positive, that was surely the best way to cope.

Rocking the baby gently in her pram, Cathie felt deeply thankful to have the child. The pair of them were also blessed with good health. As a result of all the adversity everyone had suffered on the home front, people were too easily falling sick, resistance to illness becoming alarmingly low. Cathie had recently received a letter from Brenda, tucked inside a belated Christmas card, to say she'd been struck down with a bad attack of flu and wouldn't be back for some time. She'd even slipped the key to her little bedsit into the envelope. '*Just in case you need a hideaway, darling*,' she'd written. '*The rent is paid for the next three months, so no need to worry about that.*'

She missed Brenda badly, although accepting her offer was a tempting thought.

Alex may object to taking care of a baby that was not his. Heather was not hers either, but Cathie loved the child as if she was, and no matter what problems the future might bring, she would somehow find the strength to cope. She owed it to her beloved sister, and must consider this little baby's future too, not just her own.

Her spirits suitably raised, Cathie walked briskly along the towpath to their dingy house tucked up a back street close to the river, and was astonished to discover Alex sitting in the kitchen having tea with her mother.

Heart racing, Cathie gazed upon him in wonder. It was weeks since she'd last seen Alex, and she'd almost forgotten how good-looking he was, how erect and masterful. Despite now being dressed in civilian clothes, thankfully a smart grey suit rather than the drab, too short demob one he'd come home in, he still looked every inch the soldier, right down to his polished boots.

'Ah, there you are,' he said, smiling up at her. 'We were wondering what had happened to you.' He made no move to approach her, but Cathie was holding the baby in her arms, so why would he?

'We've been taking our afternoon walk,' she said, stuttering a little over her words. Why had he come, just when she'd given up hope that he ever would? Cathie longed to ask, but couldn't quite pluck up the courage to do so, regardless of all her earlier promises to be strong. The prospect of being put down by Alex yet again was too dreadful to contemplate.

The baby was restless and whimpering a little, already nodding off in her arms, having been sitting up and taking a lively interest in the birds, passing dogs and cats, trees, flowers and ducks for the full length of the walk, as she always did. She seemed to be the kind of child who drank everything in with great gusto.

'If you'll excuse me a moment, I must change little Heather and put her down for a nap.' Cathie gathered up a bundle of clean nappies and carried Heather upstairs.

Could it possibly be that Alex missed her and wanted her back? Oh, she did hope so. Or what if he'd come to see if she'd changed her mind about adoption? If so, then he'd be disappointed. Heather was her foster child now, and would remain so.

It was a wonder her ears weren't burning, as by the way the pair had been huddled together by the fire as if they were old buddies, Cathie guessed that they must have been talking about her, and the issue of the baby. Surely Rona would have convinced him that Heather was in fact Cathie's niece, and her own granddaughter?

As she was working the six till two shift today, she'd clearly had time to change out of her work overall, turban and clogs. She was now all dolled up in a blue and white polka dot cotton frock, the kind you might expect to find on a young girl of twenty, not a woman of forty-seven. Yet she looked amazing.

Cathie felt almost jealous of her mother's good looks and glamour, but then she didn't any longer feel young and attractive herself, quite certain there must be lines of weariness on her face. Since losing Sal, and faced with all this extra work, she'd rather lacked the energy or interest to take care of herself properly, unlike Rona who took such a pride in her appearance, no matter what was happening in the world.

Perhaps that was one of the reasons Alex had dropped her, because she was no longer the pretty young thing she'd used to be, but a tired, overworked woman. And why he'd glanced up at her with only casual interest.

* * *

When Cathie came back downstairs she was astonished to find Rona standing at the cooker, stirring a pan of soup.

'Your mother has invited me for tea,' Alex explained.

'Indeed I did,' Rona said. 'I hope you don't mind, chuck, but I thought it might allow you two an opportunity to talk.'

This was the last thing she'd expected and Cathie sat down rather quickly, again feeling a tingle of nerves. She kept her head down, saying nothing, as Rona dished out tomato soup, but didn't fail to notice how her mother would give Alex the odd teasing smile or wink, as always unable to resist a gorgeous young man. Or sometimes a little shrug of her shoulders, as if in apology for her daughter's behaviour. Alex would offer a smile in return, even a covert little wink now and then. It felt as if they were exchanging secret messages.

A meat and potato pie followed the soup. 'I spent the afternoon baking this, do hope you like it,' Rona sweetly murmured, placing a portion before him with a dazzling smile.

'It's delicious,' Alex said, responding with a bewitching smile of his own.

Cathie cast a scathing glance at Rona, all too aware that her mother had never baked anything in her life. But then why would she trouble herself to cook when she'd had two daughters capable of looking after themselves and her? Caring and cooking for a man, however, she would view as another matter entirely, as it produced more interesting benefits. Guessing Rona had purchased the food from the Co-op, Cathie again dropped her gaze and said not a word, eating in complete silence. There were far more important issues to worry over than the source of a pie.

'So what is it you wanted to talk about?' she finally plucked up the courage to ask, as she laid her knife and fork down on the empty plate.

Alex paused to clear his throat, taking a swig of the beer that Rona had given him from the private stock she kept squirrelled away in the pantry. 'I wished to apologise for the way I reacted over the baby.'

'Oh!' Something seemed to melt inside Cathie. 'Do you really mean that?'

'I most certainly do, darling. Ma was right to say that I'm a little less patient than I used to be. Although it was something of a shock to learn of your plan to adopt in quite such an unexpected way.'

'I'm sure it was. So sorry about how I handled the matter.

I made a real mess of it, I know.' Cathie at once launched into an apology for not having told him earlier.

'And I apologise because I didn't feel ready to start a family so soon,' he said. 'Also for my reluctance to be responsible for someone else's child. That's probably because returning to Civvy Street is not proving easy. I have yet to find a job, a home of my own, and to settle into some sort of routine. That could take time. Nevertheless, I have no wish to lose you, sweetheart.'

'Oh, I do understand,' Cathie said, her tone somewhat breathless, even though she felt utterly bemused and startled by his sudden change of heart. What could have brought it on? 'I've no wish to rush you down the aisle, as I explained to your mother. In any case, I now have permission to foster little Heather, although obviously I would need your support in order to adopt her. Were you ever to change your mind about marrying me, that is.' She could feel a flush of heat starting up in her cheeks. Had she said too much?

'As a matter of fact I've been applying some serious thought to the matter,' Alex was saying, giving Cathie a gentle smile as he patted her hand. 'The point is, I may have been a little hasty in making such snap decisions. It's certainly the case that I do wish to feel free to get out and about more, but your mother has generously agreed to babysit for us whenever she can.'

'Really?' Cathie gazed upon the smirk of pleasure on Rona's face in astonishment. If only she was as generous towards her daughter as she was with a man.

'I do still wish to marry you, sweetheart, if you'll have me.'

'Oh, Alex, yes please! Of course I will.' Happiness exploded within as Cathie flung herself into his arms, and the pair of them kissed and made up. She felt quite unable to believe this turn in her good fortune. 'Shall I bring little Heather down so you can give her a cuddle and get to know her better?'

'If you wish,' he said, looking slightly startled by the suggestion.

On her way back upstairs to fetch her, Cathie saw how Rona turned to Alex with a seductive little smile, as was her way. 'Would you like a little bread and butter pudding?' she asked. 'I baked this, too.'

What a fantasist she was, Cathie giggled to herself. But how amazing that she now had full support from them both.

* * *

Davina sat on the edge of her bed fidgeting madly, the next minute dashing to the window to see if he was coming yet. Alex had left a note earlier, promising to be here by seven o'clock. It was already nearly half past and still there was no sign of him. Did he intend to dump her as well as silly Cathie? But why would he? They'd been seeing each regularly ever since Christmas, and not for a moment had he suspected that bringing the matter of the baby to his attention had been entirely her idea. Or that she'd lied to the manservant by claiming her to be Cathie's child.

Davina felt a small degree of guilt for the way she'd deliberately upset the infant by depriving her of food for most of Christmas Day, as well as her precious teddy bear. But some things were far more important than keeping a baby happy. She had her own future to think of, and sharing Alex with that red-headed fool was not part of it.

Hearing a knock on the door she leaped to her feet. Her landlady, Mrs Phillipson, marched straight in, as she tended to do, with no regard for a person's privacy.

'There's a young man downstairs wanting to see you.'

'Oh, thank you so much,' Davina said, making a move to rush down the stairs and fetch him that instant.

'You'll need your coat, as it's freezing cold out, and you certainly can't invite him in. I won't have any of that carry-on in my house,' the woman told her, a sour expression of disapproval on her wrinkled face.

'Oh, no, of course not,' Davina said, striving to hide her disappointment. She grabbed her coat and scarf and obediently followed Mrs Phillipson downstairs where she explained to Alex how they would have to go out, as they couldn't stay here.

Casting a furious glance in the direction of the landlady who stood with her arms folded, deliberately blocking the foot of the stairs, Alex took Davina's arm and led her out into the pouring rain. Within minutes, they were running along Bridge Street towards the Pack Horse, laughing as they bounced through the door, soaking wet.

Davina couldn't have cared less about her wet hair,

or that she hadn't properly buttoned up her coat and her dress was soaked too. All that mattered was that Alex had arrived, at last. She found a corner where they could snuggle up close, watching with her heart in her eyes as he went to order drinks at the bar.

'Sorry I was late. Been a bit busy. But I've missed you, sweetheart,' he told her, as he finally returned with a glass of wine each, and settled himself beside her.

'It feels like a lifetime since I saw you last, even if it was only a week.'

'Then let me remind you of it,' he said, giving her a quick kiss.

Davina gave a soft groan. 'I need far more than that, but Mrs Phillipson, my dictator of a landlady, would never allow it. What about your place?'

Alex shook his head. 'With Ma and Pa around? Not a chance. We'll have to think of some other solution. Perhaps a visit to the Midlands Hotel some time, or one out of town where no one will know us.'

Davina flickered from a thrill of anticipation to a puzzled frown. 'Why would that matter? We're a couple, aren't we? You aren't even engaged to that silly wench anymore, so what's the problem?'

Instead of answering, he slipped an arm about her shoulders and kissed her again, at first soft and then much harder. 'You're so gorgeous. Irresistibly lovely.'

She couldn't help but giggle with delight, wrapping her arms about his waist to hold him close, before noticing people were glancing their way and giving little sniggers. Alex also glanced about him at the crows packing the bar, and eased himself off her. 'It's a bit busy here. We'll find somewhere quieter next time. In fact, I can think of somewhere right now, once it stops raining.'

Fortunately, they found that the rain had indeed stopped as they came out of the pub later. The night was now cold and frosty, but Davina made no objection when Alex decided they should take a short walk towards the canal. Moments later, he led her down a flight of stone steps to a cobbled platform beside the lock, lit by an old street lamp. A wooden footbridge, leading to the towpath opposite, spanned the canal. But just before this was a bench set in the lea of a wall topped by metal posts. Dropping on to the seat, he pulled her to him. Davina happily straddled his lap, quivering with passion as he at once began to kiss and caress her face, neck and breasts, then quickly pushed himself inside her, gasping in his urgency.

'What would I do without you?' he sighed when he finally released himself, sinking back and giving a little shudder, although whether from the cold or the thrill of their coupling she wasn't too sure.

'What indeed?' she whispered, sliding her hand between his legs. 'Can we do that again, please, a little slower this time?' It was so wonderful that she'd won him back. All she needed to do now was to persuade him to marry her. And this was a pretty obvious way to achieve that dream.

* * *

Watching Alex scuttle out through the door of the pub with his arm still wrapped about the girl, Steve battled with himself to sit tight and not race after the fellow to punch his nose in, rather as he'd done to him that time. What a bastard! How could he treat Cathie so abominably? She was a lovely girl, so sweet and kind, if rather shy and nervous as a result of all the traumas she'd suffered in life.

Steve could sympathise with that feeling as he'd suffered quite a few traumas himself. There were days when images and memories haunted him: the sight of dead bodies lying around, the stench of burned flesh, guns blasting and the sound of explosions. They would carry him back to a time he'd much rather not remember.

Even now his leg was aching or would sometimes feel stiff with pain despite no longer being there. The doctor assured him the problem would eventually ease, he just had to be patient. Patience had never been a part of his temperament in the past, certainly not with Cathie when they were kids together. But she'd proved to be such a good friend, helping him to deal with his injuries, that his feelings towards her had changed.

Oh, how he loved her! What he wouldn't give to have her love him instead of this idiot. But what could he do? Should he tell her that he'd seen her fiancé kissing another woman? Would she believe him? She rarely believed a word he said, because of the foolish jokes he used to play on her. Yet he also understood the emotional trauma of losing someone you loved. A subject he preferred not to dwell upon.

But, as far as he was aware, their relationship was now over, and they were no longer engaged, so he was probably worrying unduly. This woman might well have been the real reason Alex had called it off, and nothing to do with the baby at all.

All he could do, Steve decided, was to keep an eye on the bloke, and watch how things developed. Then he'd make whatever decision seemed appropriate.

Chapter Eleven

Alex kicked his feet against the cold as he paced back and forth down the alley. Where was the blighter? The chap was supposed to be here by ten o'clock. Glancing at the clock through the post office window, he saw that it was almost half past. Frustration and anger pulsated through him. Maybe this had been a bad idea. What if a policeman spotted him, and arrested him for loitering? Not a pleasant prospect. He'd thought this scheme worth the risk in an effort to make some real money, which was in desperately short supply. Now he was beginning to wonder if this Eddie fellow had led him down the garden path.

Alex heard the roar of an engine and, nerves jittering, quickly stepped back into the shadows. The delivery van drew to a halt and, as the driver jumped out, he left the door swinging open before plunging into the post office. The agreement was that he would do that while he went in to ask directions.

Wasting no more time on second thoughts or doubts, Alex sprinted to the van, dragged out the couple of boxes that had been left strategically placed and, after placing a fiver on the driver's seat, carried them away at speed. Within seconds he was back in the shadows of the alleyway, and could hear the driver calling out a thank you to the postmistress, before leaping back into the van and driving off. In just two minutes, the chap had earned himself five quid. Not a bad morning's work.

Heart beating madly, Alex looked down at the two large boxes he'd tucked behind a dustbin and burst out laughing. So what had he earned? This wasn't the moment, or the place, to investigate. He lifted the boxes back into his arms and marched smartly away, heading for the allotment where his late grandfather used to grow vegetables and keep hens. In theory it now belonged to his Aunt Mary and Uncle Joe, but, being quite old now, neither of them spent much time there. Having helped himself to the key from the kitchen rack, he let himself into the shed where he deposited his booty.

When he opened the boxes up, Alex was delighted to see that they were packed with cigarettes and cigars, exactly as he had hoped. Not only that, but also a small parcel of lighters, quite pretty ones in silver.

'How easy was that?' he chuckled to himself, convinced that he could sell all of this stuff for an excellent price, with the assistance of his new mate, Eddie. Life was definitely on the up and up.

A few days later, his inside pockets stuffed with notes and the shed once more hosting only garden tools and seed potatoes, Alex decided to call upon Rona for a cup of tea, as he liked to do at this time of day. She was an intriguing and sexy woman, despite her age, most voluptuous and deliciously flirtatious. Not necessarily his type, but he did love to tease and flirt with her.

Today, when she handed him a mug of tea and a slice of cake she again claimed to have baked herself, despite it being in a box with the name Co-op written on it, he thanked her for helping him win Cathie back. 'Is she aware that you told me something of your family history, or at least the baby's, which I freely admit I found fascinating.'

Rona shook her head, giving a sly little grin. 'Nay, lad, that's just between you and me. I did think thee might change your mind when you learned of what was sitting in a bank account left by my late daughter's generous husband. The child is well provided for, so taking her on will not prove to be expensive.'

'That's something of a relief,' Alex admitted. 'Particularly considering the sad state of the economy and lack of jobs.'

'Aye, although it does work both ways. Bearing in mind the status and wealth of *your* family, I decided pairing the two of you off could bring nowt but good.'

Alex burst out laughing. 'Touché, then it's a deal, and it will be a secret well kept. I'd hate Cathie to think I was only marrying her for the money,' he said, a carefully bland expression marking his face. 'She's a lovely girl and I'm sure she'll make me a wonderful wife. I couldn't be happier.'

'Just make sure that you provide her with an equally wonderful husband. My own experience of marriage was not a good one, but I want Cathie's to be, particularly as the lass clearly loves you. I thought it might help for you to understand the financial situation with regards to little Heather. The child will cost you nowt.'

'Oh I do, I do, and will honour your wish to provide her with a good life.' At least to begin with, he thought, until I get my hands on that blessed cash. What happens after that rather depends on how I feel about being stuck with someone else's offspring. 'Now I have something for you,' he said, handing over one of the cigarette lighters as a gift. 'You deserve a present for helping to bring us together. I couldn't have achieved such a satisfactory result without you.'

'Ooh, don't mention it, lad,' Rona said, as she excitedly opened the box. 'I'm available to help at any time, in any way. Just say the word.'

'I'll remember that.'

* * *

Preparations for the wedding were progressing, if rather slowly. 'I'm afraid if you were dreaming of a rather grand ceremony, it's not going to happen,' Alex sadly informed Cathie. 'It will need to be quite a small celebration. The reason being that we'll have to pay for it ourselves.'

This came as no surprise to Cathie, as Rona certainly could not afford to finance a wedding, and if Alex's family had made no offer to do so either, there would be no other choice. Not that it troubled her in the slightest. Being Alex's wife was far more important to her than a fancy ceremony. And if his family didn't approve because of where she lived, or they still believed the baby to be hers, what did that matter? Let them think what they liked. At least Alex believed in her now.

'You should be aware that I don't have much in the way of savings, not now that I'm unemployed,' she told him. 'But I assume you still have some of your demob money left?'

'Er, I've spent quite a bit of it, as it was intended to allow me three months' leave before finding a job, which I badly needed since I've been overseas for so long.'

'Weren't you ever granted leave in Egypt?' she asked.

'Yes, we'd go to Cairo, but not very often. And, as I told you, I felt in dire need to get out and about and have some fun. But I assure you that there's sufficient money left to pay for a wedding, and a few months' rent in advance on a house or flat, once we find one.' He said nothing of the pot of cash he'd just earned from a little black marketing deal. The less said about that the better.

'We'll manage fine then,' Cathie assured him, giving him a kiss. 'We can keep costs low. I shall bake a simple, two-tiered wedding cake, and Mam has some little pottery pillars left over from her own wedding, which I can borrow to hold it in place.'

'What a talented lady you are,' he said, pulling her into

his arms to give her yet more kisses and fondle her soft breasts. She wriggled free, giving him a playful tap on the hand.

'Naughty, naughty, remember that patience is a virtue you must learn to cultivate.' She laughed. 'I also have some lengths of parachute silk to make into a wedding dress, which I've already started work on.'

Cathie thought of the way she and her mother had been using flawed parachute silk for some years to make their own underwear. But then this was the era of 'make do and mend'. She could only hope it would prove to be pretty enough to please him, when eventually he viewed her in it. 'I've dyed some of the parachute silk pale blue to make up into bridesmaid's dresses for Brenda and Davina.'

'Davina?' he asked, his eyes widening in surprise. 'Davina is to be one of your bridesmaids?'

'Of course, she's a good friend.'

He took a moment before asking, 'Even though she gave away your secret about the baby?'

Cathie frowned. 'What secret? Heather is not a secret. I just hadn't got around to explaining to you that I wished to adopt my baby niece.'

His mouth twisted into a little smirk. 'Except that Davina did plainly state the child was yours.'

'I think you misunderstood or misheard her. I explained it all to you at the time, so let's not keep going over that.' Alex looked almost relieved by this remark, which pleased her, although his comment was deeply puzzling. Surely he wasn't still suggesting that baby Heather was her child? Had he even listened properly to her explanation? It worried her at times that he seemed far more interested in kissing her than taking part in any sort of conversation between them. Was that the effect of war as well, or because of his loneliness over those long years abroad?

But, as he now seemed happy enough to walk out with her of an afternoon, even if he never touched the pram, let alone the baby, Cathie decided she would set the subject aside and concentrate on their future together. She too must be patient and allow him time to adjust to Civvy Street.

With the shortage of houses being what it was, the task of finding a home of their own was proving to be an impossible task. They walked mile upon mile, scouring every inch of Castlefield before moving on to other parts of Manchester. Here and there they might be offered a single room to rent, but Alex refused to even contemplate one of those, dismissing them all as dingy shambles. Cathie couldn't help but agree, yet that was the state of the entire country right now, a broken mess on the verge of bankruptcy.

It was becoming increasingly clear that they would have no choice but to move in with his parents. She certainly had no wish to live with Rona, particularly as she appeared to have developed a fancy for Alex. Her rapacious mother simply couldn't resist an attractive man.

'I'll speak to my parents, and let you know what they think,' Alex said. 'The house in St John Street is quite large, so perhaps they'll be willing to let us rent a couple of rooms on the top floor.'

'With the servants?' Cathie asked with a giggle.

'Possibly,' he agreed. 'Would that be a problem for you?'

'Not in the least! As long as I'm with you, darling, I really don't mind where I live. And at least your house will be clean.'

'Then assuming I get my parents' agreement, that's what we'll do until we can raise enough money to buy or rent some place of our own, which I'm sure we'll succeed in doing if we put our heads together and devise a plan. I'm working on it already. What about you? I don't suppose you have a pot of cash squirrelled away somewhere?'

Cathie burst out laughing. 'Now who's dreaming?'

* * *

'You want to bring that foolish girl to live here with *us*?' Dorothy snapped. 'Have you taken leave of your senses? I thought you'd ended that stupid engagement.'

'I'm delighted to say that it's on again,' Alex told his mother with an arrogant little smile. 'She's a very sweet girl, and does insist that the child is not hers, so I've decided to believe her.' That wasn't strictly true, but he had no wish to discuss any other reasons he might have of re-establishing their relationship, certainly not with his parents. They might be hard-working people, but possessed upper middle-class aspirations and were so greedy for money themselves that they'd always deliberately kept him short of cash. If he'd now latched on to ways of improving his own future without overtaxing himself, that was his business, not theirs.

As ever, his father chimed in with the same old question. 'Have you found yourself employment yet, son?'

'I've a few irons in the fire, so I should soon be in a better financial situation.' Not for a moment must Victor get wind of his black-marketeering schemes. Life was tough. The shortage of essential items not at all what he'd expected to find on his return. He surely had a right to a better life, not least a home of his own, a wife to care for him and a car? Neither the army nor the state had offered him much in the way of funds, so if the only way to achieve success was by taking part in these cunning little schemes with Eddie, why the hell not?

'When you do succeed in acquiring a job, let us know. We might then agree to you and your future wife moving in with us, although only for a short time until you find your own accommodation. But, as you will be required to pay us a proper rent, you'll need a job first. Is that clear?'

'Crystal,' Alex grunted, feeling almost as if he were a schoolboy again, coming home from his public school to be lectured for failing to achieve a high enough grade in his exams, or for not being top dog in the football or cricket team, debating society, or anything for that matter.

'With your background you should be head boy,' the imperious Victor would sneer. 'I certainly was.' Nothing he did seemed to please his father, who constantly accused him of being lazy and idle.

Thelma, their beloved and favourite daughter, could do no wrong in his eyes, being beautiful, married to a rich businessman, and with three children. Whereas he, as their only son, was subject to impossibly high expectations and constant criticism.

Even on the day he'd arrived home, Alex had found the house empty, with no welcome mat in place. Being a Sunday, his parents had gone off to church and then out to lunch at the Midland Hotel, ignoring the fact that their son was due home. They claimed he hadn't properly informed them of the time of his train, which may or may not be the case. Alex believed he had written to them, but couldn't be certain, as he'd long since given up worrying about pleasing his disapproving parents. Nevertheless, he should have accepted Cathie's invitation after all.

'You need to put more effort into your life, or you'll never achieve anything,' his father was now saying, his expression emitting a frown of disapproval.

He didn't seem to appreciate that Alex had nowhere to go, no home of his own, nothing to do, and little money coming in. Or that he was weary of being given orders and bossed around the entire time, as he had been all his damned life by this man, even before the army took over that role. Why should he buckle down and work his socks off for scarcely any pay? Surely he deserved more of a reward, having spent six years fighting a war, or at least being involved in one. He'd worked long and hard in a hot and scruffy mess tent in the desert, if not actually fighting and killing people. And he came home with barely a penny in his pocket. Yet the pompous Victor was not prepared to help in any way.

'Listen to what your father is saying,' his mother warned. 'In addition, do not for a moment consider adopting that child. Illegitimacy has become dreadfully commonplace throughout the war. I've heard of girls as young as fifteen finding themselves pregnant by soldiers, just because they see them as "our brave heroes".'

'Is that what you are?' his father caustically enquired. 'I somehow doubt it.'

Maybe it would be easier to stay with Rona, who, despite her obsession with herself, was far more sympathetic than his own parents.

* * *

Cathie was helping Steve organise a talent contest, his latest charity project. Feeling much more lively and happy, quite back to her old self as she lined up an excited group of children waiting to perform, she couldn't wait another minute to give him her good news. 'We're back together again,' she breathlessly announced.

Steve stared at her, stunned. 'What? How did that happen?'

Interrupted by a small boy leading his dog on stage, no more was said until the animal had performed a multitude of tricks and Cathie had helped catch it after the dog gave chase to another in the audience. This took some time and caused a great deal of laughter. Finally, directing the next entrants, two young girls on stage to sing, she then stepped back into the wings to take a rest and catch her breath.

'Mam invited Alex for tea, claiming to have actually done some cooking for once in her life. He was filled with apologies, and had clearly come round to a complete change of heart. So amazing.'

Steve could think of nothing to say, giving his attention to lining up a school choir, and indicating when the pianist should begin. 'Did you accept his offer?' he asked, as he returned to her side some moments later.

'Of course I did,' Cathie said with a laugh. 'I love him to bits.'

Steve ground his teeth, striving not to say how he'd like to see the fellow smashed into bits for being such a traitor to her. Taking a breath, his mind buzzing, he tentatively attempted to challenge her decision. 'Was that wise, after his rejection of your niece? Shouldn't you exercise a little more caution before agreeing to marry the chap?'

Cathie stared at him in bewilderment, her next comments interrupted this time by a surge of applause from the audience.

'I've just explained that he apologised,' she hissed, as she held back the curtain to allow the choir to make their exit.

'You shouldn't be too trusting.'

Three young men doing a juggling act were next in line and she quickly bustled them on stage, aware of Steve scowling disapprovingly behind her. 'Alex too has found it difficult to settle into Civvy Street,' she snapped. 'He became frustrated over the length of time it took for him even to be demobbed, just because he wasn't involved in any of the industries the government are currently supporting. Something to do with bolstering the economy, regardless of how long a man has been serving in the army. It's a policy that naturally creates resentment, so you have to sympathise with him over that. He also hates the fact that he cannot guarantee us a home of our own. He has, however, assured me of his love, so why would I not accept his proposal? Isn't everyone struggling to overcome these sort of problems?'

'That's certainly true,' Steve said, all too aware of how he blocked out his own emotional traumas. Maybe too much so at times. He started to tell the story of what he'd seen at the Pack Horse, but laughter and loud clapping from the audience in response to a young comedian cracking jokes, drowned what he was trying to say. Cathie shook her head, indicating she couldn't hear a word. There was little more opportunity to talk as the judging began, tears of those rejected had to be wiped, while those still in the competition were called in to repeat their performance.

At the end of the show Steve happily announced the winners and the substantial sum of money they'd raised for the local orphanage. But it was not until the audience had filed out to hurry off home and the pair of them were tidying up, that he quietly remarked, 'I do understand what you're saying, Cathie. People don't always react quite as you expect to problems caused by war. I remember seeing old friends cross the street rather than speak to me, perhaps not quite knowing what to say, or anxious to avoid any further sad news.'

Cathie was shocked. 'How very unfeeling of them.'

Steve gave a sigh of resignation. 'It's an attitude you have to learn to live with. You certainly soon discover who your real friends are, as you have proved to be.'

She squirmed a little, feeling she really hadn't been quite so generous or patient with him as she perhaps should have been, in view of their past differences. Yet had felt the need to do what she could to help.

'When I came home I had to wait six months for an artificial limb, at first spending my days confined to a wheelchair, my father lifting me in and out of it. That was very kind and noble of him but left me feeling trapped and very dependent. Mum would fuss over me far too much too, feeding me a constant string of meals, which also began to grate on my nerves. I'd have been as fat as a pig if she'd had her way. Finally, I started a slow recovery with a peg leg, then when I was fitted with my artificial limb no one knew about my injury, as apart from a slight limp it wasn't visible. Many people accused me of avoiding active service, of being a conscientious objector.'

'Oh, that's dreadful, almost like those women who handed out white feathers during World War One to people who'd likewise been injured.'

'Quite! They couldn't see my pain either, as it doesn't turn you purple. I'd have difficulty even getting on to a bus. Once, losing patience with the time it was taking me, the conductor rang the bell and the bus set off with me only half on. Unable to quickly jump off, I fell. He stood on the platform laughing, as if I were simply a drunken idiot.'

'How utterly heartless some people are.'

He shrugged. 'Some soldiers do turn to drink to overcome their injuries. Thankfully, I managed to avoid doing that. Once I got the hang of it, things did become a lot easier. Although now I'm treated exactly as if I were normal, which can still at times cause problems. So, like yourself and many others, I settle for not mentioning the problem. Best to keep quiet, and battle on regardless.'

'You are so brave.' Cathie was suddenly filled with admiration for this one-time nuisance of a friend. He didn't even hold any resentment against the Germans who had dropped the V1 rocket in the first place. He would say that those men were only doing their job, as he was doing his.

'And as I've said before, war can cause disruption in a relationship, which is sometimes—'

'Fortunately not in mine,' she said with a smile, interrupting him. And as she launched into a description of their plans for the wedding, Steve found himself sinking into a gloomy silence. She clearly wasn't prepared to listen and, for all he knew, it could well have been a goodbye kiss Alex had given the girl in the pub, so why upset Cathie if that was the case? What right did he have to interfere in her life? Probably none at all. 'I just want you to be happy,' he lamely remarked, hating himself for being such a coward.

'Why would I not be?' she asked with a laugh. 'I am at last to marry the man I love.'

It was not a decision Steve felt he had the right to dispute. How could he possibly say that he thought she'd fallen for the wrong man?

Chapter Twelve

'Did you really offer to babysit?' Cathie asked Rona one day, as she sat making a list of what needed to be done to prepare for the wedding. You always refuse when *I* ask you, and I have to get Brenda to babysit if Alex and I wish to enjoy an evening out together. So what changed your mind? Presumably because *he* asked you.'

'He's a lovely young man, so why would I refuse him anything?' her mother remarked with a casual shrug.

It was the kind of reply that caused a shudder to shimmer down Cathie's spine. She recalled how close Rona and Alex would sit when chatting by the fire. How her mother had made an enormous effort to produce a meal for him when she hated cooking with a venom, never having lifted a finger to help in the house in years.

Nor had Cathie failed to notice the smiles and winks exchanged between the two of them, even though Rona probably believed herself unobserved. How many times in the past had she witnessed similar scenes, when men had called round to be cosseted by her attractive mother? Wasn't that the reason why her father had left his wife, since most of those flirtations had gone on to develop into affairs? And where was her poor father now? She wished she knew. Even Auntie Evie had no idea where her brother was, as she hadn't seen or heard from him in years.

A chill settled within Cathie. The prospect of her mother engaging in an affair with her own fiancé made her gag. It really didn't bear thinking of. She took a breath to steady herself, struggling to keep her voice calm. 'I'm grateful that you're prepared to be helpful at last, Mam. So long as you remember that Alex is to be *my* husband, not a plaything of yours.'

Rona chuckled as she lit a cigarette with a pretty silver lighter. 'Are you suggesting that I might try to steal him from you?' she teased, looking gleeful. 'Now there's a challenge. If a man loves a woman, why would he look elsewhere?'

'Why indeed? He's *my* man, not *yours*. Just remember that. And please don't smoke in front of the baby.'

'I was just showing off me new lighter? Posh, eh? Expensive too, I should imagine. Alex gave it to me as a thank you gift for bringing you two back together. Ah, now isn't that generous of him?'

Cathie stared at Rona in disbelief. Alex had bought her mother a present? Yet he didn't even give her one at Christmas, beyond the offer of dinner with his family. Dear God, what was happening? Was she about to lose the love of her life to her own mother? 'You keep well away from him, right?'

'Oh, so you won't be needing a babysitter after all then?' Rona asked, her eyes wide with mock innocence.

'I don't think I'll take the risk of having you hovering around, not when I know how you ruined Dad's life. I certainly won't have you ruining mine in the same way.' And, having said her piece, Cathie picked up the baby and escaped for their regular afternoon walk, leaving her mother chortling with laughter, as if she'd found the conversation highly amusing.

Why on earth had she been blessed with such a witch of a woman?

* * *

When Cathie next returned it was to find Alex locked in conversation with her mother yet again. Their heads were nearly touching as they sat huddled together by the tiny fire flickering in the grate. It troubled her deeply to see them so friendly. How could she ever trust Rona, as she was completely without any sense of morals? But Alex seemed to call in at all times of the day, which was surely to see her, not Rona, so perhaps she was reading too much into this.

He smiled up at her. 'I just popped in to ask if we could change our plans and bring the wedding forward. Your mother thinks that is an excellent idea. Do you agree?'

'How can we do that?' Cathie said, utterly astonished by such a suggestion. 'Everything is arranged, the Co-op room booked and paid for, the church and vicar informed.

And I've really no wish to again be accused by your mother of rushing you to the altar. Why would you want to bring it forward?'

'You know that I can hardly wait to marry you, sweetie, and when we do it really has nothing to do with Ma. So let's run off and do it now, right away, with no fuss. We could elope, if you like.'

Cathie giggled as she kissed him. 'No, darling, I think we should be patient. The ceremony is but a few weeks off. Surely you can wait a little longer?'

Giving a little groan, he put his head in his hands, as if something was deeply troubling him.

'What's the problem? What is bothering you?'

'The truth is, I spoke to my parents but they have refused to offer us accommodation. Even if I managed to talk them round they would charge us the earth in rent. My imperious father is insisting that I get a job first, without appreciating how difficult that is and unwilling to help in any way. We deserve a home of our own, a real future, yet no one is doing anything to help, not the government, not the forces, not even my own parents. No one! Only the Salvation Army helps ex-servicemen by supplying them with blankets, clothes and food, and even shelter. No one else does a damn thing.'

Putting her arms around his stiff shoulders, Cathie gave him a warm hug. 'It will happen. You'll find a job soon, I'm sure of it.'

'At least you have faith in me, sweetie. I believe we'll

get lucky too, and make our fortune one day. I dream of buying a car, of moving to one of those planned garden cities. We'll enjoy a wonderfully comfortable, rich life.'

Cathie smiled as she rocked the baby on her lap, striving to go along with his dreams. 'That sounds lovely, but it might take a while. In the meantime, your father is right. We both need to find employment. What sort of job are you looking for? We have to ask ourselves what kind of skills we have. Mine has been with checking tyres, but as there are no jobs for women in that area now, I have to think of something else. I'm certainly open to offers. What about you?'

'Lord, now you're beginning to sound like him.'

She chuckled. 'Right now we can't even afford to rent a house, so we must keep searching for work. I shall go round all the factories and shops yet again, starting first thing in the morning.'

'There's really no need for you to do anything. I would prefer my wife to stay at home and be a true woman. So the sooner we marry the better.'

Giving a sad little shake of the head, Cathie said, 'Not if you don't have a job. Maybe we should postpone the wedding for a little while, if finding work or training of some sort is becoming a serious problem.'

'Good Lord, no, I can't bear to contemplate doing such a thing. I wish I had more money saved, and then we could marry tomorrow. I don't suppose you have some, by any chance?'

Cathie thought of how much she'd spent preparing a wonderful Christmas for him, and how it had all been wasted, including the precious goose. 'I'm afraid I have very little in the way of savings left. Have you been down to the job exchange recently and enquired about retraining?'

Before he could answer, Rona, who'd been sitting silently throughout this discussion, suddenly chipped in. 'You do have savings, chuck. Quite a stash of money in the bank left to you by our Sally, so why not use that?'

Cathie almost jerked out of her chair with shock. How dare her mother suggest such a thing? 'That money wasn't left to me, or by Sally, as you know full well. It's for Heather, left to her by her father. I have no right to it at all.'

'Aye, you do, if you're caring for their child,' Rona said.

'I second that,' Alex agreed, his eyes glinting with interest.

'Then you're both wrong. The money is for Heather's future, not mine. It is being saved for when she grows up and needs a home of her own. Were her parents still with us she would be living with them, in the house that Tony would have bought with the money, and then would have left to her as his heir. I certainly have no intention of stealing it from her.'

'I think you should look upon it as borrowing, not stealing,' Alex pointed out. 'Which, since my parents have refused to help in any way, may well prove to be necessary if you are to give this child a home.'

'I'm sorry, but it simply isn't possible.'

'I see, well then we'll all have to squeeze in here.'

'So be it.' Cathie glanced across at the smirk of satisfaction on her mother's face. It was plain to see that the last thing Rona wanted was to be left to live alone. She'd have to do all the cooking and cleaning for herself then. But living with her mother would not be easy. 'We'll somehow have to cope,' Cathie said, stifling a sigh of resignation.

* * *

'He must be so keen and very much in love,' Brenda said, as they sat stitching the gowns together one evening while Cathie told her friends of Alex's eagerness for them to marry as quickly as possible. They were almost finished and looking quite classy. The bridesmaids' dresses had been dyed a pretty pale blue, and the bridal gown was in white silk with a short train, each with three-quarter length sleeves and a sweetheart neckline. They were the kind of dresses that could easily be shortened into something more practical after the ceremony. As she smoothed out the gowns to admire them, Cathie was really quite thrilled with how lovely they looked. She still had a veil to make, some sort of headdress, and a posy to buy, but everything was coming along really well.

'The wedding may well be brought forward, were Alex to find himself a job.' Cathie made no mention of the slight disagreement she'd had with him about money, which she considered to be strictly private. 'It's what he wants.'

Davina made no comment to this news, being even

quieter than usual today. Cathie wondered if perhaps the prospect of attending a wedding was upsetting her friend, bearing in mind that she was still grieving for her late husband. 'Are you all right, Davina? Do let me know if this is all too much for you.'

'No, I'm fine. It's just that – actually – I have to go away for a while.'

'Oh, my goodness, you aren't going to miss the wedding, are you?' Brenda asked, sounding slightly annoyed. 'That would be such a shame after all the work we've done preparing for it, not to mention the cost of these lovely dresses.'

'I'll be back in good time, I promise.'

'Where are you off to? Have you found yourself a fella?'

'No, of course I haven't.'

'You aren't having family problems, are you? I've been suffering from those, my brother-in-law claiming he has more right to my late husband's property than I do, which is probably fair enough. But Jack did want me to have a secure future, which I no longer have despite what it states in his will. It's a legal nightmare. So what are your problems?'

Giving a dismissive little shrug, Davina turned back to her sewing. 'It's just something I have to do.' As usual, she said nothing more, giving no indication of what this mysterious trip might be about.

Brenda frowned, looking cross, but Cathie was filled with pity for her friend. 'I'll put the kettle on. It's time we had a cuppa,' she said. Whatever was troubling poor Davina it would be entirely wrong to interrogate her on the subject. Hadn't she herself suffered enough to appreciate that some problems were entirely personal? Not least the way her mother was behaving.

* * *

'I can't believe that you're really going ahead with this marriage. Are you sure it's the right thing to do?' Steve asked, feeling a curl of misery unfold within. This was yet another of their charity events, this time running a whist drive in the upstairs room at The Donkey. It had become a vital part of his life, particularly as Cathie was willing to help him and occupied such an even larger place in his heart.

'Why would it not be? I've already told you that we love each other.'

'Are you absolutely certain about that?' They'd spent the last half-hour setting out tables and chairs, but as their guests would be arriving any minute, was this the right time to tell Cathie that he'd spotted her fiancé with another girl one night in the Pack Horse? And what would be her reaction? Would it cause her to have second thoughts? Or would she be so furious with him for making such an accusation that she might banish him from her life entirely? Steve didn't dare to imagine how he would cope if that were to happen. Although how he would live with her being married to that selfish idiot was an even worse prospect. He decided to try another tactic.

'You've seen very little of Alex due to the years he's spent overseas. Not only that but you've been apart quite a bit ever since he returned home. I'm suggesting that you need to allow yourself more time to get to know each other properly again. Marriage is for life, after all.'

'How depressingly negative you are,' Cathie said. 'The war is over and it's time to be upbeat and think positive.'

'Maybe I'm just being realistic. Separation can damage and even destroy a relationship, particular during wartime.'

'Fortunately that hasn't happened with us,' she said, snapping down a pack of cards on a table.

Steve gave a puzzled frown. 'So you have no objection to him accusing you of giving birth to an illegitimate child, despite explaining that Heather is your niece?'

She stopped setting out more packs to glower at him. 'There was simply a misunderstanding over what Davina had said when she brought Heather that day. The poor girl was in a panic and probably didn't say quite the right thing.'

Stifling a sigh, Steve felt as if he was banging his head against a brick wall. Why wouldn't she listen to reason? Cathie was far too patient and tolerant for her own good at times. 'Many people are already beginning to regret hasty marriages that took place at the start of the war, so rushing off to the altar is not necessarily a good idea.'

'Now you're beginning to sound like his mother.'

'Sorry, I didn't mean to. But relationships have changed so much because of these long separations that there has been an increase in affairs, and in the number of illegitimate children.' His mind seemed to be in turmoil as he tried to decide how much to tell her. How much should he tell her?

'Are you suggesting that *I* have been unfaithful to him? That I'm some sort of slut? How dare you?!'

Steve felt the colour drain from his face. Had he said it all wrong? He hadn't meant Cathie at all. He'd been trying to broach the subject of Alex's possible affair without actually naming names. 'No, that's not what I'm saying. I'm not accusing you of any such thing. But some women left alone at home, believing they might never see their loved one again, are perhaps tempted to turn to another man for comfort. You need to remember that people have been living lonely lives in dangerous times with no certainty of survival. Affairs happen when a couple are driven apart by war. Many servicemen too have sought to satisfy their needs elsewhere, particularly when drafted overseas. Some of them consider it to be a perfectly acceptable thing to do.'

Cathie gave a snort of derision. 'It may have skipped your attention that most men are happy to remain faithful to the girl they love, and do not engage in affairs.'

'I don't deny that is generally the case, but many do stray.' Maybe he should tell her of the number of rubber sheaths automatically issued to all servicemen to protect them from VD? Somehow it didn't seem quite an appropriate subject to share with a woman, even though the authorities cared little about them. In their view it was only important that servicemen remained healthy enough to fight.

Gazing at her in a complete state of confusion, Steve struggled to decide how to deal with this problem, the list of rules he was holding in his hand quite forgotten. Was he prepared to stand back and do nothing while the girl he loved ruined her life? Even if she didn't feel the same way about him, Cathie surely had a right to happiness and to be treated with respect by the man she did love. But what right did he have to interfere in her life?

Taking a breath, he said, 'I'm just asking how you can be certain that Alex has remained faithful to you. I rather suspect he might not have been.'

'What? How dare you accuse him of such a thing!' After tossing the remaining packs of cards on to the table, Cathie stormed out.

Steve put his head in his hands and groaned. He'd said too much, or maybe not enough. He'd put forward his point of view in entirely the wrong way. Had he now lost her from his life? Maybe he should have named names, after all, or given her examples from his own experience. Sadly, thanks to the constant arguments Cathie had witnessed as a child between her own parents, she was far too wary of creating serious disputes herself. That was probably the reason she would never challenge Alex on the question of his fidelity. Dear Cathie believed that a peaceful and close relationship was essential, and was far too trusting as a result. He knew that well enough from all the times he'd teased and taken advantage of that attitude by playing jokes on her when they'd been kids, something he now regretted. Now it was him she'd deserted, not Alex.

* * *

Outside, across the street, Alex watched as Cathie walked away. So the pair of them were still seeing each other, allegedly involved in charity work together. He'd rather suspected as much. No wonder she wished to postpone the wedding rather than bring it forward. Maybe she was as much in two minds about who to marry as he was, although he really had no wish to lose her. Davina might be more voluptuous and beautiful, but Cathie would make a much better wife, being quite a domestic goddess. She could also offer other benefits, not least sufficient cash to buy them a house, even if he did have to suffer that child in order to gain possession of it.

The door opened and Steve Allenby came out to gaze after her departing figure, looking strangely sad and upset. But if this stupid man was getting in his way, he needed to be dealt with. He'd give that some thought. Right now, he had more urgent matters on his mind.

* * *

'Why didn't you tell me you were going to be a bridesmaid at my wedding?' Alex asked Davina, giving a throaty chuckle.

She stared at him in angry frustration, not quite able to take in what he was saying. 'What are you talking about?

It's true that Cathie did ask me to be her bridesmaid, when we were once having a snack at the market café, but that was ages ago before you'd even arrived home. You were still engaged then. Why would she ask me now as there's to be no wedding, and you're a free man?' She rolled over to look at him more closely, noticing how he was avoiding her gaze, although there was generally nothing Alex liked more than to study and explore her nakedness.

They'd spent the night together at the Midland Hotel, one of Alex's favourite places to dine, being rather grand and stylish, and now also for more intimate reasons. They only occasionally called at the Pack Horse these days, which pleased her greatly, as Davina much preferred making love in a warm bed rather than on a freezing cold bench by the canal. Who wouldn't, for goodness sake?

Rising from the bed Alex reached for his trousers and began to quickly dress. 'As a matter of fact I was just about to tell you that Cathie and I have made up. The wedding is to go ahead, after all. So I suppose by rights this will be our final get-together, at least for a while.'

The silence following this remark went on for what to Davina felt like a lifetime. Sitting up quite straight with her breasts erect, she stared at him. 'Are you saying that you're choosing *her* instead of *me*?'

'Cathie and I have been engaged for years. A promise is a promise, as I've explained before.'

'Even though you prefer sleeping with me, and therefore love me more?'

'As I say, that will have to stop, at least for now. Maybe we can get together again some time in the future, once all the wedding celebrations are over.'

'So you see me as mistress material, not as a future wife,' she snapped, seeing the colour rise up his throat as he quickly buttoned his shirt. Then reaching for his tie, he gave a harsh little laugh.

'What was your job, exactly, before you came to Castlefield, or even met me in London? Did it involve keeping other servicemen happy? That was the impression I got, particularly as you used to require some payment for the time we spent together, certainly at first.'

Fury ricocheted through her. 'How dare you! Are you accusing me of being a whore?'

'No, I believe you were a professional prostitute. Isn't that true?'

She grabbed hold of the pillow and flung it at him in fury, then put her face in her hands and burst into tears.

His arms were around her in seconds. 'Oh, sweetheart, I didn't mean to cause offence, really I didn't. It doesn't trouble me in the slightest if that was how you were once obliged to earn your living. We soldiers needed that kind of comfort. Besides, you are a gorgeous girl and I love you dearly, but…'

'But obviously I'm not the kind of person you'd wish to marry,' she sobbed. 'Even though I'm carrying your child?'

His arms dropped from her as he took a step back from

the bed. 'Dear God, that can't be true. Didn't I always make sure that I used proper protection?'

'Which doesn't always work, or maybe that time on the train you forgot. Anyway, I'm definitely pregnant. That being the case, I'm the one you must marry, not bloody Cathie.'

Chapter Thirteen

It was a glorious sunny afternoon and Cathie and Brenda were taking little Heather, now a lively toddler who was barely still for five minutes, out for a stroll in her pram. They'd gone along Liverpool Road, over Prince's Bridge, under the railway arches and were now walking along East Ordsall Lane heading for Peel Park.

'Have you seen Steve lately?' Brenda asked.

Cathie shook her head. 'Not for ages. I confess that I regretted walking out on him before I'd even reached the end of the street, but decided I'd no wish to return and apologise. Steve may only have been showing concern out of friendship, but really had no right to make such an accusation. Alex would never do such a thing to me. Our marriage will be a happy one, and any difficulties we're facing now are only as a result of the war.'

Cathie felt in her heart that Alex loved her. He'd told her so a dozen times since he came home, and they'd been engaged for years. Surely just by the way he was so eager to make love to her proved the strength of his feelings, although she had managed to hold him back to a safe level.

Brenda didn't respond until they'd wheeled the pram through the gates into the park, a vista of glorious green lawns and pathways opening up before their eyes. 'Even if Steve is wrong about Alex having an affair, he may have a point about not rushing into marriage too soon, Cathie, because of the long separation you've both endured. Many young wives at the rubber factory have lived to regret falling for the excitement of a hasty marriage, and are now discovering that their returning hero is not as they remembered, or had hoped for. Some of these ex-servicemen are suffering badly from nightmares or have become a bit violent.'

'Alex is the kindest of men and not violent in any way.' Even as she said these words she recalled how he'd attacked Steve, unleashing his temper in a fight. 'But we aren't rushing into anything,' she protested, desperately pushing this worry aside. 'You seem to be making the same point as Steve, and Alex's mother, and might well be right. I would be sorry to postpone the wedding after all the years I've longed for Alex's return, let alone the effort we've put into preparing for it. But in all honesty, Brenda, finding a job does feel far more urgent.'

'I agree,' her friend said, giving a wry grimace.

'Unfortunately, Alex still hasn't found employment either so I've suggested that waiting a little longer to marry might be sensible in the circumstances, and surely wouldn't do us any harm. It would also allow him time to settle back into civilian life, as well as for us both to save up a bit more money.'

'And did he agree?'

Cathie frowned a little as she struggled to remember whether he had or not. She rather thought he hadn't, as money did seem to be an issue with him, but didn't like to admit that to Brenda. She was seeing him that evening, so could surely persuade him to come round to her way of thinking. 'I'm sure he will wait because he loves me and wants a good future for us.'

Brenda fell silent as they walked over to the play area. 'I hope you're right, darling. War can change a man. Some women find that they themselves have changed, and are no longer in love with the husband they haven't seen in years.'

'That is most certainly not the case with Alex and me,' Cathie retorted, not admitting to the sense of distance she sometimes felt between them even now, after all these months he'd been home. Admittedly, the misunderstanding over little Heather had not helped.

'Some women were so lonely during the war that they did engage in little flings, often with Yanks, as Alex has accused you of doing. But then there was a huge ignorance about sexual matters.'

'Oh, indeed, including my own,' Cathie admitted with a chuckle as she sat little Heather in a baby swing. 'Rona never did explain anything about sex or contraception. Whatever I've managed to learn over the years has come from chatting with you and other friends at school or work.'

They were both laughing now, and even the baby joined

in the fun, although thankfully due to the joy of the swing as she didn't comprehend the joke.

'I remember warnings that you could get pregnant just by sitting on a man's lap,' Brenda chuckled, 'or climbing into a bath previously occupied by your brother or father. Even a French kiss was said to be dangerous.'

'But then others claimed that the first time you had intercourse with a man, you couldn't possibly get pregnant.'

'I do so wish that was true,' Brenda said, a hollow sound in her tone of voice now as she leaned against the frame of the swings.

'Why do you say that?'

'Don't ask. It's a long story with a heartbreaking end as I lost my husband as well as my child.'

'Oh, Brenda, I had no idea.' With her constant toing and froing she'd been fully aware that her old friend was suffering from family problems, but this was the first indication that she'd lost a child. 'How dreadfully sad.'

'Such is life. As I say, it's a horror story best forgotten.' She forced a smile back on to her round face. 'Judging by the number of girls who suddenly go off to spend time with some unknown aunt, that has most definitely been proved to be a complete fantasy.'

Listening to her friend with a growing sadness in heart at this small glimpse of her grief, Cathie made a private vow never to be so stupid. Nor did she believe Alex would cheat on her, despite what Steve might suspect, or her stupid mother's obvious efforts to flirt with him. He was an attractive man and a brave soldier, so girls, even an older woman, might well fling themselves at him. Rona's own passion for affairs was well known, but that didn't mean Alex would engage in one with her. At least Cathie sincerely hoped so.

Shaking her head in despair, she lifted a wriggling toddler out of the swing to let her run about on the grass, all too aware that her lack of trust in her own mother had built up over a lifetime. Maybe she should speak to Rona again to make sure she behaved properly.

As they each played with the lively youngster as she ran round and round, Cathie remembered the key Brenda had sent her with the belated Christmas card, and fumbled in her pocket for it. 'I forgot to return this,' she said, holding it out to her.

Her friend shook her head. 'No keep it, just in case you ever need it. I have to go away again.'

'Why would I? I'm to be married soon.' Seeing the doubt in Brenda's gaze, she said, 'All right, I'll be married before too long, and I accept that the question I must now face is should I ask Alex for assurance that he has indeed remained faithful while serving overseas.'

'Would he give you an honest answer if you did?' Brenda softly asked. 'Or might he assume you are simply taking retaliation for the fact *he* accused *you* of an affair with Steve. After all, he did punch him pretty hard in that fight.'

'Goodness, I hadn't thought of that. I really have no wish to create any further argument between them. I hate disputes. And that's the last thing I want when we should all be hoping for peace and happiness in life.'

'Steve, too, will be feeling a bit hurt as a result of your quarrel. He was only thinking of your happiness, darling. Wouldn't you miss him as a friend if you didn't make up?'

Cathie was surprised to feel a bleakness overwhelm her at such a prospect, although why would it matter if they didn't? Steve Allenby had teased and played tricks on her for years, so why should she listen to his advice now? Maybe because it made a certain sense. 'I suppose I would miss him, as an old friend, but he really had no right to say such things.'

'So will you ask Alex about his fidelity, or not?'

Cathie's only reply to that difficult question was to run and pick up little Heather who was chasing a pigeon across the lawn, then suggest they buy an ice cream before visiting the art gallery.

* * *

Alex was at the Co-op, where he asked to speak to the manager. 'I'd like to apologise for that fracas the other week, which was entirely personal but did get a bit out of hand,' he said, as he was shown into his office.

'Steve is a good man, and an excellent worker.' Mr Leeson frowned at him, looking most disapproving, which irritated Alex somewhat.

Alex gave a wry smile. 'Perhaps you've been fooled into thinking so. Were you aware that as a driver he allows spivs to help themselves to boxes of stuff from his delivery van?'

'What? That can't be true. Steven Allenby is as honest as the day is long.'

'I'm afraid not. He's in collusion with black marketeers. I witnessed such an event with my own eyes.' The man's expression, Alex noted with satisfaction, changed instantly.

Leeson closed the office door and offered him a seat. 'Tell me exactly what it was you saw.'

'Gladly.'

Alex proceeded to relate the incident of the delivery van pausing outside the post office, accusing Steve of being the driver and placing goods that belonged to the Co-op on the passenger seat, leaving the cab door open so they could be stolen. It was a complete fabrication, of course, the driver in question being someone entirely different. Nor did he reveal his own part in the operation or admit that he was the one who had robbed it of the two parcels left waiting for him. But the manager wouldn't know that. Alex could see that Leeson was convinced by the tale, as his jaw had tightened and his eyes narrowed with fury.

'Thank you for this information, Mr Ryman. Let's keep it confidential between ourselves, shall we, while I look into the matter? I've no wish for the Co-op to lose its excellent reputation.'

'You can be assured of my discretion.' As he was politely shown out the door, Alex thought he could not have wished for a better result.

* * *

Later, feeling rather pleased with himself, Alex sat with Davina on the bench by the canal, generally a quiet spot at this time of day, his mind racing as he compared the two women who occupied his life. He wondered which one he wanted the most, not easy to decide. Cathie was sweet natured and intelligent, and Davina stunningly beautiful and very sexy. Yet she was as poor as the proverbial church mouse, while Cathie had a stash of money tucked away that he fully intended to take control of one day. Once he was her husband he would have the power to do that. She would also be a much more caring wife. But what should he do about Davina?

How on earth she'd fallen pregnant he couldn't imagine, when he'd always taken the proper precautions. Maybe she was right, and he'd been so desperate for sex when he met her on the train home that he'd forgotten to protect himself.

But, as money was tight and difficult to come by in these post-war times, he had no intention of allowing her to spoil his plans.

'Are you sure marriage is what you want, sweetheart? You never used to show any interest in a domestic life when first we met. You were very much a gadabout girl.' She might claim to be a widow, but Alex had seen no proof of her ever having had a husband. When he'd first met Davina in a local pub close to the base in Salisbury, she'd been a young girl of eighteen, and the one to approach him. She'd asked if he was lonely, making it very clear by the way she'd smiled so seductively at him, what it was she was offering.

'One who jumped on the bandwagon to find myself a fella?' she cried. 'Don't insult me, Alex. I love you, and thought you loved me. And I'm pregnant, remember?'

'I do have sufficient funds to pay for an abortion, should you prefer.'

'Abortion is illegal.'

'It does still happen though, if a person can afford to pay, which would surely be the answer.'

'As you can see, I'm way beyond the point of that being possible. Time is running out as I'm nearly four months gone.' Pouting beguilingly, she began to stroke him, as he so loved her to do. 'But I'm still capable of a bit of loving, or are you saying that you no longer want me?'

'No, of course not.' He gasped as desire flushed through his loins at her touch. Dear God, what a temptress she was. How could he resist her? After quickly unbuttoning his flies, he whipped up her skirt and thrust himself inside her, satisfying his urges with lustful grunts and groans. There was something about the solitary terror of war that had made him need this sort of comfort more and more.

Afterwards, as they snuggled up together on the bench, still kissing and caressing, Davina licked her lips enticingly as she gazed into his eyes. 'If you have a bit of spare cash, I could do with some to buy myself one or two items for our coming wedding. Is that possible?'

Alex rummaged through his pockets and counted out a

few notes into her outstretched palm, thinking he'd need to do a bit more black market work in order to finance this problem he was now facing.

'Thank you, darling.' Then, wrapping her arms about his neck, she murmured, 'I knew you were only agreeing to go along with the wedding to Cathie out of a sense of duty, because of a promise you made years ago. But that was before you and I met, and it upset me greatly to think you still felt bound by it. Everything is different now and, as I say, time is of the essence. I'm doing my utmost to disguise my condition, Alex, but some folk are already beginning to give me funny looks.'

Panic hit him as he considered the ramifications of that. Not only his own reputation would be ruined if her condition became widely known, but that of his imperious father who'd be sure to disinherit him. He could lose everything, not only access to Cathie's bank account, but his right to inherit a share of his parents' wealth, which was considerable. It really didn't bear thinking about. 'Don't worry,' he quickly assured her. 'I'll call off the wedding with Cathie, and get a special licence so that you and I can marry quickly.'

What on earth had made him say such a thing? Was that the answer? Surely not. But what was the alternative?

Davina was squealing with delight. 'Oh, that would be wonderful! I do love you so much, darling.'

'And I you,' he said, starting to unbutton her blouse so he could make love to her all over again. Surely he deserved that, at least.

Later, when he'd fully satisfied his lust, Alex tidied himself and offered to take her home. 'I'm supposed to be meeting Cathie this evening, and the sooner I tell her this change of plan, the better, wouldn't you say?'

'Oh, yes, I do so agree.'

For once Davina made no excuses to linger as he walked her back to her lodgings, the excitement of his proposal making her skitter along excitedly beside him.

'Where will we live, darling?' she asked. 'Will your parents allow me to move in with you?'

The prospect of making such a request to them brought a shudder rippling down his spine. 'I think not. We'll find somewhere of our own to rent, I'm sure.'

'You could always stay here with me. Once we are wed, that is,' she giggled. 'Otherwise, Mrs Phillipson would never allow it.'

That didn't appeal to him either, his mind still buzzing about whether he really wanted to call off the wedding with Cathie. He did still feel a certain affection for her, even if she had been guilty of an affair with this Steve character. Although he should bear in mind that the pot of money the infant brought with her might prove she was indeed Cathie's niece. It was certainly a useful compensation for the unexpected addition of a child, and a good reason for marrying her. Why would he risk losing the possibility to gain such a benefit? Yet how on earth could he resolve this dilemma?

At the door of her digs, Alex gave Davina a lingering

goodbye kiss. She was hugging him tight, giggling with joy as he held her close to his chest. It was then that the door opened and the landlady appeared.

'I'll have none of that palaver on my doorstep. What would the neighbours think?'

'We've just got engaged,' Davina burst out. 'So surely that deserves a kiss or two.' After planting a quick goodbye kiss upon his cheek, she flounced past her landlady, chin held high, and marched briskly along the passage and up the stairs.

Turning back to Alex, the woman said, 'By heck, so a young man like you, whose bow-legged with brass, is willing to wed this little tart? Why would thee do such a thing?'

Alex could feel his face growing warm with embarrassment as she glared at him. The woman must know who he was, even if she was wrong about him personally being rich, since his father had always kept him short of cash. But she could easily be one of Victor's patients, which would do him no good at all. It was then that a possible solution popped into his head, almost out of nowhere. Having dealt with the problem of Cathie's ex-lover, he now needed to deal with his own.

He gave the landlady a sad little smile. 'I'm afraid I have no choice in the matter, Mrs Phillipson, since she's pregnant. We all make foolish mistakes under pressure of war, so thought I should do the right thing by her.' He watched with satisfaction as the woman's jaw dropped open with shock, even as her eyes melted with sympathy.

'I thowt there were summat wrong with her. Nay, lad, don't land yourself in even deeper water. Why should you pay the price for her stupidity? She got herself into this pickle. There are places for silly madams like her, and that's where she should go.'

'If it were possible for me to find her such a place, I would do so. Although I doubt it would be quite appropriate in the circumstances.' He gazed at her with a sad appeal in his eyes.

'Leave it to me.'

Then, lifting his hat in a polite goodbye, he turned on his heel and walked away. If he judged her right, the landlady would evict Davina without delay. And her remark about a home for unmarried mothers, which is presumably what she was referring to, was most interesting, although not something he should involve himself with. Fortunately, she seemed to have got that message, so it might be wise to make himself scarce for a little while, if that was at all possible. He'd have a word with Eddie, who would be sure to know of some place he could kip down for a while.

* * *

Cathie sat waiting at home with increasing anxiety. As the hours passed it became clear that Alex was not going to come this evening, as promised. Perhaps he'd been held up somewhere. When a knock came to the door, she ran to open it only to find a young boy standing fidgeting on the doorstep. He shoved a note into her hand, then scuttled off. Cathie quickly opened it and read the letter, torn between disappointment and relief.

'Sorry to let you down, sweetie, but I've heard of a few possible job vacancies that might be worth investigating, so may be away for a week or two. This might mean we will have to postpone the wedding for a little while, as you suggested. I'll be in touch later.

All my love,

Alex.

Goodness, the possibility of a job. How wonderful! Cathie felt a little disappointed that Alex hadn't come to tell her this news personally, and even that the wedding was indeed going to be postponed, after all. Yet a good job was exactly what he needed, as did she, and she intended to spend the extra time continuing with her search for one.

Chapter Fourteen

The next day, being a Saturday, Cathie went as usual to Campfield Market. A man walked by carrying a tray of fish on his head, which brought a pang of hunger to her belly, reminding her how tight money was right now. She couldn't afford to do much shopping, but it was a good idea to search out a few bargains. How she used to love coming here as a young girl with Aunty Evie when good food was easy to come by. They'd explore all the stalls then Cathie would help her aunt carry home shopping baskets loaded with onions, potatoes, carrots and cabbage, a string of shiny red polony sausage, pork chops and meat and potato pies, not to mention all manner of feathers and ribbons to trim one of her favourite hats.

If only she had the funds to do the same today. Oh, and what she wouldn't give for an orange or a banana, which were still rarely seen anywhere. She needed to buy wool to knit little Heather a cardigan, and soon she'd be needing new shoes, but Cathie knew she couldn't afford to do either of those things. She'd been tossed aside like a used dishrag just because the war was over. But why was employment so hard to find, even for Alex? Cathie could only hope that this interview he'd gone to would pay off, then the future would look rosy again.

Today she mustn't spend too long browsing as little Heather was a bit fretful, perhaps starting with a cold or yet more teething. If only Rona would do her bit to help it would make life so much easier. She could then have left the little one at home. Cathie also hoped to meet up with Brenda before she went off yet again to visit her late husband's relatives. Sadly, she seemed to have left already, as there was no sign of her.

Davina, however, arrived at the market café looking even more gorgeous than usual, and much more cheerful. As they ordered their usual Welsh rarebit and found themselves a table, her face was alight with a bright smile, quite unlike her normal gloomy expression. 'I'm really rather surprised to see you here, Cathie?'

'Oh, why is that? Don't we meet most Saturdays for a snack and a chat?'

'Yes, we do, but didn't you speak with Alex last night?' she asked, looking slightly puzzled.

Davina was wearing a beautiful beige woollen dress with beads and braiding across one shoulder. It looked brand new, not at all the usual shabby style of second-hand clothes she generally chose for her working day at the market. The smartness of the outfit appeared to give her a new air of confidence.

'Actually, he sent me a note to say that he'd unexpectedly

heard of some job vacancies, so he's gone off to apply, which is good news.'

Her friend's beautifully arched brows rose even higher. 'I think you must have been misinformed, or else your cunning fiancé is making an excuse in order not to upset you.'

Something froze inside of Cathie as she heard these words, but as little Heather began to wail she lifted the toddler from her pram to hold her close and pat her gently against her shoulder. 'Why, is there some sort of problem he's been keeping from me? Isn't he well?'

'He was perfectly well when I saw him last.'

'*You* saw him? When was that exactly? I don't quite understand what you're trying to say.' The wails were increasing in volume and, after quickly finding Heather's dummy, she popped it in the baby's mouth, which thankfully soothed her. Feeling slightly flustered, Cathie said, 'There's no problem so far as I am aware. Alex has been searching for a job for several weeks now, and I'm hoping he strikes lucky this time, then we won't have to postpone the wedding for too long.'

Davina burst out laughing, as if she'd made some sort of joke. 'He clearly is reluctant to confess the truth. Your wedding isn't going to be postponed, Cathie, it is to be cancelled.'

'*Cancelled?*'

'Yes, Alex is going to marry me instead.'

The silence following this statement seemed to go on for ever. Even the baby appeared to be struck dumb.

'Did you hear what I said?' Davina asked. She took a cigarette out of her bag and lit it with a silver lighter that looked identical to the one Rona had claimed Alex had given her as a present. What was happening here?

Cathie stared in disbelief, struggling to take in what she was seeing, let alone hearing. Did this mean that Steve was right? It would seem that his suspicions were entirely correct and Alex had indeed been involved in an affair. Although maybe it wasn't Rona Alex fancied at all, but Davina. Drawing in a sharp breath, she struggled to find her voice. 'Perhaps you would care to explain.'

'With pleasure! Alex and I have been lovers for some time. Not simply months, but well over a year, ever since he returned to England and was at first stationed down south. That was, in all honesty, the reason I came to Castlefield some months ago, to be near to him. I didn't like to mention that fact, in the circumstances of your long-standing engagement. He has admittedly been torn between the two of us for some time, but has now come to the sensible decision that I am the one he truly loves. He has no wish to lose me. His engagement with you, Cathie, is most definitely at an end. He and I will be married by special licence quite soon, as I'm already carrying his child.'

* * *

Davina was still chuckling to herself as she strolled home to her lodgings late that afternoon after the market closed. The shock on Cathie's face had been a delight to see.

Her supposed friend hadn't even hung around to eat her cheese on toast that the waitress had brought moments later. She'd bundled the screaming child back into her pram and almost ran in her eagerness to get away. It must have occurred to her what a naïve idiot she'd been, and how she would now need to bring up this allegedly orphaned child by herself. Alex would be raising his own son or daughter, not somebody else's, a fact that made Davina's heart sing with joy.

She could hardly wait to see him this evening, when they would start making plans. No doubt it would be Monday before he'd actually get his hands on a licence, but they could be married within days. Excitement pulsated through her. Things couldn't have worked out better.

Mrs Phillipson was waiting for her in the kitchen when Davina arrived, and quickly placed a dish of Scotch broth before her, as she did every Saturday evening. Her menu never changed. Sunday was generally shoulder of lamb, leftovers on a Monday, pie, rissoles and chicken mid-week, with fish on a Friday. But she was a good cook and Davina had no complaints.

She ate the broth quickly as she was in a hurry to get ready for her evening out with Alex, reminding her landlady as she dashed upstairs to let her know the moment he arrived. Hours later, he still hadn't appeared and Davina spent a lonely evening pacing her room in complete bewilderment. Nor did he call to see her the next day, despite it being a Sunday. She spent the entire day searching for him in all their favourite places: down by the canal, Peel Park, the Pack Horse, and the Midlands Hotel. Davina even hovered outside his house in St John Street for a while, although couldn't quite pluck up the courage to knock on the door.

Where had he gone? Could what Cathie told her about him going off to apply for a job really be true? If that were the case then she would just have to be patient. He would no doubt be back in a day or so, and then they'd start to make their plans.

That evening, as she ate the expected roast lamb with very little appetite, Mrs Phillipson informed Davina there was someone coming to see her later.

Her heart leaped. 'Alex?'

'No, it's a lady. She'll be here shortly.'

Stifling a groan, Davina assumed it must be Cathie coming to create a fuss, which would get her nowhere, silly girl.

She was wrong. The woman, when she arrived half an hour later, was tight-lipped, grey-haired and with the kind of sour expression on her grumpy old face that did not bode well. 'Are you Miss Davina Gibson?' she asked.

'I am.'

Her landlady having made a swift exit, Davina found herself left alone to deal with this woman, whoever she might be. Placing herself on the chair beside her, she clasped her hands across her plump stomach.

'I work for a charity run by the church,' the woman announced. 'And, as I understand it, you are in need of new accommodation in view of…' here she paused for a moment, her stern gaze sliding over the hint of a bump that Davina was doing her best to hide '…your condition.'

The teacup she'd been about to sip almost dropped from her hand as Davina jerked with shock. 'Who told you…' she began, but got no further.

It was at this point that Mrs Phillipson reappeared, carrying Davina's small brown suitcase, which she placed on the floor beside her, together with her coat and hat. She then handed her an envelope. 'Since you've paid up to the end of the month, here's a rebate for the final two weeks.'

'What are you saying? Are you throwing me out?'

'I made it very clear when you first moved in that I have strict standards of behaviour in my house, which you have broken in a most shameful way. You must leave now, this minute, girl. Thankfully, Mrs Mitchell here, who I spoke to this morning in church, is willing to find you a hostel for unmarried mothers. They will offer accommodation and take full responsibility for you and your child.'

Looking from one to the other of them in stunned dismay, Davina let out a spurt of laughter, although she felt more hysterical than amused. 'You've got it all wrong. I'm about to be married.'

'There's no proof that will happen, although you can send your new address to your man-friend in the hope that it does,' the stern-faced charity worker briskly informed her. Then getting to her feet, she added, 'We'd best be going, as I've managed to get us a lift and we mustn't keep the driver waiting.'

'I'm going nowhere,' Davina snapped, firmly folding her arms, scarcely able to believe what was happening to her.

'I'm afraid you have little choice. Either you come with me to this hostel, or sleep out on the streets. Unless, of course, you can move in with your alleged would-be husband right now?'

Seconds ticked by as thoughts whirled in Davina's head, going over her endless search that day for Alex, which had resulted in complete failure. And if the damn landlady was throwing her out, she had to stay somewhere tonight. She certainly had no wish to sleep in the streets, or a damp air raid shelter, even were she able to find one still open and available. Taking a breath, as reality began to sink in, she convinced herself that Alex would be bound to return within a few days, and everything would then be resolved. Turning to Mrs Phillipson, she conceded this fact to her.

'I'm sorry if I've let you down. It was not my intention.' This was not strictly true as getting pregnant had seemed like the best way to catch him, but Davina felt the need to defend herself. 'However, my boyfriend, Alex, is currently away applying for a job, so when he returns and comes looking for me, please do inform him where I am. I will, of course, write to him at his home, but I would appreciate your help in this matter.'

'Should he ever turn up, I'll refer him to Mrs Mitchell

here,' her landlady agreed with a brisk nod before ushering her to the door.

Moments later, Davina was driven off into a cold, dark March evening, wondering where the hell she was going, and how she'd come to find herself in this mess.

* * *

Cathie was utterly heartbroken, quite unable to take in what she'd been told. How could Davina have made herself out to be such a good friend, when all the time she was sleeping with Alex? This was a nightmare! Her first instinct was to seek out Steve, to tell him that his suspicions had been entirely correct, although why that would help she'd no idea. In any case, he'd be at work right now so she'd have to wait till he took a break.

Cathie delivered little Heather to the nursery before setting out on her usual trek around shops, businesses and factories. The fees were small, but with no job, and her savings rapidly running out, she could only afford mornings to allow herself time to enquire about the possibility of work. She called at various motor companies, factories, hotels, cafés and bakers, various shops including Kendal Milne, even one or two breweries, being perfectly willing to spend her days washing bottles, only to be turned away by them all.

Come lunch-time she hurried back to the Co-op, hanging about outside in the hope that Steve would come out as usual for a breath of fresh air and to eat the sandwiches he generally brought with him. When he still hadn't appeared after half an hour of waiting, she slipped into the shop in the hope of finding him. Spotting Mr Leeson, the manager, she hurried over. 'Is Steve out doing deliveries? I was hoping to just ask him a quick question.'

'Sorry, Cathie, but Steve no longer works here,' the manager coolly informed her.

She stared at him in astonishment. 'Really, why is that?'

Mr Leeson cleared his throat. 'I'm afraid we came up against a problem and I had to let him go.'

'I'm sorry to hear that. What went wrong? It wasn't because of that stupid fight, was it? That definitely wasn't Steve's fault.'

'No, it had nothing to do with that incident at all. But I'm afraid there's a limit to what I can say on the subject. He made a mistake and let me down badly. I believe he's gone to work in Birmingham, or maybe Northampton. I can't quite remember. You'd need to ask his parents. Sorry I can't be of more help.'

After thanking him, Cathie walked out in a state of dazed disbelief. Goodness, what sort of bad mistake could it have been to cause Mr Leeson to sack him, and after keeping his job open for years during the war? Why hadn't Steve told her about this? The answer to this rang in her head like a tolling bell of doom. Because he believed that she was about to be married, and they'd fallen out, this time more firmly than ever before.

It was now that she realised how important his friendship

had been to her. She needed him and would miss him so much.

Cathie considered contacting his parents, but there seemed little point if he was in Birmingham, Northampton, or wherever. If he was so far away it wasn't as if they could sit down and chat over a cup of tea, or while they organised some charity event, as they'd so liked to do. He was gone from her life, perhaps fore ver. Tears filled her eyes at the thought. She'd lost him and must somehow work out how to face this bleak situation on her own.

Finding a job suddenly became more important than ever. By the end of the day, Cathie had taken on a cleaning job to work early mornings at the umbrella factory. It was only part-time and the wages were poor, not what she'd hoped for at all, but better than nothing.

She was also rather worried about a rumour that the nursery might be closing soon, due to lack of financial support from the government and women losing their jobs, now that the servicemen were flocking home in droves. Things seemed to be going from bad to worse, certainly so far as she was concerned.

More importantly, in view of what she'd learned from Davina, what would she say to Alex when he finally returned after his own search for a job? Being betrayed by the man she loved really didn't bear thinking about. She'd lost everyone who mattered in her life, and now she was about to lose Alex too.

Chapter Fifteen

'Who is this woman who claims to be pregnant by you?' Victor roared.

Alex stared at his father, stunned. How the hell did he know about Davina? Had her landlady spoken to him? He felt that all-too-familiar surge of resentment whenever Victor addressed him with such contempt. His mother was sitting in her armchair beside the fire, ashen-faced.

'I don't know what you're talking about,' he said, struggling to keep his tone of voice calm and reasonable.

Alex felt slightly guilty about lying to Cathie, if not his so-called betrayal. Most of his comrades had done exactly the same thing. How could men be expected to remain faithful to their womenfolk at home while finding themselves stuck out in a desert in the middle of nowhere with a war raging all around them, even if they weren't the ones to be actually holding a gun? They surely had the right to seek relief somewhere, so why not in the arms of a willing woman? Nor could they be certain that their sweetheart or wife back home would remain faithful to them. Weren't women more likely to be tarts than Madonnas? Certainly in his experience.

Not for a moment did Alex blame himself for what happened on his return to England either. He'd still been a lonely serviceman with needs, which Davina had offered to fill. She was the one who had taken the risk, not him. Where the hell she was sleeping right now he had no idea, nor did he care. As her landlady quite rightly said, she'd got herself into this pickle and must live with the consequences.

It hadn't been easy to decide which woman he really wanted, not helped by the fact that his parents, in particular his mother, refused to accept Cathie's story that little Heather was her niece and not a bastard child. But then he wasn't entirely convinced by her claim of innocence either. Just when he'd finally made up his mind to marry Cathie, for the money she could provide as well as the fact she would make a much better wife, even if she might prove to be less exciting in bed, circumstances had changed. He'd found himself facing the equivalent of a shotgun wedding.

Now, having returned home a week or two later to collect some fresh clothes, he half feared his father might wield his own gun against him.

'Don't lie to me, son. You know damn well. We've received this from some woman called Davina Gilbert,' he yelled, snatching up a letter from the coffee table to flap it in his face. 'The woman is begging us to help her as you are apparently ignoring her letters. There's a stack of them on the hall table, which I had definitely ignored as you were away, supposedly seeking work. But then she addressed this one to me. So, what have you to say for yourself, boy?'

Rage rose within him. How dare the stupid girl do such a thing? Revealing her condition to his parents was the last thing he needed, as it would only make the problem worse. But having said that, what business was it of theirs, anyway? 'I would remind you, Father, that I'm no longer a *boy* but a man of almost twenty-six, so can do what the hell I like.'

'Can you indeed? Then I assume you are now going to marry this little tart, instead of the other one.'

'Indeed not,' Alex calmly stated. 'I've no intention of marrying the girl simply because of a wartime affair, of which half the forces are guilty of. She made her choices and must now be the one to pay the price, not me.'

'*Any son of mine should do the honourable thing!*' Victor roared.

'I'm afraid life is no longer that simple.'

'Have you even found yourself a job yet? Have you even *looked*?'

'No, Father, I'm not yet quite up to the stress of such responsibility.' Fortunately, he'd made another pot of money, although not in a way he wished to reveal to his parents. Nevertheless, it would allow him to please himself as to what he did in future. 'In the circumstances I think it best if I leave home, then you will no longer be troubled by my allegedly shocking behaviour.'

'Yes, damn you! Get the hell out of here.'

At which point his mother burst into floods of tears. Alex kissed her goodbye and walked proudly out.

All this time he'd believed that he'd got away with his lies. He thought he'd managed to convince everyone that he'd been faithful to his fiancée, and that he was genuinely seeking work, but seemingly not. The prospect of being tied down to marriage and caring for a child, even one of his own, let alone becoming embroiled in a long tiring working day, did indeed feel quite beyond him. He'd had enough of following rules and working to a strict regime.

Returning to the miserable dive that Eddie had found for him, Alex read the letters to see what it was Davina wanted from him, and his fury escalated. The blasted woman intended to create even further problems for him by declaring to the entire world that he was the father of her illegitimate child. Not only had she ruined his reputation, he was also in danger of losing Cathie too, and of his father cutting him out of his will and disinheriting him. And money, when the country itself was on the point of bankruptcy and the government not helping ex-servicemen quite as much as it should, was in his opinion essential if he was to survive and build a future for himself. And he'd certainly no intention of succumbing to his father's bullying ever again. Blast the woman; he'd make her regret she'd ever met him. He just had to decide exactly how to achieve that. First of all, he needed to find out where she was living.

* * *

Davina was housed in a cockroach-infested dormitory with a dozen or so other young women, in what they amusingly called 'a prison for naughty girls'. It certainly felt like that at times. She spent her days scrubbing floors, cleaning toilets, sweeping the huge spiral staircase, or working long hours in the steam laundry without pay, and hating every minute of it. When first she'd arrived she'd been locked up in solitary confinement in what had once been a nun's cell in this part of the convent. For the better part of a week she'd had no contact with a living soul, save for the stern-faced nun who delivered her food.

'Let me out of here. Why am I locked up?' she would cry.

'It is to allow you time to pray and repent of your sins.'

Instead, Davina paced back and forth in anguish, her mind going over and over everything that had happened to her in life. First her beloved mother had died of tuberculosis, and then her father had abused her since he no longer had a wife to satisfy his needs. This had led her to run away and find young men who were at least prepared to pay for the privilege of sleeping with her. By good fortune she'd met Alex and dreamed of escaping a degrading existence to become his wife. It had seemed like a glorious and very real solution to all the traumas she'd endured. Now he'd vanished from her life and she was locked up here like a prisoner in jail.

'I need writing paper and a pen to contact my fiancé and

tell him where I am,' she insisted. 'I am not a prisoner and surely have some rights.'

'You have committed a crime against God and society,' the nun starkly informed her.

Paper and pen were, however, duly brought and Davina sat and wrote countless letters, day after day. Unfortunately, she received no replies to any of them, not even Alex's own father when in despair she'd finally confessed her situation to him. Even when she was later allowed out of solitary and moved into the dormitory with the other girls, she continued to write a letter each and every day until all her money was gone and she could no longer afford to buy stamps from the nun who acted as postmistress.

A doctor had come to examine her during those first few days, and confirmed she was four months pregnant, but she hadn't seen him since. What would happen when she actually gave birth? Davina felt traumatised with terror at the thought. If you needed assistance when in labour you were supposed to pay for it, otherwise you were expected to work for *three more years* to pay off the debt. A horrific thought to be locked up here for that long, very much like serving a prison sentence.

And what would happen to her child? If she kept it, assuming she had a job and a home to go to, she'd be ostracised by society. But the thought of handing it over to the nuns for adoption filled her with anguish. This was her baby, hers and Alex's. How could she give it away?

Every night as she lay in the hard, uncomfortable bed,

Davina would pull the blanket over her head and weep silently into her pillow, hoping she might wake up and discover that this was all a bad dream and Alex had not deserted her.

Fortunately, she'd made a new friend, a girl called Barbara Cartwright who had also fallen foul of society by getting herself pregnant by a Yank. As he was a married man there would be no wedding ring for her, whereas Davina still lived in hope. Surely one day Alex would turn up and rescue her. Oh, but where was he, and why didn't he come for her? She could but hope and pray that he finally would.

When one morning she found a letter waiting for her she could hardly believe her good fortune. Alex apologised for being absent so long, but had needed to go in search of a job, just exactly as Cathie had told her. So he hadn't abandoned her, after all! Even more wonderful, he asked if they could meet. Oh, thank goodness for that! But towards the end of the letter came the news that he was not prepared to visit her at the Home, as he dare not take the risk of offending his parents any further.

He finished by saying, 'Their reputation in the local community, and at the church, is very important to them. You will have to come to me, darling, perhaps at our usual meeting place by the canal on Friday evening? I do hope you can make it. I look forward to seeing you.'

That evening, when her chores were done, Davina sat down to write a quick response. She explained how she'd been locked up for days, and even now was not permitted to go beyond the grounds, guarded as they were by high walls and a locked iron gate. 'But I'm sure there must be some way out,' she wrote. 'I can hardly wait to be in your arms again.' Agreeing the date and time, which Davina vowed to keep, she gave the letter a kiss, sealed the envelope, and handed it over to be posted.

'Many girls do attempt to escape,' Barbara, her new friend, told her. 'So long as they have the courage to risk hurting themselves on the spikes that top the walls. Even those who do manage to get over the wall are more often than not caught and brought back.'

'Why is that?' Davina asked in alarm.

'Probably because they have nowhere else to go or anyone to help them.'

'Or because they went about escaping the wrong way. I certainly intend to investigate possibilities, as I'm desperate to get out of this dreadful hole. But I have no wish to be caught on a spike.'

'Me neither, love. We'll investigate the possibilities together,' Barbara agreed.

What did she have to lose? No matter what the risks involved, she'd already lost her freedom.

Over the next few days, Davina kept a careful watch on the routine in and around the Home. Standing at the sink in the laundry each morning she would steal quick glances through the window, soon noticing that the milkman came and went at the same time every morning. He left his horse and cart at the gate while he carried a crate through the side door. Did someone lock it after him? she wondered. Rinsing the sheets as she watched, Davina saw a nun walking over to do exactly that, opening and locking the door as he came and went. She clicked her tongue in annoyance. How irritating, just when she thought she'd found a solution to her dilemma.

'She could be distracted,' her friend Barbara whispered, coming over to help put the sheets through the mangle. 'If we managed to do that, then we could easily slip out while no one was looking.'

Davina blinked. 'In broad daylight? I don't think so. Far too risky.'

'With a little careful planning we might work something out. We'd need to make sure the nun didn't lock the door again, or else we somehow got hold of the key. Why not? It's worth a try, don't you think?'

Excitement welled in her. 'I agree. Let's give it a go.'

Whenever they had a moment alone the pair of them spent the rest of that week talking the plan through, as well as recruiting help from the other girls. So eager was she to escape that Davina felt she'd never known a week drag by so slowly, save for the one she'd spent in solitary. No more weeping in her pillow now though, only blissful dreams of marriage with Alex. How fortunate she was.

'Where will you go if we do get out of here?' she asked her friend.

Barbara shrugged. 'Hopefully to my sister's as she didn't

approve of Dad chucking me out. But I'd sleep on the streets rather than here. They gave my baby away so I'm just serving time paying my debts.'

'Give me her address then I can invite you to my wedding.'

'Lucky you,' Barbara said, as she scribbled it down on a piece of cardboard torn from a packet of washing powder, and handed it over. 'We should bear in mind that we won't be able to take anything with us. No bag, no clothes, no ration book, nothing, so stuff this in your pocket or brassiere, along with anything else of importance.'

'Don't worry,' Cathie said, doing exactly as she was advised. 'I'm happy to walk away from everything and start afresh.'

'Me too!'

When Friday eventually dawned, the moment the young nun placed the key in the lock to open the side door to let the milkman out, having finished his deliveries, Davina scampered across the yard and shouted to her. 'Sister, there's a fight starting up in the laundry, and the other Sisters there need help to stop it.'

The sound of screams and yells resonating from behind closed doors proved this to be the case, and, picking up her skirts, the nun immediately ran to assist her colleagues, forgetting all about the key still sitting in the lock. Davina quickly grabbed it, stuffed it down her bra then ran to catch up with the nun. The next half-hour she and Barbara kept well away from the riot, not wishing to find themselves blamed in any way for it. Fortunately, all the nuns were far too busy calming down the fight in the laundry to remember the key.

It proved to be an anxious day as they kept glancing over at the door, worried someone might remember and go in search of the key, which was still nestled by Davina's breast. But finally dusk fell, supper was over and, as routine dictated, the girls were sent quite early to bed. Once everyone was settled, Davina and Barbara crept out of bed, still fully dressed, and tiptoed downstairs and across the yard. To their huge relief they unlocked the door with ease and slipped quickly through it. Once out on the pavement they hugged each other in delight and said their goodbyes.

'You have my address,' Barbara reminded her.

Davina pulled it from her pocket to wave it in the air. 'I do,' she laughed, tucking it back in as a wind blew up.

'Good luck.'

'You too.'

'Stay in touch.'

'I will.' Then each went their separate ways, Davina running hotfoot to meet the man of her dreams. How gloriously easy that had been. She was free at last.

* * *

Alex was waiting for her down by the canal in the shadow of the bridge, as planned, constantly glancing at his watch with a degree of impatience and anxiety. But when he saw her come running towards him, he smiled to himself and gathered her close as she flew into his arms. 'My darling, how wonderful to see you,' he cried, instantly smothering her with kisses.

'Oh, Alex, I can't tell you how I've longed to see you too. I've had the most dreadful time, locked up like a criminal, all thanks to that prissy landlady.'

Wrapping her arms about his neck, she responded with equal passion, so much so that Alex couldn't resist savouring her beautiful body one more time. Despite the slight swell in her stomach, she looked as gorgeous as ever, even if the rest of her was a little thinner. Perhaps she'd hadn't been very well fed in this so-called Unmarried Mothers' Care Home.

Pulling her on to his lap, he eagerly set about kissing her, feeling no inclination to waste too much time caressing her, or any desire to lick her nipples as she stank of dust and washing powder. But, locked in his tight embrace, she arched her back in ecstasy, clearly relishing the passion of the moment as he thrust himself inside her, pounding hard and fast. His intention had been to pay her off with a large wad of cash, then put her on a train back to where she'd come from. But, as a climax burst within him, he rose from the bench to lift her high, her legs still wrapped about his waist. Then, taking a step forwards, he jerked them free and flung her backwards into the canal, almost out of instinct.

Her scream echoed for some moments as she flapped and floundered in the water, madly splashing about with her arms, legs, feet and hands. Not that there was anyone to hear at this time of the evening, and Alex knew full well that she couldn't swim. He made no attempt to save her, any more than he had when so-called mates had treated him like dirt back in the desert. Disposing of them during a war had been easy too, and the canal was deep at this spot so close to the lock. She sank very quickly. Once she'd entirely vanished from sight, he gave her a final salute of farewell.

A sound from behind made him glance quickly around, anxious for a second or two, but all he saw was a cat stalking a mouse and Alex chuckled to himself. He wished the animal as much success with catching its own prey as he'd had with his.

Now life could return to normal.

Carefully straightening his tie, which she'd loosened, he walked away, whistling, and headed straight over to Rona. And she, dear lady, welcomed him with open arms.

Chapter Sixteen

One evening in early April, Cathie arrived home following a meal with her Aunt Evie to find Alex yet again seated with her mother. More significantly, on this occasion, they weren't simply chatting over a cup of tea by the fire in the kitchen. They were seated on the couch in the parlour and Alex had his arms about her, with Rona resting her head against his chest as she gazed up at him with adoration in her eyes. Just looking at them cuddled up together like that made Cathie want to vomit.

'What are you doing?' she cried, struggling to disguise the catch of a sob in her voice.

'Ah, there you are, chuck,' Rona said, gently disentangling herself from his hold. 'Why are you looking so cross? I thought you'd be pleased to see that he's back.'

'*I* certainly am,' Alex agreed with a grin. 'Not only have I happily returned with money in my pocket and the prospect of earning a good income, but I've actually moved in.'

'What?' Cathie stared at him in shocked disbelief.

'Having suffered further dispute with my parents, and unable to find anywhere else to live, Rona has suggested that I stay here, with both of you. I was just thanking her, as it is so kind of her to offer. But don't fret, I'm quite content to sleep on the couch here in the front room, as is only right and proper,' he said with a laugh. 'It's so good to see you again, sweetie.'

But, as he reached for her, Cathie slapped his hand away. 'Stop it! Davina has told me all about your plans to marry her instead of me, so go and live with her, why don't you?'

His smile instantly vanished, and he was silent for some moments as he slowly drew in a breath. 'Ah, I hadn't realised she'd told you. However, she's very much mistaken. I've no intention of marrying that girl. It wouldn't be right, as it's you I love.'

'Utter rubbish!' Fury rose within her as Cathie recognised an expression of guilt mingling with embarrassment in his face.

'Never listen to gossip when…' Rona began, but Cathie put up a hand to silence her.

'Don't take me for a fool, Alex. Whether or not you marry Davina is of no concern to me. But it's perfectly clear that you have been lovers for months as she is apparently pregnant with your child. So it's Davina you should be moving in with, not *me*! And if you also fancy an affair with my mother, then feel free to do that too. I really couldn't care less, but I refuse to have you living in this house, so please leave. *Now*!'

'This house is mine,' Rona snapped. 'At least, I'm

responsible for paying the rent, so *I* decide who lives here. And if this lovely young man wants to stay, he can.'

'Right, then I'll be the one to leave.'

It took only moments for Cathie to pack an overnight bag, and a few essential things for the baby, then saying she'd call back for the rest of her belongings later, she gathered little Heather up in her arms and walked out. It was only when she was standing outside on the pavement in the cold of the evening that she stopped to ask herself where on earth she could go.

* * *

Alex found it strange to be sleeping in his ex-fiancée's bed, and really rather irritating that she wasn't lying beside him, as he'd planned. Wasn't it around now that they'd planned to marry? If only he'd managed to persuade Cathie into bringing forward the date of their wedding then things may not have gone so badly wrong. But having spent some weeks sleeping in what could only be termed a rubbish dump that stank of urine, alcohol and vomit, he was at least grateful to be cosseted in a warm bed between sheets that smelled sweetly of her.

He'd certainly no intention of letting the girl go, not when she had so much to offer, and felt highly confident that he could win her back with a few kisses. He'd always found women easy to seduce.

Over the coming days, he set out to acquire more cash, which he'd need if he was to successfully win her back, if only to take her to the Ritz. Trying to think of a way to do that he recalled his visit to the release centre, very much like a quartermaster's store with bundles of clothes stacked everywhere as men were kitted out in preparation for their demobilisation. He'd walked away to be instantly approached by a spiv. The fellow had offered him ten quid for the box of clothes and shoes he'd been issued with. It was a tempting sum, but Alex had declined to accept. Later, watching some of his mates smugly pocket the money, he'd come to regret his refusal, particularly considering he'd been fobbed off with a demob suit that didn't even fit.

Taking a leaf from their book, he now stationed himself close to Victoria railway station in Manchester. Trains arrived daily, packed to the gunwales with soldiers, sailors and airmen, some of them obliged to sit on their suitcase in the corridors for lack of space. As they poured off the train, he made similar offers to these returning ex-servicemen, who were equally desperate for hard cash. Alex forked out fifty pounds on purchasing parcels of clothing from them, some of which included trilbies and greatcoats. But he then went on to double his money by selling them off to folk who were in desperate need of clothes but short of coupons. You needed sixteen points just to buy a coat these days.

Following the success of that little scheme, he then bought a stack of clothing coupons from Eddie, asking no questions about whether or not these were legal or perhaps stolen. He bought a couple of thousand for fifteen quid, and happily went on to sell those too at a good price. He bought other kinds of coupons, as the demand was insatiable, telling potential customers that it shouldn't trouble them in the slightest what they were actually intended for, as clothes coupons could be exchanged for sugar and eggs, if their grocer or butcher was of a mind to be flexible.

'You are so kind,' people would say, not only grateful for the opportunity to buy extra coupons, but excited at having to pay a pittance for them as they could cost as much as two shillings per coupon on the black market. Kindness played no part in his character, but Alex settled for one shilling, and still made a tidy sum.

Back in Cathie's bed, he would tuck the wad of cash he'd earned that day into the envelope that he kept under the mattress, then turn over with a contented sigh to sleep. Not only was he at last free of his dictatorial father, and other irritations in his life, but had also found a way to make easy money. Long may it last.

As for Cathie, he'd win her round in the end, he was quite certain of that. And marriage with her would provide him with the opportunity to acquire even more. He really was much more clever than people gave him credit for.

* * *

That first evening Cathie had returned to Aunt Evie, who kindly offered her a bed, or rather a blanket and pillow on the floor in the living room. The night had seemed endless, and although little Heather slept contentedly in her pram beside her, Cathie herself had barely slept a wink.

She felt that her much-hoped-for future was at an end, as if all her dreams and hopes were dead, along with her sister. How could she have been so naïve as to trust Alex? Why hadn't she exercised a little more common sense instead of fussing about wedding plans, gowns and baking cakes?

Even making a Christmas cake and buying a goose had been a complete waste of time, as those plans too had been ruined. She really must stop being so trusting and learn to rely upon that sense of independence Steve had told her she'd acquired during the war. If only she'd listened to him more. Oh, how she missed him. His absence had left an unexpectedly great hole in her life. Who was left for her to turn to for help and support?

At least her aunt loved her, even if her own mother couldn't give a toss what happened to her. Finally, Cathie had fallen asleep out of sheer exhaustion. But the following morning her aunt confessed that she was not in a position to offer her permanent accommodation.

'Sorry, love, but things are a bit tricky for me right now with Donald and the kids back home at last, and none of them getting on too well. Even accepting me as their mum after years living as evacuees in the Lake District is not proving easy for them. But they don't seem to remember that he's their father, and after years as a POW I confess he doesn't look or act like the same man.' She paused, distress all too evident in her woeful expression, so that Cathie put her arms around her aunt to give her a warm hug.

'I'm sorry to hear that. Then I won't get in your hair, Aunty, I promise.'

'So where will you go, love?'

'Don't worry, I can stay with a friend,' she said, explaining about the key Brenda had sent her, and insisted she keep. 'I'm deeply grateful for her generosity.' As she fed Heather her breakfast porridge, Cathie risked repeating a question she'd asked several times before, with little success. 'I can see why it will feel odd for your children coming home to a father they haven't seen in years and probably have little memory of. You have my sympathy over that, Aunty. I remember feeling equally deserted when Dad left home. Do you have any idea what happened to him?'

Evie let out a sigh. 'I wish I did. Frank just vanished one day. He told me he'd had enough of Rona's cavorting and was leaving her. You were about six or seven at the time, I seem to recall. He gave me a hug then just walked out. I haven't seen or heard from him since.'

'Why is that? I thought you two were close. And why did he have no wish to contact me, his own daughter?'

Evie plonked herself down in the chair beside Cathie to stroke and tidy her somewhat unruly hair. 'He did love you to bits, but had a strong yearning to emigrate. I suspect he went to Australia, or maybe Canada. He did promise that he would send for you once he was settled. The fact we haven't heard from him since must mean that he never did settle. He's no doubt spent his entire life roving around the world. But then he too was a soldier during the First World War, and it affected him badly. He never settled back home in Manchester. His best mate was shot for desertion, and Frank himself suffered from shell shock. He was riddled with problems, and as a result it was never a happy marriage.'

'So there's not much hope of me ever seeing Dad again?'

'I very much doubt you will, love.' Glancing at the baby with porridge pasted across her chubby cheeks, Evie gave a soft little chuckle. She began to wipe them clean. 'My advice, Cathie, would be don't look back, look forward. Plan a lovely future for little Heather here. She's such a darling.'

'She is indeed,' Cathie agreed, brushing away the start of tears from her eyes. She'd lived most of her life without a father, and with a witch of a mother, so it would be a joy to provide a more loving home for this little one. Wishing her aunt well and offering every hope of recovery from her own troubles, Cathie took herself off to what Brenda always dubbed as her 'miserable little bedsit'.

* * *

It proved to be actually quite a pleasant little flat overlooking the canal, with two bedrooms, a combined kitchenette and living area, and a small bathroom. Perfect, if rather sparsely furnished with only the odd chair, no wardrobe or set of drawers. But each bedroom possessed a comfy bed, and there were hooks on the wall to hang her clothes on. It looked rather in need of a good clean as her friend had been absent for a week or two, constantly being called back by her late husband's family. Cathie set to at once to give everywhere a good sweep and polish, a task with which she'd had plenty of practice since taking on her new job as a cleaner at the umbrella factory.

Once that was done, she wrote a quick letter to Brenda to explain that she was here in her flat, and to thank her for her generosity.

'Do hope you'll be home again soon, as I miss you greatly,' she finished. Then as a PS, added, 'And Steve too, of course. I called on his parents to ask where he was and they said he was working at a printing works in Birmingham. They gave me his address so I do intend to send him an apology, once I decide what to say.'

It took her a few days to settle in and pluck up the courage to write to Steve. Having finally done so, she decided to post it there and then. Knowing that Rona would be at the cotton mill, and Alex hopefully out looking for a job, this might be the ideal moment to slip back home for the rest of her belongings. After that she'd collect Heather from the nursery around lunchtime, as usual.

* * *

Carefully checking that the house was indeed empty, Cathie let herself in and hurried straight upstairs. Flinging open her wardrobe doors and dressing table drawers, she quickly gathered up clothes, shoes and other personal possessions to stuff them into a small brown suitcase and a large carpet bag.

When she was done she glanced about her, just in case she'd missed anything. Seeing the rumpled sheets, she realised that Alex must have actually slept in her bed last night, and her throat tightened with pain. It could well have been their wedding night, in which case she should have been here with him. Or had her mother joined him instead? She felt sick at the thought.

Instead of celebrating their wedding she'd had no option but to walk out, finding herself all alone in a bleak world.

It was bad enough that in recent weeks just walking up the street pushing the pram would bring forth sly, disapproving glances from neighbours and so-called friends. Some had begun to avoid her, clearly assuming little Heather to be her child, and with no ring on her finger they considered this quite shocking.

Sal would be heartbroken if she knew.

Cathie almost wished that she'd never met, let alone fallen in love with Alex Ryman, but sadly he'd captured her heart and nothing could reduce the pain, as it seemed to disintegrate within her. But if he'd truly felt the same way about her, why had he betrayed her? Did he chase any woman who winked or smiled at him? Or was she being unreasonable to expect a man to be faithful through such difficult times? Remembering what Aunt Evie had said about how her own father had suffered badly as a result of the First War, perhaps she was. Fighting a war thousands of miles from home, family and loved ones, could not be easy.

Wiping the blur of tears from her eyes, Cathie tossed her last few precious belongings into the bag. Whatever the reason, she had to put all this behind her and think of the future, as Aunt Evie had advised. She needed to be strong and determined, and not allow herself to be put down by gossip.

Dropping to her knees she peeped under the bed, just in case she'd left the odd sock or an old pair of slippers lurking beneath. It was then that she spotted a brown envelope tucked under the mattress. Curiosity struck her and she couldn't resist pulling it out to take a look. She stared at the contents in utter shock and disbelief. Alex had claimed his demob money was almost used up, yet here was evidence to the contrary. A whole wad of cash. Or had managed to find himself a job, after all. If that was the case, why hadn't he told her?

Perhaps he'd said nothing because of the growing distance between them. They were no longer a couple, so why would he share such good news with her? Tucking the envelope back exactly where she'd found it, she started to gather together all the baby stuff, then quietly let herself out of the house; her heart once more plunged into misery.

Chapter Seventeen

Using one of his spare ration books Alex bought some lamb chops for himself at the butcher's shop, which he intended to grill on the old paraffin stove in his shed at the allotment. 'Do you have any problems finding enough meat?' he asked the man.

'Course I do. It's hard to come by and, unlike some butchers, I don't pass horsemeat off as stewing steak.' After stamping the coupons, he handed the ration book back. 'I see this belongs to a woman. Is she your sweetheart?'

'A friend, she's not feeling too well so I'm doing her shopping for her,' Alex lied, as he picked up the parcel of chops. 'If you were interested, I might be able to help you find more meat, as I do have contacts with a few farmers.'

There was silence for a moment as the man quickly glanced at the queue piling up behind Alex. Then leaning closer as he handed over his change, he murmured, 'Were you to acquire some, then you can generally find me round the back.'

Nodding and smiling, Alex bid him good day and strolled out. It was always useful to find possible new customers.

Now, he just had to find the necessary supplier, as that tale of knowing a few farmers was yet another lie. He wondered to himself if he were ever capable of telling the truth. But he was quite sure he'd find someone willing to supply him.

Admittedly, some of the men he associated with were a bit hot-headed and reckless, as many had come close to death on more than one occasion during the war. Others had deserted and were living under an assumed name. Flirting with danger seemed to be an essential part of their lives.

Once he'd enjoyed his lunch, he did a bit of digging in the potato patch to justify his reason for being at the allotment. After that, Alex spent the rest of the day prowling around factories and chatting to workers, as he so often did. He was ever on the lookout for possible candidates who could provide him with pilfered goods. If they didn't want to risk trying to smuggle these out through the factory gate, he'd arrange to hover outside the lavatory window at an agreed time, and they'd chuck a bag out to him. He'd collected a sizeable stack of cigarettes as a result of this little scheme.

His stash of food was also growing, almost as big as his wad of cash. He kept it hidden away either in the shed, or buried in metal boxes in the potato patch, comprising tins of beans, ham, sardines and salmon, packets of chocolate biscuits, as well as soap, perfume, cigarettes and alcohol. And as bananas were now back on sale, if he got his hands on some of those, he'd sell them for anything up to two shillings each. Eggs too would fetch almost as much.

To his delight he did find a pig farmer willing to supply him with pork and sausages. Money seemed to be falling into his pockets as easy as riding a bike downhill. But what Alex most coveted were petrol coupons. If he ever got his hands on some of those, he could surely make a small fortune in no time.

He'd rather thought that the black market might die, now the war was over. But with rationing still in place, and even getting worse now that bread and potatoes were rationed, quite the opposite was the case. Instead, this illicit trade was growing, probably because folk were sick of a dull wartime diet. The government must be turning a blind eye because they were unable to provide the necessary amount of food needed.

At least his time working as a cook helped him to judge what to buy, and was making him far more money than toiling in a sweating kitchen, peeling spuds and scrubbing floors. Which was one good thing to come out of it, despite having been pilloried and used like a slave.

It began to occur to Alex that he should perhaps widen his scope and start seeking out more profitable goods than eggs and bananas, or even coupons. Maybe he'd do a bit of snooping around jewellery shops, in case some more enterprising project sprang to mind. If he could get his hands on a lovely diamond ring, Cathie would surely come rushing back to him. Then once he'd walked her down the aisle, he could buy them a house with that pot of money she had stashed away. Alex smiled to himself at the thought.

But first he had to persuade her to return home. He had one or two ideas on how he could achieve that. It was all about control, and he fully intended to keep a close watch on her over the coming weeks to help make up his mind. In the meantime he called in at a tailor's shop on St Ann Street and had himself measured for a new suit. He likewise deserved such a treat for all his hard work.

***

Cathie heaved a sigh of resignation as she let herself back into Brenda's small flat, accompanied by the taxi driver whom she'd hired to help. Seeming to guess her problem, he'd generously carried everything up to the first floor for her. She'd even thought to bring Heather's cot and high chair, and the man had kindly folded them up and transported those for her too. The pram was parked downstairs in the hall, and Cathie hoped that none of the other tenants would object to her leaving it there.

After she'd thanked and paid him, costing far more than she could really afford, Cathie sat little Heather on the rug with her teddy and wooden bricks, and began to unpack her suitcase and various bags.

The flat felt cold and unlived in, rain lashing down the windows, quite grey and miserable as the lights didn't seem to be working either. Was there a power cut, or had Brenda forgotten to pay the electricity bill? With money so tight and few jobs around, Cathie worried about how she would find sufficient cash to cope with such problems.

When Brenda had first sent her the key she'd told her that the rent was paid for three months, but that had been back in January and, as it was now the first week in April, it could be due soon too.

Oh, how she wished her friend was here right now, then they could work out some solutions together.

Cathie shivered as loneliness overwhelmed her and, settling into bed that night, still wearing her coat and socks as it was so cold, tears rolled down her cheeks. Could she even contemplate facing life without Alex? Yet no matter how stark it might be living here all alone, Cathie sternly reminded herself why she was here. Something had changed between them as a result of the war, or the years of separation, and despite her best efforts to understand and help him overcome whatever traumas he was suffering from, he'd still betrayed her. He'd also shown little interest in Heather. But then why would he when Davina was pregnant with his child, and he intended to marry her instead?

As Heather beamed across at her from her cot set close beside the bed, Cathie's heart swelled with love. The child was utterly adorable. Despite the pain Cathie felt, she had most definitely done the right thing. There was no help for it now but to buckle down and work hard; although how she would manage to earn enough money to bring up this little one alone she had no idea. But she'd do her best to cope, as hundreds of other women were having to do right now.

Cathie spent the coming weeks working harder than ever

while she diligently searched for a better job with more pay. There were very few around, and nurseries were starting to close now that the war was over, although fortunately not little Heather's. But she worried that childminders might also prove to be a problem if it did.

There were days towards the end of each week, before her next wage packet was due, when she would barely have enough cash or coupons to feed them both. On those occasions Cathie would go without food herself in order to feed the baby. Even at the start of the week, she would buy the cheapest she could find: tripe and trotters, kidneys, potted meat and brawn. Sometimes she would treat herself to a black pudding, or oatcakes and baps from the muffin man who would come strolling down the street, carrying his basket on his head.

Fortunately, little Heather continued to thrive, even if Cathie herself began to feel increasingly weary and lacking in energy. But the task of caring for the baby, bathing her each evening in the sink with water she'd warmed on the small gas stove, then tucking little Heather up in her cot to sing her a lullaby, brought joy to Cathie's heart.

'What a little sweetheart you are,' she would say, loving the sweet baby scent of her.

'Mm-m-m,' she'd say in response, almost as if she was trying to say 'mummy'. Cathie hoped that was how this little angel would view her. She was her legal foster mum, after all. And she would give her all the love she would have received from Sal, had things been different.

Should she use the money her daddy had left her? Cathie hoped that would never become necessary, quite certain she would find a job in the end, and earn a decent income to secure the child's future.

The question buzzing through her head right now though, in addition to why he'd failed to be faithful to her, was how Alex had come by that wad of cash she'd found tucked away under the mattress. She did recall him saying that after years of obeying orders the prospect of being his own boss held strong appeal, so maybe he'd started up a small business on the quiet. Or else it was a gift from his well-to-do father?

However he'd come by the money, he would spend it on Davina and their child, certainly not on her, or this little one. Cathie would need to find her own source of income. She'd even begun to question who she missed the most: Alex or Steve. Her old friend had certainly shown far more sympathy and understanding for her than her alleged fiancé, and she'd greatly appreciated the time they'd spent together on the charity work, particularly while Brenda was away. But at least she could live in Brenda's miserable little bedsit, as she called it. A justifiable description right now as there was no hot water, no electricity and no spare cash to buy coal. How would she survive?

* * *

A day or two later, Cathie went to collect little Heather from the nursery, as usual, following her shift at the umbrella factory. She stood waiting in the yard, becoming increasingly alarmed when she saw no sign of her niece among the children running into their mother's arms. Panic robbed her of breath as she hurried to the door. Catching sight of the nursery nurse tidying away the toys, she politely asked, 'Please, miss, where's Heather? I can't see her anywhere.'

The young woman turned to look at her in surprise. 'Your fiancé collected her, half an hour ago. I rather assumed you'd know that.'

Cathie gasped, then spinning on her heels began to run, vaguely aware of the woman calling out her apologies as she chased after her.

'It's all right. I think I know where she'll be,' Cathie yelled, not pausing to explain that Alex wasn't her fiancé any more. Why would he do that, and where would he have taken her? Home to Rona, she hoped.

She was running so fast, and the sense of fear was so strong in her, that Cathie felt almost as if she'd slipped back in time to when she'd dashed to their house in Duke Street to collect those dratted blankets for her mother, and been bombed as a result. She could only pray that whatever was waiting for her today would not be anywhere near as bad.

It was as Cathie reached for the sneck of the kitchen door, heart pounding and gasping for breath, that it suddenly opened and Alex appeared. He was holding baby Heather in his arms as he stood before her, a smile lighting his handsome face.

'Cathie, sweetie, how wonderful that you've come home at last. Does this mean that you've changed your mind?'

'No' she said, vigorously shaking her head. 'I came looking for Heather. What right had you to pick her up, and without even asking me?' She reached forward to take the child, but Alex took a step back, shaking his head as he gave a little smile.

'I have every right if I'm to be the child's father, darling, and I've made up my mind that is what I'm going to be. So I thought it time I took some responsibility for the little one.'

Cathie gazed up at him in amazement, hardly able to take in what she was hearing, and deeply aware of the nervous expression on the baby's face that looked about to dissolve into tears. 'I… I don't quite understand.'

'Of course you do, sweetie. You've been most patient of my problems, and the mistakes I've made as a result of the war. It was foolish of me to lie to you. I regret that greatly. I should have been more upfront about things and confessed the truth. You are my little treasure, after all.'

A part of her was trembling even as she struggled to calmly smile. Could she believe a word he was saying? Oh, she so wanted to. Maybe she shouldn't risk losing him just because of a foolish affair that he clearly regretted. How could she even contemplate life without the man she'd once thought of as the love of her life? But then how could she ever trust him again after what he'd done? As Heather began to wriggle and cry, reaching out her small chubby arms to Cathie, she said, 'Please give her to me. She's rather shy with people she doesn't know.'

'I'd put the child in her cot but it's no longer here, so I'll pop her down on the rug while we talk. Is that all right?'

Noting the determination in his face, Cathie chose not to argue. Had it not been for the fact that he placed the child some distance behind him, well out of Cathie's reach, she would have grabbed her and walked away. As it was she felt trapped, quite unable to do anything. Then the memory of the rumpled sheets and him cuddling Rona hit her, and she faced him with fresh fury in her eyes. 'How can you assume I'd return to you when you've not only engaged in an affair with a friend, but I saw you embracing my own *mother*?'

He stepped in front of her, arms folded, a flicker of a smile on his face. 'I assure you that my relationship with Rona is purely platonic. I was only thanking her for her generosity as she urged me not to leave. I really have no wish to lose you, Cathie. I'm only using your bedroom because my parents threw me out for no sensible reason. I'm quite happy to sleep on the couch if you want your room back. I swear I did not sleep with Rona. Nor have I any wish to do so. It's you that I love.'

He was so earnest and in such obvious anguish that Cathie was sorely tempted to believe him, particularly as she knew what a flighty piece her mother was. Even Rona's own husband hadn't been able to tolerate living with her. Of course, Frank had suffered as a result of the war, according to Aunt Evie, as had Alex. He might declare that he loved her, yet how could she be sure?

As the baby's wails grew louder, she took a step forward. 'She needs a cuddle. Please, get out of my way.'

Alex reached the baby first, sweeping her up in his arms and Cathie watched in dismay as he settled himself on the sofa with the little one on his lap. 'Have you considered how you would cope bringing up a child on your own?' he asked.

She thought of the problems she had at the flat, not least her lack of money and with the rent due soon, but chose to make no comment on this as things would surely improve, given time.

'And why would you wish to when I've declared myself willing to adopt it.'

'*Her*. Heather isn't an *it*!'

'Sorry, sweetie, I'm not used to babies yet, but I'm heart-broken that everything has gone wrong for us. I admit it was my fault. I accept now that I was wrong about this child, about lots of things. Such is war and, as I said before, I have no intention of marrying that tart. Please forgive me, darling, and give me another chance. I promise you will never regret it. Believe me when I say that you are my one and only true love, and will be forever. Now why don't you put the kettle on, then we can enjoy a cuppa and make plans for our future together.'

Did his behaviour indicate a return to the charming man he'd appeared to be when she'd first fallen in love with him, or some sort of ploy to win her over? She certainly had no wish to be made a fool of. What game was he playing? This was much worse than the ones Steve used to play on her. Cathie had always thought Steve to be a bit reckless and irritating, but now he'd grown into a caring and attractive man who expressed genuine concern for her. He certainly showed no sign of attempting to control and manipulate her as Alex now seemed intent upon doing. And using a baby in order to do so was beyond belief. Anger simmered within her as Cathie struggled to find a way out of this muddle.

Setting the screaming infant down on the sofa, Alex came to slide a hand tenderly over her cheek. When his lips touched hers, Cathie offered no resistance as something inside of her crumpled. Did she still love him? Or was the emotion she felt down to nervous tension? Was it fear of Alex, or of coping alone that was troubling her? Right now it was very clear that she didn't possess either the power or the courage to defy him. He was very much in charge, and not for the world would Cathie risk any harm coming to her lovely niece. She could but hope that time would resolve this issue.

Chapter Eighteen

'So you've stopped fussing at last, and come home? Thank goodness for that,' Rona said, when she arrived home from the mill later that day.

'Your tea is in the oven, Mam,' Cathie said with a sigh, knowing her mother's relief was more to do with the fact she'd be spared housekeeping duties rather than being pleased to see her daughter. 'I'm back for now, to see how things go.'

'So you're hoping everything will eventually come right between you, then you can marry after all, eh? Happen it'd help if you agreed to release the child's pot of cash. Money is tight these days, remember, and he has every right to share it.'

'Don't start on that again, Mam.' Cathie made no mention of how Alex had picked up little Heather from the nursery, or the doubts growing in her about his controlling behaviour. Was marriage what she truly wanted, or was she only thinking of the child? She couldn't quite decide. As she helped little Heather spoon stewed apples into her eager little mouth, it felt as if she was standing at a crossroads in life, unable to make up her mind which route to take. In a way it had felt a wonderful relief to hear Alex apologise so humbly to her and be back in his arms, but learning to trust him again would not be easy. Perhaps that's why there still remained a slight distance between them, one that would take time to bridge.

'Stop being so bossy,' Rona was saying as she helped herself to a portion of liver and onions. 'And don't ask too many questions of the poor chap. He needs time to acclimatise to everyday life.'

'I do feel sorry for him in a way, as he still seems restless, and not at all settled into Civvy Street. Maybe I have been a bit too condemning and independent-minded. But I hate the fact that men seem to have double standards. They consider it perfectly acceptable for them to play around while wives and sweethearts aren't even allowed to be friends with another man.'

'That's life.'

'It's entirely unfair. I have not spent the war entertaining the troops as Davina apparently did. I would love for things to return to the way they were between us, although it does feel a bit odd to have him living here.'

'If he's to be your husband, lass, why shouldn't he?'

Cathie said no more. Perhaps Rona was right, and she was fussing too much. She was at least finally convinced that Alex was not engaged in an affair with her own mother, or had any wish to be.

* * *

Over the coming days and weeks, Cathie applied all her attention upon caring for little Heather. As a lively toddler, she happily spent her time running about and playing with her wooden bricks, her teddy and a rag doll that Cathie had stitched for her. She loved her so much, as if she really were her own child.

Every now and then, Cathie would encourage Alex to play with her too, so far with little success. She once placed Heather on his lap with her favourite teddy in her arms. The toddler pressed its nose against Alex's mouth as if Billy the bear was giving him a kiss, making Cathie laugh. Alex, however, was not amused. He whipped the toy from her hands and tossed it across the room. Heather instantly began to cry, which infuriated him, and he handed her back to Cathie as if she were a dishrag he really had no wish to touch.

'Shut that child up *now*!' he snapped.

Little Heather gave a startled jerk and screamed all the louder. Cathie rushed to pick up her precious teddy, and quickly handed it back to the child for her to cuddle. 'That is really no way to react. She was only having a bit of fun with you.'

'She cries the whole damn time.'

'No, she doesn't, only if she falls down, feels hungry or she's having a bit of a paddy as children do at this age. But it soon passes. It doesn't help if you take away her favourite teddy.'

'The noise grates on my nerves.'

What had happened to his resolve to be like a father to her? His attitude towards the child troubled Cathie deeply, as it did not bode well for the future. Perhaps his reaction to her noisy screaming was a result of his fear of guns going off during the war? Cathie immediately set about trying to calm the toddler down, which did not prove easy, so she took her upstairs for a nap.

Heather also had a passion for opening bags, drawers and boxes. Anything she could lay her chubby little hands on she would search and empty. But when she explored Alex's gas mask pack, scattering papers, letters, notebooks and other stuff all over the rug in the front parlour, he flew into a rage. Cathie had never seen him so angry.

'Get that child out of here,' he roared, so loud and furious that Heather's little mouth compressed with shock then opened wide in yet another piercing scream, her panicked gaze turning at once to Cathie for help.

'Please don't shout, you're frightening her,' Cathie cried, rushing to pick her up. If it was noise that troubled him, why did he make so much himself? 'She was only playing, and hasn't damaged a thing, at least I don't think so.'

Staring down at the letters, she could see that some of them had been torn in half, although she couldn't imagine Heather managing to do that with her tiny fingers. She'd no idea who they were from. Perhaps his grumpy father. Cathie could also see one or two ration books, and a few loose coupons held by an elastic band, which seemed odd, as Alex had handed his over when he'd moved in.

'Whose are these?' she asked, but as she reached down to investigate he snatched them up.

'I'm looking after them for a mate of mine. Nothing to do with you, or that damned infant.'

Remembering the advice she'd received, not only from her mother but also on the wireless from members of the Salvation Army and the WVS, explaining how ex-servicemen could be very obsessive over their privacy, she gave him a polite smile of apology. 'Sorry, I'll go and put the kettle on. I think we could all do with a cup of tea.'

'If we had a decent home of our own we wouldn't be so crushed for space,' he growled. 'But you selfishly refuse to share your pot of money with me.'

Cathie decided not to indulge in a dispute upon this point either.

* * *

And then her worst fears came true when one morning she took Heather as usual to the nursery only to be told that it was closing down.

'Sorry, dear, but this is our last day,' the matron told her. 'No more government funding available, and fewer children seeking places as mothers return home, so that's it. I'm afraid this nursery, like most others, is to close.'

'Oh, no, so how am I supposed to cope now?' Cathie felt sheer panic flood through her.

'Maybe a friend with a child of her own would help, or perhaps your mother?'

Cathie didn't know whether to laugh or cry at this suggestion. She didn't have any close friends around right now. And she certainly had no intention of leaving little Heather with Alex, even if he showed himself willing to babysit. Could persuading Rona to finally take some responsibility for her grandchild be the only answer, assuming childcare could be fitted in with her shifts? Rona made it very clear that it wasn't.

Fortunately, Cathie's new boss at the umbrella factory kindly agreed she could take the little girl with her, so long as she was kept in her pram. Poor Heather did not enjoy being so confined and would wail and howl, struggling to free herself, so that once again the dummy had to be brought into action, and the apron and harness fixed firmly in place. But what else could she do as Rona had point-blank refused to help? Besides which, she had her own shift work to deal with.

Every morning, Cathie would dash to the umbrella factory to clean their offices before they started work at nine. Around half past ten, she'd pop in the Co-op to do the day's shopping, always keeping an eye out for Steve, in the hope he might have changed his mind and returned home. Then she'd clean their own house, fetch in the coal, wash, iron, scrub floors and cook, an endless raft of domestic duties that greatly bored and exhausted her. There must surely be more to life than this.

Alex was generally absent during the day; although where he went and what he got up to Cathie had no idea.

He seemed to take long walks along the Rochdale canal towpath or by the River Irwell, but also claimed to be seeking work. What kind of employment he was seeking she did not have the courage to ask.

No questions, that's what the WVS also advised, which suited Cathie greatly.

But it still puzzled her slightly that if he hadn't already found a job, how was it that he never seemed to be short of cash? Now that he was sleeping on the couch, the envelope of cash had disappeared from under the mattress, and not for a moment did Cathie dare mention she'd found it there, let alone ask how he'd come by so much money. But he certainly had enough to go out drinking every night, living life to the full, as he liked to call it. Rarely did Cathie go with him, even when invited, although on occasions Rona would surprise her by offering to babysit. At last prepared to take some responsibility for her grandchild. On those occasions they'd go to the Gaumont cinema, or back to the Ritz.

It was such a treat to be able to go out together. Cathie came to enjoy sitting beside Alex at the flicks, holding his hand or feeling his arm about her shoulders. She loved dancing with him and enjoyed his kisses, although she was careful not to allow him too much leeway. After all, they were no longer even engaged, and Cathie wanted their relationship to grow at a modest rate. To be fair, he seemed perfectly happy with that, so perhaps things might work out for them in the end.

Oh, but how she missed her work at the tyre factory, and the companionship of the other women she used to work with, not to mention Brenda who was still with her relatives. She'd written to her friend, explaining that she'd now moved out of her flat as she and Alex were giving it another go.

Oddly enough, Cathie even missed Davina, and would sometimes wonder how or where her erstwhile friend was, and whether she'd given birth to her baby yet. Although not for a moment dare she mention this fact to Alex. He might take it to mean that she wasn't in the least bit jealous and he could continue his affair with her, which was the last thing Cathie wanted.

As for Steve, she ached to know where he was too, wishing he would answer the letter of apology she'd sent him. But it was not something she dare repeat, fearful of what Alex would do to her if he found out they were still in touch.

* * *

Cathie was making herself a mug of hot chocolate one night when she heard the front door bang. Most evenings Alex went out alone and would often come home late, having clearly overindulged himself on far too much alcohol. She should have been in bed herself but had been kept awake by Heather having another of her screaming tantrums.

Thinking that perhaps she was suffering from a bad

dream, Cathie had sat with her for some time, singing gently to her: *Hush little baby don't say a word, Momma's going to buy you a mocking bird…* until she fell asleep again.

Now about to take her drink upstairs to bed, she realised Alex was home. Strangely, instead of feeling pleased, her heart sank, partly because he might demand that she make him some supper, and she was so exhausted. She was also fearful of his reaction if Heather woke up crying again. Just as the sound of thunder and sirens would upset her, crying and screaming seemed to badly affect him.

Before Cathie could escape up the stairs, he entered the kitchen and, from the bleary expression on his face and the way he staggered, she realised that yet again he must have drunk an excessive amount. Reaching for the cake tin and handing over her own mug of chocolate, she managed a smile.

'There you are. Help yourself. I'm shattered and off to bed.' But as she moved away, he grabbed hold of her to pull her into his arms.

'Aw, come on, girl. Stop avoiding me and give me a kiss.'

'I'm not avoiding you,' Cathie said with a gentle little smile, even as she struggled to free his hold upon her.

'If you really want me, why don't you show it?' His eyes were glazed and, lifting her in his arms, he half carried her to the old horsehair sofa in the living room where he started to kiss her with passion. His mouth and hands seemed to be everywhere, as if he were devouring her. But instead of feeling that surge of desire she used to experience at his slightest touch, fear and revulsion cascaded within her. Being made love to by a drunk was not what she wished for at all.

'*Stop it!*' Cathie cried, striving to push him away.

'Why are you resisting me?' he slurred.

'It's late, and I'm tired.'

'We're about to become man and wife, so I've every right to make love to you.' He had her pinned beneath him, one hand fondling her breast while the other slid beneath the waistband of her skirt to explore the nakedness of her stomach. Cathie sent up a thankful prayer that she'd been sensible enough not to venture downstairs in her pyjamas or nightgown, a feeling that didn't last long as his hand slid up her leg to caress her buttocks and private parts.

'Not like this,' she cried, slapping him. 'Leave me alone. *Please!*' Even the smell of him was revolting: the beer on his breath and the stink of sweat made her feel sick. Fearing that at any moment her virginity could be taken from her, and not at all in the romantic way she'd envisioned, she fought to push him away. But the weight of him on top of her was overpowering. It was then that Heather let out a heartrending wail of distress and began to scream and cry all over again.

'Let me go, please. She's having bad dreams.'

But he only laughed as he began to unbutton his flies.

'That bloody child can wait. You can't be doing a good job as a mother if she cries all the flaming time.'

'How can you say that? She's just a baby.'

'I'm sick of listening to her screams and yells,' he shouted.

'Then let me go to her. *Now!*'

'Not till I've had you first,' he hissed.

'What's going on here?' Rona's voice rang out. 'This isn't the place for such a carry-on, or an argument, not when that flipping child is ruining my night's sleep.'

Within seconds Alex had rolled off her, and Cathie was on her feet and rushing upstairs, for once grateful for her mother's intervention. Dear God, what had she been thinking of to stay here? Had she completely lost her senses? As she cradled the sobbing baby in her arms, soothing and kissing her and feeling Heather rub her little head into her neck for comfort, she was even more surprised when Rona came to join her.

'Is the little lamb all right?'

Goodness, it almost sounded as if her mother actually cared. 'I'm not sure. She may still be teething, or suffering from bad dreams. Thanks for coming for me, Mam. Alex is as drunk as a lord, yet again, so I was most grateful for your help. I really don't understand why on earth he drinks so much, night after night.'

'That's what ex-servicemen do, chuck. It blocks the horrors they've suffered from their minds. Happen he'll get over it, given time. As to whether he'll agree to father that child, I still have me doubts. Anyroad, goodnight. I need my sleep.'

So do I, Cathie thought, taking Heather into her own bed, and cuddling up beside her. There were times when her stupid mother did speak sense, even if those last words had filled her with fresh doubt and fears. Perhaps what Alex had suffered in the desert was causing him to drink. How long would it take for him to recover from whatever was troubling him? And her hopes that he might come to adore little Heather didn't seem to be working either.

* * *

It was as Cathie changed the bedding in the baby's cot the following morning that she came across a scattering of dust and plaster beneath the bottom sheet. How on earth had that got there? Looking up at the ceiling she wondered if it had rained down from above, but could see no sign of any cracks. Hadn't she given the entire place a coat of whitewash just a few months ago? No wonder the poor love had woken up screaming and crying, and been quite unable to settle. She must have felt so uncomfortable with bits of plaster and rubble sticking into her back and little bottom. It was most odd. And why hadn't she noticed this while singing her to sleep?

'Have you been messing with Heather's bedding?' she demanded of Rona as she slapped a plate of toast and jam on to the table before her. Alex, fortunately, was still asleep, so Cathie felt free to challenge her mother. 'I found plaster and dust in Heather's cot. Have you any idea how that could have happened?'

'Nay, why would I?'

'I've no idea, but you've rarely shown any interest in her, despite the fact she's your grandchild.'

'Mebbe that's because I can't bear to remember her real mother is dead.'

Stunned by the sadness in Rona's eyes, Cathie sank on to the chair beside her, then quietly murmured, 'Oh, I'm sorry, Mam. I should allow for the fact that you too are grieving for our Sal.' This may well account for Rona's black moods, although she'd never been the most affectionate of mothers, even when they were young. She was always far too obsessed with her own needs, and having a good time. Cathie wished she understood her mother better, and then she might feel closer to her. Yet Rona did love Sally; there had never been any question about that. In a way she was her favourite daughter, and would often say to Cathie: 'Why can't you be more like your sister?' never quite appreciating Cathie's own strengths and qualities. Rona must miss Sal greatly, as did she. And everyone had their own ways of grieving; anger being a major part of the pain involved.

'I'll admit you've been much more helpful lately, allowing me some time off now and then, although I did wonder if that was more to please Alex rather than any love you feel for little Heather.'

'It's not that I don't care, chuck. I never was the maternal sort, and it's too late for me to change now.'

'It would seem so, as you aren't even prepared to adjust your shifts to share the job of childcare.'

'I can't. I need the income if I'm not going to be a burden to you as I get older. Anyroad, it's not *my* lack of help for this little lass you should be worried about, it's the reactions of the man you are keen to make into her father.'

This remark stunned Cathie into silence as she concentrated on assisting Heather's attempt to feed herself, while nibbling her own toast. Was that the reason she hadn't returned to Brenda's flat? Her indecision and dread of struggling to cope alone sending her demented? And possibly the reason for the rubble in the baby's cot lay in this ramshackle house they were renting. All of which should encourage her to try all the harder to find a better job. She needed a good income too. But on the plus side, for the first time in years Cathie felt something akin to a closeness with her mother.

A day or two later, Cathie received a letter from a local orphanage thanking her for her enquiry and saying they did now have room to take her sister's child.

Chapter Nineteen

Cathie stared at the letter, perplexed. What on earth were they talking about? She hadn't made any such enquiry. Had her mother done this? Dear God, she'd give her a piece of her mind if she had. When challenged, Rona denied any knowledge of such a letter.

'What are you accusing me of now? None of this has owt to do wi' me,' she responded indignantly.

'Are you sure?'

'I never chucked you in an orphanage, did I, even though I had to bring the pair of you up all by myself?'

That was certainly true, even if she hadn't been the most wonderful mother, Rona had always provided them with a comfortable home.

'There must be some mistake then.'

So what was going on? When Cathie called round to the orphanage later that day to inform them she had made no such enquiry, the young woman in the office looked somewhat puzzled.

'We did indeed receive a letter. Here it is.' And opening

her filing cabinet she drew out a sheet of paper, which she handed to Cathie.

Reality dawned, rather like a shower of cold ice sliding over her. This wasn't her handwriting, or her signature. Nor was it her mother's. Nevertheless Cathie recognised it instantly. Hadn't she received a number of letters written in this hand over years, not as many as she would have liked and often in batches with long pauses in between, with some of the words blocked out by black pencil? There was no mistaking the sender. What had possessed Alex to do such a thing?

When asked he looked stricken with guilt. 'I thought that was what you wanted, to be free of the responsibility of being the foster mother to a child that is not yours.'

'I've never said that. I *love* her. Heather *is* my child, in every respect but one. I did not give birth to her.'

'I'm sorry, sweetie, I didn't understand. Bit confused. Will you forgive me?'

It was difficult to find it in her heart to do so. As he took the child from her arms to give little Heather a cuddle, fear escalated inside her yet again, instinct warning her not to irritate him further. He was so impulsive, his moods unpredictable and irrational, much as he might claim to love her. It was as if he was jealous of this little one's demands upon her attention. Perhaps she should encourage him to spend more time with Heather, and learn a little more about childcare. But would that work? Could she trust him? Cathie sent up a silent prayer that he'd come to love the child as much as she did. Finding a solution to this problem was going to take time.

* * *

Parenting, Cathie discovered as little Heather's independence grew, was not simply a job but more a way of life, and one that would last for ever. Oh, but she loved the bones of her, and was gaining increasing confidence as a mother. She had established a good routine, knew not to overexcite the child as bedtime approached, and when and how to put her down to sleep. She'd even disposed of her dummy yet again as she didn't want the toddler to damage her teeth. Instead, the little girl would chatter away using her own made-up words, or sing herself back to sleep, which was a delight to listen to. And whenever she threw herself into a tantrum Cathie would stand by and let her get on with it, finding that she generally grew bored after a few minutes and would start playing with a toy instead, as if to distract herself.

But, as Rona had predicted, persuading Alex to take an interest in the child was not proving to be easy. He showed very little patience. On one occasion when Cathie had left him in charge for no more than ten minutes while she slipped out to the corner shop, she'd returned to find he'd plonked her into a cardboard box under the stairs, just because she'd started crying the moment Cathie had gone. They'd had a furious row over that.

'If children don't behave they need to be punished,' he snapped.

'But not locked up in the dark,' Cathie shouted back. 'Don't *ever* do that again.'

'Don't you tell me what I can or cannot do!' He'd stormed off, but had returned later with a bunch of violets, looking most contrite. 'Sorry, sweetie, I'd had a tiring day so lost patience.'

Doing what? she wondered, but didn't dare enquire. He was far too unpredictable to argue with. Cathie accepted his apology with good grace, but doubted she would ever leave Heather alone with him again. Although if that were the case, how could she even consider marrying this man? Their relationship seemed to be going from bad to worse. What was it that made him lose his patience so easily? On other occasions he could be the sweetest, most generous person, often providing her with unexpected gifts of clothes and cash. One minute he could be raging with temper, the next loving and caring. Was that genuine or a ploy on his part? Or perhaps all part of the healing process. Maybe she just needed to be patient too.

Today he'd brought home some fillets of haddock, which a fisherman friend had apparently given him.

'Oh, how wonderful,' Cathie told him as she happily set about cooking it. 'You're so clever the way you keep finding us good food, and something different to eat.'

Heather, however, was less impressed and refused to eat it, spitting out every mouthful with a sour expression on her little face. Alex was not pleased.

Cathie merely laughed. 'She's never had haddock before,

or fish of any kind. I expect it takes time to acquire a taste for it. Never mind, I have one or two eggs left; I'll boil one of those instead. She loves boiled eggs.'

'No, she must eat this. She's a silly child, and has no right to waste perfectly good food,' he barked. He picked up a spoon, scooped up a morsel of fish and attempted to shove it into her mouth. Heather stubbornly resisted, clamping her plump little lips together and turning her head away. 'You naughty girl!' he yelled, standing over her and jabbing a finger in her chest.

'Stop that!' Cathie cried, pushing him away, utterly horrified by such behaviour. 'You'll hurt her.'

'She must learn to do as she's told.'

For once Heather did not start crying. Instead, she seemed to have frozen, her little mouth still clamped shut, an expression of wary distrust in her blue-eyed gaze. Cathie found this reaction even more disturbing.

'Please, Alex, as we've already discussed, you need to exercise a little more patience. You're expecting her to behave like a five-year-old, but Heather isn't even eighteen months yet. Right now she needs loving comfort; rules and punishment can come later when she's old enough to understand.'

'She never will understand if we aren't firm with her.'

'You are *too* firm.'

'Nonsense, you should have seen how my father behaved towards me.'

'Then don't repeat his mistakes upon Heather.'

'I'll do as I damn well please!'

'No, you won't,' Cathie patiently responded, stifling a sigh. 'As I am her foster mother, she is *my* responsibility, not yours.'

Almost as soon as the words were out of her mouth, she instantly regretted them. Hadn't she once agonised for months over how to tell Alex she wanted him to help her adopt the baby? Now his mouth twisted into a curl of sarcastic amusement, and he laughed. 'We'll see what good that does you.'

Finishing the rest of his meal in silence, he then picked up his hat and marched off to the Pack Horse, as he did most evenings. Cathie heaved a sigh of relief, even though she knew he would no doubt come home the worse for drink. Rather than settling into a civilian way of life, Alex seemed to be battling against it.

* * *

The next day Alex was out and about, as usual. This time hovering close to various jewellery shops, trying to decide which one to try. Perhaps the smartest part of the city would not be a good idea, certainly not St Ann Street, as he was too well known by the shopkeepers there. He had, however, adopted a disguise of sorts by wearing a large pair of spectacles and a false beard, plus the kind of bowler hat he would normally never wear. He walked along Deansgate, and various roads and streets leading off it, and then wandered over to Piccadilly, which was something of a blitzed site still, as most of the warehouses had been damaged or destroyed by bombs.

The city was bustling with activity, and he quickly dashed across the road as a cart passed by, loaded with great churns of milk. Stalls and hawkers' carts lined Oldham Street but it was a prosperous shopping area with many fine shops, popular with Mancunians. And in one of the streets just off it, he soon found what he was looking for: a small shop selling new and second-hand jewellery.

The bell rang as he strolled inside, and a grey-haired stockily built man with a ruddy complexion emerged through a curtain at the back of the shop. He was cleaning a pair of spectacles, which he then perched on to his long nose.

Alex kept his own glasses firmly in place, squinting at him through narrowed eyes. 'Good morning,' he said with a polite smile. 'I'm seeking an engagement ring for my fiancée. In theory we've been engaged for some time but because of being sent overseas during the war I never got around to buying her a ring.' Not true, but this man had no way of knowing that. 'Sorry, I don't have too much money, I'm afraid, but wondered if you could help.'

'Be happy to,' the shopkeeper said, and instantly began pulling trays of rings out from under the counter. 'Would she like a sapphire, ruby or…?'

'Diamond. She loves diamonds.'

A few trays were set out before him and, as he examined each one, Alex made a careful note of the prices, which were reasonably low. 'Perhaps I could see some rings with stones a little larger and more valuable. Actually, I'm not totally without funds and this lady is the love of my life.'

A couple more trays were brought out, at a much higher price. 'If these are too expensive, sir, I could show you some priced between the two,' the man assured him.

They were indeed far too expensive, but, giving a wry smile, Alex lifted one or two rings to examine them more closely under the light of a lamp. 'I can see why. They are quite beautiful, but perhaps something a little less costly would be more sensible. Have you a solitaire, perhaps?'

'Of course,' he said, pulling out yet another tray. It was as Alex reached for it that he managed to 'accidentally' knock one of others on to the floor. 'Oh, I'm terribly sorry,' he cried, instantly bending down to start gathering up the rings scattered about.

'Yi, yi, yi!' The old man threw up his hands in horror and came scuttling quickly round the counter to help. It took no more than a matter of moments to collect up all the rings and set them back upon the tray, then Alex chose one of the cheaper imitation diamond rings. 'I think I'd better stick with this one,' he said with an apologetic grimace.

The chosen ring was swiftly put into a box, the shopkeeper informing Alex as he handed over the money that if he brought his fiancée in the ring could be resized to fit her finger.

'Thank you, you've been most kind.' Then, glancing at the trays on the counter, now in something of a muddle, he again apologised profusely and calmly left. Once outside, he slipped his hand into his pocket to find the ring that had just happened to fall into it. It was amazing how foolishly trusting some people were. Cheating, he'd discovered, was so easy and extremely profitable. But then he'd always had a talent for deceit.

Chuckling to himself as he turned the corner back into Oldham Street, Alex quickly removed the bowler hat, spectacles, beard and even his raincoat, and dumped the lot into a dustbin behind a hawker's cart, just in case it dawned on the shopkeeper that he'd been robbed. Then he strolled into a pub for a pint of beer to celebrate.

* * *

It was a beautiful sunny spring day and Cathie was walking along Back Irwell Street towards Deansgate, thinking she might enquire at Kendal Milne to see if they had any vacancies, when she spotted Brenda approaching. Her friend was smartly dressed in linen trousers with a tailored jacket, a broad grin on her face and her arms outstretched. Cathie instantly raced over to give her a hug, the baby bouncing in her pram. 'Oh, there you are, Brenda, how lovely to see you back. How I've missed you.'

'Good to see you too, darling. Shall we go and find Davina to enjoy our usual cup of tea and a gossip?'

'I'd rather not, if you don't mind. I've so much to tell you. You wouldn't believe what I've been through.'

Brenda frowned. 'Not more problems?'

'I'm afraid so. What about you, are your family legal problems resolved?'

Brenda pulled her face. 'I hope so. Come on, let's go and eat.'

It took no time at all for Cathie to pour out her heart to her best friend as they linked arms and headed for their favourite café on Campfield Market. She was as ever loyal, supportive and deeply sympathetic.

'I always thought there was something fishy about that girl,' Brenda said with a snarl of ill temper. 'She turned up out of the blue one day, yet never said a word about her past, not even where she'd been born or anything about her family, let alone the war. What a madam she must be.'

'She took such pleasure in revealing their affair, and telling me she was carrying Alex's child, with not a word of apology even though I'd always looked upon her as a friend.'

'You poor darling, that must have been awful. Have you seen her since?'

'No, not a sign.'

'There's no sign of her today either,' Brenda said, glancing over at the second-hand clothes stall where she normally worked. 'You order tea and a sandwich for us while I go and ask.'

Cathie watched as Brenda bustled over to chat with the owner, who seemed to be shaking her head. Did she even need to know what had happened to Davina? she asked herself.

'The stallholder says she's no idea where she is. Davina didn't even bother to hand in her notice, just disappeared, maybe back to wherever she came from.'

'Well, it's of no interest to me where she's gone,' Cathie said with a sigh. 'All that matters is that Alex and I are back together, well almost. Possibly. I'm trying my best to put all this mess behind me and see if it will work. Admittedly, it isn't easy as he's still not at all himself, and a bit too impatient with little Heather here,' Cathie said, stroking the toddler's fluffy blonde hair as she lifted her from the pram to sit her on her lap, then quickly told Brenda about his attempt to find Heather a place at the local orphanage.

'Oh, my goodness, that's dreadful!' Brenda said, giving the baby a comforting pat and kiss.

'Don't worry, I've no intention of allowing that to happen. I just can't understand why he would imagine it to be a good idea.'

Brenda gave a sad shake of her head, her normally cheerful face looking doleful. 'I doubt he's thinking things through properly. The psychological effects of war can be very damaging.'

'I do realise that. Aunt Evie was telling me about my dad, and how the First World War affected him so badly that he couldn't settle, then disappeared to explore the world, never to be seen or heard from again. I'm wondering if that is partly the reason why my mother became such a selfish queen. Being locked up with her husband's problems obviously didn't appeal.' Cathie was silent for a moment as the possible truth of this notion hit home. Maybe she should show more compassion towards her mother. Rona can't have had an easy life, losing a husband and having to bring up her daughters alone, then losing Sal whom she loved so much. Her losses in life had sadly turned her into a bitter and selfish woman. How Cathie hoped and prayed the same things wouldn't happen to her.

'Has Alex found employment yet?' Brenda asked, interrupting her troubled thoughts.

'Not that I'm aware of.'

'That's a shame. I believe the British Legion has been attempting to achieve priority for ex-servicemen in getting jobs, so far with little success as the new Labour government insists on equality for all. They say this is because civilians too have been on the fighting line.'

'That's a fair point, but I still think ex-servicemen deserve better treatment than they're getting. As for Alex, oddly enough he doesn't seem to be short of money, which is a bit of a puzzle to me, particularly considering how he keeps demanding I hand over little Heather's inheritance, which I refuse to do.'

'And what's happened to Davina is a mystery too, but then that girl always was. Maybe I'll ask around, see if anyone knows where she's living now,' Brenda said.

Chapter Twenty

Alex was eating his breakfast in peace and quiet one morning, as he so liked to do after both women had gone off to work, when to his horror he found a piece in the *Manchester Guardian* reporting a theft at a jewellery shop. He quickly read it, instantly recognising the story as that of his own. To his great relief, the description given by the shopkeeper of the person he suspected of the crime was of a man with a beard, who wore spectacles and a bowler hat. Alex chuckled to himself as he recalled how easily he'd disposed of this simple disguise. It was highly unlikely that he would ever be recognised or implicated as the thief responsible.

The word 'thief' resounded momentarily in his head. Is that what he'd turned into, as a consequence of this dratted war and a need for hard cash? Dismissing the crime as unimportant, as was what he'd been obliged to do to Davina, he tossed the newspaper aside. His family had largely disowned him because his fancy public school had never regarded him worthy of high regard. Nor had the army. His future now lay very firmly in his own hands, and allowing his plans to be ruined by some tart was never on the cards. He was not the idiot people might think.

He'd also attempted to dispose of that irritating child, but had sadly failed, which annoyed him enormously. Nor had he yet managed to lure Cathie back into his arms, as she was still resisting him with obstinate stubborness. He would need to exercise his charms a little more in order to completely win her over. Maybe he could begin tonight by taking her out for the evening. Didn't he deserve to enjoy life after years of hard work, not to mention bullying from army commanding officers as well as his own father? Now it was his turn to rule the roost.

Before he left the house that morning on his usual round of factories and deals in the black marketing world, he tore the offending page from the paper and threw it in the fire, just to make sure that Cathie never saw it.

That evening, Alex took her to the Ritz dance hall, their favourite place, leaving the child in her grandmother's care. He'd made it very plain to Rona that if she really wanted him to ever get back together with her daughter, she would need to play her part. Happily, she'd agreed. He so enjoyed holding Cathie in his arms, smoothing his hand over her slender back and waistline and gently kissing her soft cheeks and lips. Even though he longed to go much further, he carefully held himself in check. There would be ample opportunity to explore her delightful body once he'd got a ring back on her finger.

A few days later, they went to the Palais on Rochdale

Road, and the following Saturday to see 'The Harvey Girls' at the Odeon. Life was looking up, so far as Alex was concerned. He had a pocket full of cash and a girl on his arm. What could be better? Having her in his bed, of course, which was the next and most important step.

But Cathie was not Davina, and would never entertain such a move until she'd agreed they had a future together. And before that could happen he needed to appear to reconcile himself to this so-called niece of hers.

* * *

'How about a visit to Belle Vue?' he suggested one Sunday. 'The sun is shining as summer is almost here. I thought perhaps the little one might enjoy a day out to see the elephants and monkeys.'

'Oh, that would be lovely,' Cathie cried, clapping her hands with joy. 'You'd love that, wouldn't you, sweetheart?' she asked Heather, who giggled and laughed with a nod of her little head, shouting "Yes, yes," not knowing what she was agreeing to but loved to join in the fun. Cathie felt a surge of joy that at last Alex was beginning to take a proper interest in the child.

They caught the number thirty-four tram to Belle Vue, and Heather did indeed squeal with delight at seeing the monkeys playing on their rocky hill. She was utterly entranced by the way they cuddled and groomed each other, pointing first at one monkey and then another, her chubby little face aglow with happiness.

'Look, look. Want a cuddle.'

'What about taking her for an elephant ride?' Alex suggested with a smile.

'Ooh no, I think she's far too young to sit on such a huge animal, but perhaps on a donkey.' And keeping a firm hold around her tiny waist, with the donkey's owner controlling the animal, it worked a treat with Heather chuckling with excitement.

It was a wonderful day. The sun shone, the sight of bombed factories, rows of damaged houses and shops not evident for once. Belle Vue felt like a magical wonderland of fun and entertainment with its zoological gardens and amusement park, musical concerts, dancing and even a circus at Christmas time. Today there was a band playing out on the lawns, and they sat for some time listening to 'Have I Told You Lately That I Love You?' Alex held her hand, gazing deeply into her eyes as he sang along with the music. And when he put his arm about her to give her a tender kiss, she felt as if her heart was melting. Perhaps she did still love him. How could she not?

Cathie even raised no objections to him taking them to watch the racing on the track at the corner of Hyde Road and Hunter's Lane, even though the sound of the engines roared in her ears as the bikes tore around the track. Surprisingly, they didn't seem to bother him, despite his protests that he hated noise.

'It must be a hugely dangerous sport,' she said. 'How very brave those men must be.'

'Or maybe a bit mad,' he laughed. 'You get that way after fighting a war.'

Alex bought some candy floss for the toddler, and a dish of vanilla ice cream each for Cathie and himself. What a generous and kind man he was turning into, she thought, as later he took her to a tea dance at Joe Taylor's Dance Hall, where he held the baby in his arms while they danced together. Cathie smiled up at him with delight. He must be on the road to recovery at last, and soon everything would be just fine between them.

'At one time we could have taken this little one to see the fireworks,' he said, as they enjoyed ham sandwiches, tea and cakes together. 'Unfortunately, they haven't started yet, all because of that dratted war.'

'I wonder sometimes if we'll ever get over it,' Cathie groaned, taking a sip of the sparkling wine he'd also ordered as a treat, and feeling her cheeks glow with happiness.

'Of course we will, sweetie. You and I are meant to enjoy a wonderful life together. Which reminds me of the rather special reason I invited you out today.' He placed a small box on the table before her. Cathie's eyebrows lifted in startled surprise as she looked at it, a part of her guessing what it might be. 'Go on, open it.'

After taking it gently in her hands, she did so, and stared in disbelief at the beautiful solitaire diamond ring set within a pad of blue velvet. 'What is this?'

'What do you think? A brand new engagement ring to replace the cheap second-hand one I got you during the war.' He took it from the box and slid it on to the third finger of her left hand. He had to push it slightly, but it did go on. 'Wonderful, it fits perfectly. A new ring for a new life between us.'

'Oh, it's beautiful. Are you sure you can afford it as you don't even have a job yet, do you?'

The smile slid from his face as his eyes flickered with annoyance. 'What are you suggesting? That I don't have two pennies to rub together, let alone buy you a mark of my love?'

'No, no, sorry.'

'So will you marry me, darling?'

Gazing up into his eyes and still feeling joy at the kind and loving way he'd treated little Heather, who was even now sitting on his lap, how could she refuse? She'd forgiven him for his past misdemeanours, and did still love him, didn't she? Even as she told herself this, an image of Steve drifted into her head, as if challenging that belief. Stifling a sigh, she blocked it out. Steve had gone and, according to his parents, would be unlikely ever to return to Manchester. Besides, this man was her future, not Steve, who had been a good friend to her, once they'd got over their childhood battles, but never any more than that.

* * *

Cathie felt so delighted that at last things were as they should be between them. Alex's profound apologies had helped, but now he'd gone a step further by proving his acceptance of her lovely niece. The future suddenly looked bright. Perhaps it was the happiness on her smiling face that did the trick when a day or two later she called at the Christmas card factory to ask about a job. The forewoman, who introduced herself as Mrs Woolton, said that she did happen to have one or two vacancies available.

'Summer is our busiest time of year as we have all the orders coming in for Christmas, so aye, we are looking to take on new recruits. Some of the work involves collating cards into boxes; other tasks are dropping said boxes on to a conveyer belt to be filled. We set a limit and if you go beyond that number of cards, you win a bit of a bonus,' she said with a wink. 'How would you feel about that?'

Cathie's eyes shone with new hope. 'I'm a hard worker, Mrs Woolton, but there is just one problem. I have a small niece to care for, as her parents are not with us any more, thanks to the war, and her nursery has closed down so I'll need to find someone to mind her.'

'Ah yes, that's been happening to all our women workers. The government is good at ignoring us ladies, despite all our hard labour throughout the war, so we've set up a crèche here. Bring her along, she'll be very welcome.'

'Oh, thank you so much. That would be wonderful!' All her problems resolved in one go, thanks to this lovely lady. 'You can rely on me to do my best to try and meet those targets.'

Mrs Woolton chuckled. 'I'm sure you will, love. And

if you make good progress, there are other tasks such as using machines to add glitter or gold dust to the cards, which are more demanding but better paid. You just have to prove yourself first.'

'I'd love to do that.'

'Right then, chuck. You're on. We'll give you a month's trial, if that's agreeable to you.'

Cathie assured her that it was, even though it meant giving notice to her cleaning job without absolute proof that this one would last. But she had every hope it would. The chance of being back working in a factory again with the opportunity to be part of a team and make new friends felt like a joy to her heart. How she'd missed all of that. On top of which she'd be earning much better wages, and with the chance to improve them over time.

Cathie went straight to Brenda's flat to tell her the good news, mentioning that there appeared to be more than one vacancy. 'Why don't you apply too?'

'Really? I'll go and speak to the lady right now,' her friend said, jumping up and grabbing her coat from the hook behind the door.

'I'll come with you and wait outside while you go in and ask.'

By good fortune, Brenda too was offered a job, and the two friends did a little jig together on the pavement outside. Life was looking up for them both, at last.

The pair of them quickly settled in to their new job, being used to a factory system of clocking in, targets to be met and a long working day. Cathie loved every minute of it. She couldn't remember feeling this happy in months. The task of dropping the boxes on to a conveyor belt was rather boring but she would hum little tunes to herself as she worked. She soon got the hang of sitting at a bench collating the Christmas cards, counting and sliding off a dozen from the various piles and popping them into the boxes.

By the end of the first week both were suffering from an aching back, and would rub liniment into each other's shoulders, giggling as they did so.

'Are we turning into old women?' Cathie chortled.

'Never.'

But over the coming weeks the pain eased and her speed gradually improved. Cathie felt quite certain she would soon reach the required target to ensure she kept the job. Getting beyond that level to earn a bonus might take considerably longer but she was delighted to be employed again and happy with the progress she was making.

Alex, however, was less impressed. 'You won't need to work at all once we are wed,' he said, watching with a sniff of disapproval as she left off peeling potatoes to set little Heather on her potty; then gave her shoulders a quick massage before dashing to check the sausages in the oven. 'There's no reason to wait, and you could then devote your time to being a good wife and mother instead of running round in circles like a mad thing.'

Cathie stifled a sigh. She'd been thrilled by his change of

attitude towards little Heather, and his loving proposal. But because of all the ups and downs in their relationship, and remembering what Steve and Brenda had both said about the effects of separation during war, felt the need to take things slowly. Perhaps a month or so to allow herself time to be absolutely certain she was making the right decision.

'I'm happy to be engaged to you, Alex, but still have no desire to rush you to the altar, or give up work even when we do marry. We agreed we needed time to save up. Beside which, I do like my independence.' And pecking his cheek with a kiss to brush away the sour expression on his face, Cathie then bustled off to pin a clean nappy on the toddler, wash her hands, and go back to peeling the potatoes.

* * *

Saturday was now the only time Cathie could take little Heather out in her pram, although at eighteen months old, it was obvious that the child was itching to be free of such confinement. But not here, or right now, as Cathie was walking along Oldham Street, which as usual was thronged with people milling about. The area was a strange mix of cheap bargain stalls and a most prosperous range of fine shops. She loved browsing at the hawkers' barrows that jostled the length of the street as far as Stevenson Square.

Hearing the sound of an organ grinder, she strolled over to listen. He was playing a Perry Como hit: 'Prisoner Of Love'. She understood perfectly how that felt. Hadn't she been trapped by her feelings for Alex, even when there was no proof that he felt the same way about her? Now there was, following that wonderful day out together at Belle Vue, and his proposal. Happiness soared through her at the memory and her dream for a happy future together about to be fulfilled. Everything was looking wonderful, at last. The war was over and even Alex was beginning to settle.

Perhaps she'd walk over to Shudehill fruit and vegetable market later, and see if she could find any bananas for little Heather. She'd heard tell that there were now some available, if you were lucky. As the music ended, she swung the pram around and went bang into a man who'd obviously been standing right behind her. 'Oh, goodness, I'm so sorry. I hope I haven't hurt you.'

'Nay it's my fault, dearie. I were standing too close.'

Alarmed by the man's age and the way he was bending down to hold his knee, Cathie helped him away from the crowds to sit on a low wall just off the main street, dragging the pram behind her as she did so. Then she began to gently massage the knee for him. He was grey-haired, stockily built with a ruddy complexion, and quite old. Cathie didn't have the nerve to ask him to pull up the thick tweed trousers he was wearing to examine the knee for any bruising, but she did help him to stretch and bend his leg to check it was all right. 'Is that helping or making it worse?'

'Much better, dearie, thank you.'

'Maybe you should go to the chemist or a doctor to get it

checked, or I could run and fetch one for you?' Panic and guilt was overwhelming her, and the baby was beginning to moan and whine, as was her wont when ignored..

'There's really no need. I'll be fine in a moment, once I've had a bit of a rest. That's a beautiful ring yer wearing.'

Cathie smiled as she flipped up her hand to admire it again with pride. 'Isn't it just? It was given to me by my fiancé when he proposed. Such a thrill.'

'You look a right bobby-dazzler. Expensive too, by the looks of it.'

Cathie laughed. 'I very much doubt it.'

'Congratulations on your engagement, and thanks for your care of me. You've been most kind. What's your name, dearie?'

Cathie smiled as she told him, but then little Heather began to cry and wail even louder, perhaps feeling hungry as it was well past her dinner time. She rushed to give her a little cuddle and try to settle her.

'And your young man?'

No longer able to hear him over the hubbub little Heather was making, she gave a little smile and a sigh. 'Are you sure you're going to be all right? It's time for my little niece to be fed, so I must be on my way.'

'Ah, of course. She's a lovely little thing. I'll be fine, you go and feed her.'

'Good day to you, sir, and take care.'

And giving him a cheery wave, Cathie bustled off, aware that he continued to sit on the wall watching her for some time, or maybe still resting his knee. But what a nice old man he was.

* * *

It was early one Friday evening as she was getting baby Heather ready for bed that there came a knock on the front door. Rona was out with her mate Tommy at The Donkey, and Alex on his usual pub crawl.

'Now who can that be?' Cathie asked the small infant, sitting her down on the rug as she went to answer it. It was unusual for anyone to knock. Some folk might give a light tap, but generally they'd walk straight in saying, 'Hello, it's only me.'

This time a complete stranger was standing on the doorstep, a woman of about fifty in a smart coat and hat. She glanced at a piece of paper in her hand. 'Are you Miss Catherine Morgan?'

'I am, can I help you?'

'My name is Marjorie Simpson, and I'm a social worker. May I come in?'

'Of course.' Cathie dutifully led her into the living room, feeling slightly puzzled about why this woman was here. 'Would you like a cup of tea?' she politely offered, showing the woman to a chair by the fire.

Instead, she went straight to the baby and picked her up from the rug. 'I take it this is your niece.'

'She's our little Heather, yes, and quite adorable, don't you think?'

The woman did not respond to Cathie's question. 'I've been informed that you are living with a man to whom you are not married. No foster mother is allowed to behave in such an immoral manner, so I'm afraid that has to end now.' And giving a brisk nod of her head she walked out the door, taking the baby with her.

Chapter Twenty-One

As the woman carried Heather away, Cathie dropped everything and scuttled after her. 'What are you doing? Where are you taking her?' she shouted. But there was a Ford motor car waiting at the door with its engine running and, within seconds, the social worker had climbed in and the driver roared away. Cathie ran after it the entire length of the street, screaming for the car to stop, much to the curiosity and alarm of neighbours who all came out to see what was going on.

She was running so fast she tripped over one of the ruts in the road and went flying, bashing her knee on the cobbles. Utterly devastated, Cathie limped back home, too distressed to speak to anyone or explain what had happened. Besides, it could have been any one of these neighbours, or so-called friends, who had reported this alleged immorality.

It was midnight by the time Rona arrived home, and Cathie was still sitting sobbing in the kitchen. 'This is all your fault,' she yelled at her mother, after she'd explained what had happened. 'Now she's been taken from me because someone has reported I'm an immoral woman who is sleeping with him. *Which isn't true!* If you'd never invited Alex to come and live here, Heather would still be safely tucked up in her cot.'

Even Rona looked shocked. 'Nay, chuck, I were only trying to help you two get back together, and look at that ring, it worked.'

'No it hasn't,' Cathie snapped, anger pulsating through her.

She was seriously beginning to question whether she still wanted to be his wife. If asked to choose between marriage with Alex or keeping little Heather, she would surely choose her lovely niece, wouldn't she? But she hadn't been given that choice. And why did she feel so torn?

She spent a sleepless night in floods of tears, her anger mounting to more ferocious levels, as Alex didn't return until the early hours. 'What am I do to?' she cried, rushing into his arms when finally he did appear at well past four in the morning.

Holding her close, he gently stroked her face, leading her back to a chair to draw her on to his lap. 'Hush, sweetheart. Do stop crying and tell me what has happened.'

He listened with sympathy as she told her tale, wiping the tears from her eyes with his handkerchief. 'You need to calm yourself as this could well be for the best.'

'How can you can say that when she's been taken away? And it's a *lie*! You and I are not having an affair, or living as man and wife, which is how that woman described it.

I've done nothing immoral at all, but how can I prove that?'

'By marrying me, sweetie, quite quickly. Why don't we get wed now?'

Cathie felt her heart lurch as she gazed into his eyes. 'Oh, Alex, why didn't I think of that? Of course, we are engaged to be married. I should have told the woman that fact. And you have agreed to adopt Heather.'

'Were we to be man and wife in actuality then indeed I would, if that's what you want.'

'Of course I do. I love her.'

'But do you love me?'

Cathie hesitated, asking herself the same question. 'It is possible to love more than one person at a time.' These words brought another image bursting into her head, which she quickly blocked out, as was her way. Her fondness for Steve had increased in recent months, but only after he was gone from her life had she appreciated how much he meant to her. She'd lost a good friend. Nothing more, she reminded herself. 'But I hate the fact these people have made judgements against me that are entirely untrue. I must do something about that.'

Alex stroked her strawberry blonde curls from her damp cheeks.

'Give yourself a rest first,' he urged, giving her a tender kiss on the lips. 'You've been working so hard caring for that child that you are utterly exhausted, particularly now that you have a job too. That's far too much responsibility for a young woman to cope with. The child will be well looked after and once we are married there'll be no difficulty in claiming her back. Then you can give up work and concentrate on being a real woman and mother.'

Cathie rested her head against his neck, conflicting emotions ricocheting through her as he kissed her some more. It seemed to be the expected behaviour nowadays for a woman to give up work on marriage and devote herself to domestic duties, so why didn't she feel any joy about that prospect? Was there something lacking in her as a woman? And how could she bear to be parted from that darling child, even if it was only a week or two until the ceremony took place?

'The poor love will be heartbroken without me around to love and care for her. She'll be feeling lost and abandoned. I can't allow that to happen to her.'

'You are her loving aunty, I know that now, and once we are married she may well be safely returned. You can then also start having some children of your own.'

Cathie could hardly believe what he was saying. How very kind and sympathetic he was now, marking an end to all his earlier anguish and distrust. And in a way marriage would be the most sensible way of securing little Heather's future. Yet she did need to make her situation clear, and start things moving in the right direction. 'Thank you so much for your support. But before rushing into anything, I intend to find out exactly where Heather is, and when and how I can get her back.'

He looked faintly irritated by this remark. 'I've just said that you don't need to do that. Once we are wed it will happen anyway.'

'I must and I will,' Cathie insisted, her sense of independence again coming to the fore as she dismissed his scowl of disapproval with a smile.

* * *

Cathie caught a bus the moment the clock struck six that morning, unable to wait another minute even though she'd barely had more than an hour's sleep at most. Thankful it was a Saturday and she didn't have to go into work, she knew that nothing would stop her from going in search of little Heather. Her plan was to go straight to the orphanage, where she assumed they would have taken her for the night. The sooner she got there the better, before they had time to hand Heather over to some other foster mother who would be a complete stranger. It would no doubt be necessary to prove her innocence, perhaps by showing them this ring. But she could do that now that she had Alex's full support.

The orphanage was some distance from the bus stop, and rain began to beat down upon her as she half walked, half ran along a seemingly endless medley of streets off Liverpool Road.

On arrival at the old Victorian building, she hammered on the door, feeling rather damp and out of breath. It was opened by one of the young nuns, and Cathie could see from her expression that a visitor so early was not welcome. Had she intruded upon their early mass?

'May I please see the matron?' she politely asked, heart pounding with anxiety and exhaustion.

'Mother Superior is still having breakfast. Can I help?'

Cathie quickly related what had happened. 'This is all a big mistake. I am not doing anything wrong or immoral, although we are about to be married. My fiancé is simply renting a room in our house, having returned from the war. The child is my niece and I was granted the right to be her foster mother until Alex and I marry, after which we fully intend to adopt her. I really need to speak to her *now*. Please.'

'One moment,' the young woman said, and marched off.

After waiting for ten fretful minutes, the young woman returned, shaking her head. 'Sorry, we have no child of that name here.'

Cathie's heart sank. 'Then where can she be?'

'Possibly in any one of several orphanages in Manchester, or already placed into foster care. I'm afraid you'll have to visit children's services.'

'But it's a Saturday, they won't be open.'

'Then you'll just have to wait till Monday morning, or else visit them all.'

Deeply distressed, Cathie turned to leave, but then it occurred to her that she didn't even know where all these orphanages might be. 'Do you have a list?' she asked.

'Well, yes, but I'm not sure I'm allowed to hand it out.'

Perhaps moved by Cathie's tears, and glancing over her shoulder to make sure no one was around, the kind nun dashed into the nearby office and returned with a sheet of paper. 'Here you are. Good luck.'

Cathie spent the rest of that day, and the next, searching the entire city, the cost of the bus and tram fare required quickly disposing of far too much of that week's wages. She visited orphanages on Deansgate, Ducie Street, Hanover Street, and then moved on to more distant parts of the city, including Salford, Cheetham, Ancoats and Hulme. Some of these homes turned out to be only for boys, not baby girls, while others had closed following the war, or the children had been evacuated. It was not an easy search.

She felt bone-tired and starving hungry, as she'd barely had a thing to eat all weekend, as well as increasingly anxious. Where could Heather be? The poor child must be frightened and upset at having been removed from her home. What if she wasn't in Manchester at all but taken over to the Fylde coast to Lytham or Southport, down to Cheshire, or up to the Lake District? She could be anywhere, even in the Yorkshire dales, as Manchester was central to so many places. How could Cathie hope to find her without the help of that Marjorie Simpson woman, the social worker?

Reaching the next orphanage on her list, Cathie knocked on the door and was shown into the office where she came face to face with a robust, stern-faced woman she took to be the matron. Indicating that she should be seated, Cathie at once launched into telling her story yet again, which she'd done countless times. 'I need to find her. Is she here?'

'Ah yes, that child is with us and perfectly well.'

Cathie almost jumped out of her chair in delight. 'Oh, thank goodness for that! I've been searching for her all weekend. Can I please take her home?'

'I'm afraid that's not our decision to make. That's up to children's services.'

'But she should be with *me*. I am her aunt, and innocent of these charges. And I love her to bits.' Cathie found herself again close to tears as she struggled to remain calm. 'Who has made this false accusation against me? It is all just malicious gossip.' Even as she asked this question Cathie felt her heart lurch as a worry lodged at the back of her mind.

'Proving the source of this information will not be easy,' the matron warned. 'As I say, you will need to speak to children's services.'

'I will do that first thing tomorrow. In the meantime, can I at least see her?'

The matron shook her head. 'I don't think that would be wise. It might only upset her. Come back when you have the necessary permission.'

Cathie walked away in a daze of despair, to spend yet another sleepless night, this time with no comfort offered by either Alex or her mother. She felt utterly bereft and alone.

The following morning she arrived early at the Christmas

card factory to ask if she could take some time off in order to pursue this matter further.

'Sorry, but we're far too busy to allow anyone time off work right now. You can go during your lunch break,' said the forewoman. 'So long as you're quick about it and clock in again on time.'

That would not be easy, but considering how difficult it had been to acquire the job in the first place, Cathie had no wish to risk losing it. As luck would have it she was shown in to the social worker's office without delay.

'Ah, I thought you might call in, Miss Morgan. No doubt you are about to assure me that you are actually married,' the social worker remarked caustically.

'That would be yet another lie, in addition to the one that caused you to take Heather away from me in the first place. Alex and I are engaged and do intend to adopt my niece,' she said, and then went on at some length to explain their situation in a desperate attempt to prove her innocence. 'Please, may I have your permission to take her home?'

'It's a charming romantic tale, but why would I believe you? I need far more proof, probably in the form of a marriage licence, or better still a certificate.'

'The thing is, we aren't yet married because we've had problems, due to the war, but things are improving between us.'

'What kind of problems?'

'I'd really rather not discuss it.' The worry that had been needling away at the back of Cathie's mind now reasserted itself. She was quite convinced that it was Davina who'd spread this evil gossip about her, in a bid to take revenge over losing Alex. But his affair with one of her best friends was not something Cathie wished to reveal to this woman. It might only make only matters worse.

However, the social worker began to fold up her papers and rose from her chair. 'Then I wish you good day, Miss Morgan.'

'Oh, please, don't send me away.' Cathie took a deep breath, making the decision that like it or not she must come clean, otherwise she would never discover the truth or get little Heather back. 'All right, Mrs Simpson, I'll tell you everything. If my suspicions are correct then the person who has been trying to steal Alex from me, my one-time friend, could have told this lie. They had a fling but in the end he came back to me, which has no doubt infuriated her. If that is the case then surely I have the right to know.'

Marjorie Simpson returned to her seat, sitting in silence for some moments as she considered these comments with a speculative frown on her wrinkled brow. Then reaching into a filing cabinet she brought out a file, withdrew a sheet of paper and handed it over. With a sinking heart, Cathie read the anonymous letter that related her alleged crime in a few short vicious sentences, seeming to imply they were having sex every five minutes without the benefit of a wedding ring.

'Dear God, this is even worse than last time.'

'Last time, what are you talking about?'

Cradling her face in her hands, it took Cathie a moment to recover her composure sufficiently to speak. 'A little while ago I spoke to someone at a local orphanage who told me they'd received an enquiry from me, asking for a place for Heather. That wasn't true, I definitely made no such request. I love her and wish to bring her up as my own child. I can't remember the lady's name but she showed me the letter in question, and I'm sorry to say that I instantly recognised the handwriting.'

'Who was it from, this one-time friend of yours?'

Cathie met the social worker's curious gaze with anguish in her own, feeling as if a knot had been tied around her throat, choking her. 'No, the letter was written by my fiancé. Alex has been badly affected by the war, which is the reason I didn't rush into marriage with him; and why my mother allowed him to rent a room off us when he developed problems with his own parents. He did apologise for sending that letter, and promised most sincerely he would never make such a mistake again. But one glance at this tells me that he was broken his promise.'

'Ah, I see.'

The discussion that followed was both lengthy and heart-rending, so much so that the woman's attitude towards her changed entirely and the social worker became increasingly sympathetic. After several phone calls, it was agreed that once Cathie had resolved these difficulties she probably would be allowed to take Heather home, although she'd be rigorously checked for a little while to make sure all was as it should be.

'It's not my place to advise you, Miss Morgan, but if I were you I'd give the fellow a piece of my mind then turf him out.'

That was exactly what Cathie intended to do. As soon as her shift was over, she marched home, her anguish now turning into a fizz of fury. As usual, she found Alex in the living room happily gossiping with her mother. She whipped the ring from her finger and slammed it on the table before him. 'How dare you do such a thing?'

'What are you accusing me of now?' he asked, lifting his gaze from the ring to consider her with resigned patience.

'You know damn well!' She slapped him across the face with the flat of her hand.

'Hey up, what's all this about?' Rona asked, jumping up to grab her.

'Ask *him*! He was the one who arranged for little Heather to be taken away from me. God knows why he wrote yet another dreadful letter to the authorities, except that he's a selfish bully who imagines he can control me!'

This time when she collected her things and walked out, Cathie knew it would be for good.

Chapter Twenty-Two

Cathie moved in with Brenda, who welcomed her with open arms, having heard the story in full as they'd stacked boxes of Christmas cards together that afternoon. 'Men can be such devils,' she said with a groan. 'You've done the right thing by walking out on him.'

'But will it help me to get little Heather back, that's the worry?'

'She's your niece, why would you not?'

The very next day Cathie called at children's services yet again during her lunch break, but Mrs Simpson was out doing calls. Cathie explained to her secretary that she needed to speak to the social worker quite urgently, and finally managed to arrange an appointment to see her on Friday afternoon at six-thirty, after she'd finished work.

'What do you think I'll need to do to prove myself?' she kept asking her friend as the week dragged by.

'Just be yourself, honey,' Brenda assured her, 'and let your love for that little one shine through.'

But once seated before the stern-faced social worker, it

felt so nerve-wracking that Cathie could barely concentrate on a word the woman was saying as she briskly leafed through a file on her desk. She spoke at some length about new rules and regulations, how children used to be accommodated in workhouses but now more care was taken to ensure a better future for them in orphanages.

'I don't want Heather put into an orphanage, certainly not for ever,' Cathie said. 'She has a family to care for her and, as agreed, I've broken my relationship with my fiancé.'

'So you won't be getting married, after all?'

Cathie shook her head, suddenly feeling nervous that if she was no longer about to marry she might never get little Heather back. It felt very much a no-win situation. Within moments, she found herself dealing with a whole barrage of questions.

'Have you built a good relationship with the child?' the woman asked.

'Of course! As I explained to you before, she's my niece and I love her to bits.'

'Do you have her birth certificate, to prove who she is?'

'I'm afraid not,' Cathie said, with a sad shake of her head. 'My sister hadn't got around to registering the birth by the time she was killed, less than a month later.'

'Then why didn't you do that?'

'I never gave it a thought. I was too shocked over what had happened to my beloved sister. The war was still going on, close to the end as it turned out, although I didn't know that at the time. Just looking after the baby was more than enough to cope with, and being swamped by grief.'

Was that a flicker of sympathy in the woman's gaze? Her next question destroyed such a hope. 'I understand the infant has been left a large sum of money by her father, could that have anything to do with your wish to foster her?'

Cathie stared at the woman, shocked to the core. 'How can you suggest such a dreadful thing? My only concern is that the poor child has lost both her parents, her family destroyed. I never gave the money a thought. I haven't touched a penny of it, nor will I ever, as it is meant to provide a secure future for Heather once she grows up. That is what her parents would have wished.' A new thought occurred to her. 'How did you know about Heather's inheritance? Was it mentioned in that letter Alex sent?'

'There was a second little note pointing out the money may well provide the motive behind your actions.'

'Goodness, that man is beyond belief! More likely it was *his* motive for choosing to marry me, and not that he loved me at all.' The thought filled her with fresh anguish. He could have planned this all along in order to force her into a hasty marriage. Why hadn't she paid more attention to the pressure he'd applied on her to release that pot of money, as he called it? Once he was her husband with full control over her and the child, he could easily have helped himself to Heather's inheritance. Why had she been so naïve as to keep on trusting him? Was it out of love or foolishness on her part? There seemed to be so much about Alex's behaviour that she hadn't understood, possibly not as a result of war at all, but a difficult childhood or simply a flaw in his nature.

'Can you afford to support and bring up this child all alone?' the woman was asking her now.

'I certainly can,' Cathie proudly stated, straightening her spine as she explained about her job at the Christmas card factory, with its crèche facility, and a decent wage coming in with every possibility of increasing it.

After further grilling, which covered pretty well every aspect of childcare, the child's daily routine and diet, as well as Cathie's entire family history, Mrs Simpson finally sat back and closed the file with a snap. 'Very well, you may now pay the child a visit.'

'Oh, thank you so much. Can I take her home?'

'That depends on how the child responds to you. She seems to be a very quiet little girl.'

Cathie frowned. 'Not really, I always find her to be very lively.' But a part of her was worrying over whether her niece would even remember her after being apart for over two weeks. She was but a toddler, after all. Little Heather was a child of some intelligence and with an increasing sense of independence, who might well blame her aunt for allowing her to be taken away by a stranger. Her resentment could well show itself in sulks or a tantrum, which surely wouldn't go down well.

With some trepidation, Cathie climbed into the Ford

motor car, as ordered by the social worker, to be driven to the orphanage. They rode out past the flattened warehouses in Piccadilly, along Market Street and Blackfriars, her mind in such turmoil that even the bright sunny June day failed to warm her.

On arrival, the matron led the pair of them along the passage to the playroom, Cathie's gaze lighting upon little Heather the moment they entered. The toddler was sitting in a corner all alone, her arms wrapped about her knees and her plump little face a picture of sadness. Hearing the door bang shut behind the visitors, she glanced up to gaze across at her aunt in startled wonder. She at once jumped to her feet and came running across the room, squealing with delight.

'Mummy, mummy, mummy!' she cried, and flung her arms around Cathie's legs.

Never had Heather called her by that name before, and the feel and sweet smell of the beloved child as Cathie sank to her knees to gather her in her arms made her weep with joy.

Mrs Simpson, along with the matron and the rest of the staff, stood watching with huge smiles on their faces.

'Mummy has come to take you home,' she announced, and Heather buried her face into Cathie's neck, clinging to her so tight it was as if she never meant to let her go.

* * *

Alex had been keeping a close eye on Cathie ever since she stormed out, his rage increasing as he silently stalked her from a safe distance. He needed to check what exactly the stupid woman was up to. He watched as she visited the office at children's services time and time again, eventually to be driven off in a car by that social worker person. Irritated that he couldn't follow, not yet being able to afford a car of his own, he hung around by the River Medlock instead, in case she returned home. Eventually, it dawned on him that he was waiting in the wrong place, but by the time he reached the area around Brenda's flat, it was almost dusk. Losing patience, he took himself off to the Pack Horse for a pint of bitter.

If only women would do as they were told, life would be so much simpler. He was infuriated that she'd discovered his ploy. That flaming social worker had no right to show her his letter, which was quite obviously what the woman had done.

As he spent the next morning lying in late, due to an indulgent evening with his mates at the pub, it was late afternoon when he finally spotted her. She came walking out of the Christmas card factory with her friend, holding the child by a rein, as she trotted along beaming with happiness. That was exactly how the kid should be treated, like a dog on a lead.

Holding out her arms, she cried, 'Carry, carry,' and laughing, Cathie picked her up to sit the child astride her hip as she walked away.

So now Cathie had managed to get the baby back without

marrying him, which meant all his efforts had been in vain. His rage escalated all the more.

He'd never intended to keep the child for ever, just long enough to get his hands on her bloody money, which he was far more in need of than some waif and stray. Once Cathie had fallen pregnant he would have used that as an excuse to pack this alleged niece off to some orphanage or other. Unfortunately, that wasn't going to happen now, so he'd need to devise some other plan to get his hands on the cash. Ever a man with ideas, he was quite certain he'd think of something. In the meantime, he would continue to keep a close eye on her every move.

And he could at least sell off that diamond ring she'd tossed back at him.

* * *

It was as the two girls were sitting down to supper one night that Brenda brought up the question of Davina. 'Did you ever find out what happened to her?' she asked.

Cathie shook her head. 'I've no idea. Why?'

Brenda was silent for a moment as she tucked into her sausage and mash, then gave Cathie an apologetic little smile. 'I appreciate the fact you may not be interested, but in view of what Alex has done to you, I'm wondering if he had anything to do with the fact that Davina has vanished.'

Cathie felt something lurch inside her, like a shaft of guilt or fear grasping her heart. 'I did wonder where she might be, and if she's safely given birth. But what are you suggesting?' Was Brenda hiding something from her? she wondered. 'What have you found out?'

Heaving a little sigh, her friend said, 'Actually, I called on her landlady to ask if she knew where she was living, and discovered that Davina had been taken to a home for unmarried mothers.'

'Oh, well that's all to the good, isn't it? At least she would have been somewhere safe and protected when the baby was born.'

'Those are not always terribly friendly or happy places to be, often ruled by a rod of iron, and they allow women little say over what happens to their child once they do give birth.'

Cathie wondered how Brenda knew this. She had once mentioned losing a child, but not quite how that had come about. She'd rather assumed it had been stillborn, but what if it had been adopted? It didn't seem her place to ask. Cathie was all too aware there were some matters her friend preferred to keep secret. 'She surely wouldn't stay there fore ver though, so why are you so concerned for her?'

'I wondered if perhaps she might be regretting having fallen for Alex's charms, as much as you do. Also, Cathie, wouldn't you like to know exactly what happened between the two of them, and how she ended up in such a place even though she'd been led to believe they were about to be married?'

'I believed I was to marry him too, until she told me otherwise,' Cathie said, a swell of worry starting to grow within her despite the devastation that had caused. 'It's certainly possible that Alex may well have used Davina too, if in a different way. Maybe we should check that all is well with her.'

Brenda smiled. 'What a lovely, kind person you are. I have the address, so why don't we pay her a visit?'

'Yes, let's.'

* * *

Strangely, the nuns did not welcome them. 'That young lady is no longer with us,' said the sister, rather tartly when they asked to speak with Davina.

'Oh, she has left then. Where did she go?' Brenda politely enquired.

'We have no idea as the silly girl did a bunk with a friend. A most foolish thing to do with the baby due only a few weeks later.'

'I wonder why she did that. Wasn't she happy here?'

'I wouldn't know,' came the sharp reply. 'She was certainly showing little remorse for her sins.'

Cathie quickly interjected, sensing Brenda could say something she might later regret. 'So who is this friend? Do you know where she lives?'

'She lived here,' snapped the nun. 'Now they've both left and are no longer our responsibility,' whereupon she closed the door in their faces.

They looked at each other in dismay. '"Curiouser, and curiouser," cried Alice,' Brenda remarked dryly.

* * *

Life settled into a pleasant and orderly routine with Cathie and Brenda working happily together at the factory, sharing the housework in the flat, as well as the cost of rent and shopping. They enjoyed little in the way of a social life, apart from the odd Saturday matinee at the flicks, as Cathie devoted herself to the care of her beloved niece.

'Do feel free to go out with other friends. There's no reason for you to be tied to this little one,' Cathie assured her, but Brenda would generally shrug her shoulders and insist she was quite happy. 'After all the harassment my brother-in-law has given me, right now I feel in dire need of a little peace and quiet.'

The pair of them would sometimes walk by the Rochdale or Bridgewater canal, enjoying a lovely day out in the summer sunshine, as they were doing today, being a Sunday.

As they strolled along the towpath, smiling at the waterhens bobbing about, Cathie said, 'Did you know that the building of this canal began way back in 1759 by the third Duke of Bridgewater? He employed a famous engineer, James Brindley, to build it for him, as he needed these waterways in order to transport coal from his mines. It crosses the River Irwell, and links up with the Manchester Ship Canal as well as with the Rochdale Canal and others. It was the first of many. So began the start of the canal age and a profitable industrial period for Manchester.'

'I'm aware the canals have a rich history, but how do you know so much?'

'My dad told me endless stories when he used to take me out in his barge. His job was to transport goods from the docks to the warehouses. More and more warehouses had been built, although on occasions they'd be damaged by fire. He always had a fire in the bow of his barge, which he would put out when he sailed underneath a warehouse to unload. Not good on a cold January morning, but it was the rule. You had to be safe. After he left, I missed going out on such trips with him,' she said with a sad smile. 'I bet he's still sailing a boat some place or other. And I still love walking along the towpaths, and looking at barges and narrowboats. Perhaps it helps me to remember him.'

'That's lovely,' Brenda said, then with a shiver added, 'but maybe not when there are clouds gathering. It looks like rain and the wind is whistling towards us under the canal bridge. Time to go home, I think.' As a spatter of rain began to fall right on cue, Brenda spun around. Unfortunately, her foot slipped on the damp path, and she might well have fallen had not one of the boatmen busily tethering his boat nearby, managed to catch her.

'Whoops, take care. We don't want another accident.'

'Sorry, silly me,' Brenda said, thanking him.

Cathie added her own thanks, then asked, 'What do you mean by another accident, has there been one already today?'

'Nay, not today, thank goodness, but a young lass was found a month or so ago under a bridge on the Rochdale Canal. She must have fallen in and drowned, poor soul.

So do take care how you walk on these slippy towpaths. And learn to swim, just to be safe.'

'Goodness, and there was me thinking canals were lovely safe places,' Brenda said, giving a wry smile as they walked on. 'But after what you and that boatman have told me, I can see they are not at all safe. Fortunately, I can swim. How about you?'

Cathie shook her head. 'Never felt the urge to learn, but maybe I should. In fact, Heather and I could learn together at the Corporation Baths on New Quay Street.'

'Good idea. I'll come with you and teach you.'

This became one of their regular weekly jaunts, sharing the cost of threepence for the baths, and twopence for a towel, since money was still a little tight. Cathie felt deeply grateful to have a good friend like Brenda, even if her other one-time friend, as well as her fiancé, had betrayed her. At times she would stand staring bleakly out over the bomb-sites as sadness swamped her. Their on and off engagement had been an absolute nightmare, and all because of that dratted war. Now, her hopes for marriage with the man she'd loved were quite dead. Alex had cheated on her, used and abused her, then attempted to deprive her of this precious child for unspeakably selfish reasons.

There could be no question of her ever forgiving him for such callous behaviour. However sad that made her feel in her heart, their relationship was most definitely over.

But then Cathie would watch little Heather chuckling as she played, and her heart would swell with love and happiness. The little girl would shout, 'Mummy, look,' chuckling with delight as she showed off something she'd built with her bricks, or drawn with crayons, or how she could make her precious teddy dance across the rug. Cathie could barely let the child out of her sight. Marriage, she decided, was most definitely not for her. But what did that matter when she had this adorable child to love and cuddle?

Chapter Twenty-Three

It was early August and Cathie had called in at the Co-op on her way home from work one Friday afternoon to do a bit of shopping, as she liked to do. It was a hot, sultry day and she was trying to decide whether she could afford to buy a tin of salmon to go with the salad for tea. It was a miracle to see such an item on the shelf, as shortages were still common. Would it ever end? 'We have tins of tuna if that price is too high,' a familiar voice behind her said.

Whirling about in startled delight, she could hardly believe her eyes. 'Steve, is it really you?'

'I'm afraid it is.'

She felt an urge to give him a hug, but managed to restrain herself. 'Oh, how lovely to see you again. I thought you were working for a printers' in Birmingham.'

'I was, but now I'm back.' He laughed.

'You're looking well,' she told him, feeling a strange shyness ripple through her at the sight of his smiling face. He looked different somehow, no longer as pale or as thin as he'd been when last she'd seen him, nor his blue-grey eyes quite so bleak.

Mr Leeson, the manager, came to stand beside him, giving him a playful slap on his shoulder. 'Hello, Cathie, it's good to see your old friend again, eh? I remembered what you told me about that fight not being Steve's fault, so I've given him his job back.'

Steve grinned. 'Actually, it's only for the summer, as I've gained myself a place at a teacher training college, starting September.'

'Oh, Steve, that's wonderful. I'm so pleased for you.' The joy that had exploded within her on seeing him began to instantly fade as Cathie realised this meant he would be leaving again soon.

He glanced about him. 'Where's little Heather?'

'With Brenda at the flat.'

He frowned. 'Not with your husband then?'

'Ah, I think you are a little out of date on my news.'

'Can't wait to here it.'

They went to sit in their favourite café just a few doors down to enjoy a cup of tea while Cathie filled him in on recent events. 'I can't say I'm surprised by what you've told me,' he admitted, when she reached the part where Alex had written an anonymous letter to children's services accusing her of immoral behaviour. 'Although I'm seriously appalled and angry on your behalf, particularly for his betrayal. I always thought the chap was a liar, so it doesn't surprise me that he's also a cheat and a fraudster. Think yourself fortunate to have found out before he actually put a ring on your finger.'

The mention of a ring brought back the memory of her bumping the pram into that dear old man on Oldham Street, and she smiled. 'Certainly not a wedding ring, and I gave him his engagement ring back. So yes, you're right, life would have been much more difficult had I been stupid enough to marry him. What was I thinking of to be so naïve?'

'Love does strange things to people,' he said, with a wry smile.

'I suppose that's true. What did you mean when you said you knew that he was a liar?'

'Ah, well, the fact is that I saw him with another woman in the Pack Horse one night.'

Cathie blinked as she stared at him in shock. 'Who was it?'

'No one I recognised.'

'It could have been his sister, Thelma.'

Shaking his head, Steve said, 'It obviously wasn't, as he was kissing her quite thoroughly, and not in a way a man would kiss his sister.'

Cathie's heart plummeted yet again. 'Then it must have been Davina. So why didn't you tell me?'

'In retrospect, I can see that I probably should have done, but I wasn't sure it would be the right thing to do at the time. You were very defensive of him as you quite rightly felt you were helping Alex to recover from the traumas of war. However, he lied about that too.'

'In what way?'

'He may have been stationed in the desert out in Egypt, but not on the front line. He was a cook in the mess tent. I found this out when I met one of his old mates at the British Legion. Ryman resented being treated as a mere labourer, but apparently had no hope of promotion because he was deemed to be a coward at heart. He wasn't even a good cook, spending most of his time peeling potatoes, chopping veg and scouring pans.'

Cathie stared at Steve in stunned silence for some seconds. 'But he's a bully who feels the need to be in control.'

'Bullies are often cowards when faced with real danger. That's why they enjoy lording it over women whom they view as inferior, or they attempt to make them feel as if they are. In my opinion that shows how little he really knew you,' he said with a grin, leaning closer so that Cathie could feel the warmth of his breath against her cheek, which sparked a ray of happiness to light up within.

'It's true that he did seem to rob me of my confidence with the way he gave orders and attempted to control me, behaving rather like a sergeant major at times. He was constantly demanding my pity while making out he was traumatised from fighting, not peeling spuds. Lord, what a fool I've been. I should have questioned him more, although we women are advised not to do that. So how did he come to find himself in such a menial position?'

'Apparently he never made any effort to improve his skills, being far too self-obsessed to care about others, or take any risks.'

'So his father was right about him. He's certainly a puzzle,' Cathie admitted. 'For some time I've been wondering where he's getting his income from, since as far as I'm aware he still doesn't have a job.'

'Really? That's interesting. Judging by what he told the Co-op manager, I have some suspicions on that score, which may or may not be correct. I'll make a few enquiries on the quiet and see what I can find out. Now let's stop talking about that idiot. Tell me more about yourself, and this new job of yours.'

He was gazing into her eyes so deeply that Cathie felt as if her heart was doing cartwheels. 'Oh, it's great to have you back, Steve. I've missed you so much.'

'That's good to hear,' he said, the husky tone of his voice resonating within her. 'I've missed you too.'

'But you'll be leaving again soon, I take it?' she asked sadly.

Giving a throaty little laugh, he gathered her hands in his to give them a gentle squeeze. 'As a matter of fact the course is right here at Manchester University, so I'm going nowhere.'

'Oh, I'm so glad.'

* * *

Outside, in the blistering August heat, Alex stood growling to himself as he watched the young man grasp Cathie's hands in such a loving manner. What right did he have to touch her? The thought of some other man's hand possibly caressing her breasts made him grow hot with rage. Cathie belonged to *him*. She was his property. Admittedly, they were somewhat at odds right now, but he fully intended that to change. He would win her back one way or another, or at least savour the delight of her body if he failed to do so. He deserved that much, at least.

He certainly wasn't interested in her stupid mother. Rona was now proving to be something of a problem, blaming him for losing her daughter's company, and, more importantly, her help around the house. She even kept insisting that he should leave. What complex creatures women were.

As for this idiot, his presence in Cathie's life had always been a hindrance. How infuriating that despite having successfully scuppered the fellow's job at the Co-op he was now back, no doubt hell-bent on creating yet more havoc. Alex decided that he'd make bloody sure Allenby regretted coming back home and didn't stick around too long.

Savouring a beer at the Pack Horse, he went over various possibilities of how he could achieve this. Much as he'd like to strangle the chap with his own tie, engaging in another fight held no appeal. But there were others ways of dealing with him, maybe by getting the damn fellow arrested.

Alex had built himself some useful connections among the dock workers, and as the Co-op had large quantities of goods delivered straight from supply depots at the docks, including meat, which was still in short supply, he could very easily arrange for orders to this particular shop to be cut down, or even go missing altogether. As nothing had gone wrong before Allenby had returned, it should be easy enough to lay the blame on him. With the right word in the right ear, he could ensure that Cathie's old friend received his due comeuppance.

Later that evening, when darkness fell, he walked over to the docks to make the necessary arrangements. He knew he could trust these new mates of his, as they were poorly paid and would lose out on a large share of the deal if they ever revealed what was going on. Alex smiled at his own cleverness. Revenge could be so sweet.

* * *

Cathie and Steve quickly fell into a routine of meeting up regularly, even though he was not currently engaged in any charity work, since he was about to start a teaching course. They would enjoy the odd evening at the Crown on Byrom Street, often known as the Top Hamer, named after the lady who had owned it back in the thirties. Cathie never felt she could stay long as she'd left Brenda in charge of little Heather, but it felt good to spend even a little time with him, and to find their friendship flourishing.

There was the odd occasion when he didn't turn up, as promised, and feeling far too embarrassed to enter a pub alone Cathie would wait outside for a little while, then sadly go back to the flat alone. She would feel deeply let down as just seeing how fit and well he was now, and really quite good-looking, filled her heart with joy. The next time he would be there as usual, apologising for not being able to come before but giving no indication about what exactly had kept him away.

She did once risk asking if something was troubling him.

'To be honest, there is. I've been put in charge of sending and receiving deliveries and something is going wrong. There are too many occasions when we don't receive the right quantities of goods in an order, but I can't quite put my finger on why that is.'

'Where are these orders coming from?' Cathie asked.

'Our supplier down at the docks. I've had a word with him and he insists they are all sent out correct: meat, fruit and veg, everything. He seems to be accusing *me* of getting it wrong, but I'm no idiot and do check that we receive the required pounds of potatoes we ordered, shoulders of lamb, sausages, pork chops or whatever.'

'Might it have something to do with shortages?'

'I thought that might be the case at first, yet time after time the actual quantity delivered does not match the amount charged on the invoice.'

'Oh, dear! That won't do you any good at all, Steve, having already been sacked once from the job.'

'I'm fully aware of that, and did go to see the boss at the warehouse, which resulted in a blistering row as he furiously defended his staff. I wish I could work out exactly what, why or who is getting these orders wrong. Anyway, how are things with you?'

Their friendship developed over the days and weeks following and they became increasingly close. Steve would often pop into the flat for a chat, although sometimes it would simply be to apologise that he couldn't make it for their usual meet-up, and, as Cathie knew he was having difficulties, she didn't like to press him. She was always glad to see him, and the moment he walked in little Heather would run to grab him with a squeal and a giggle, as he was always ready and willing to happily play games with the toddler. One evening. he even offered to babysit when Brenda and Cathie expressed a wish to see Humphrey Bogart and Lauren Bacall in *The Big Sleep* at the flicks.

'He's so kind,' Cathie said, as they walked off together arm in arm.

'He'd stand on his head for you, darling, but it's him you should be going to see this movie with, not me.'

'Don't say that. I've no wish to get involved in anything serious right now, perhaps never again.'

Brenda burst out laughing, her round face a picture of good humour. 'That's a big decision to make at just twenty-three. I can't quite see you living as a nun for the rest of your life.'

Cathie found herself giggling at this too. 'So what about you, Bren? Have you anyone in mind?' And, as the smile slid from her friend's face, she wished she hadn't asked.

'Maybe one day,' she said, after a long silence. 'But like you, I'm in no rush.'

The following Friday when Steve asked if she'd like

to go to flicks with him, Cathie couldn't resist accepting his offer. Sitting beside him in the dark of the cinema did bring to mind the occasions she'd been to the Gaumont with Alex, and how instead of watching the movie he'd spend most of the time kissing and petting her. Now, she and Steve sat side by side without even glancing at each other, let alone touching, which made her feel slightly disappointed. Perhaps he didn't see her in any other way but as a friend.

He asked her out the following Saturday too, and she gladly accepted, but then he backed off at the last minute, which greatly disappointed her.

'Sorry, but something urgent has come up that I have to deal with.'

The number of occasions when he let her down seemed to be increasing. Too often he would fail to turn up, or else leave early. A suspicion began to grow in her mind that Steve too might be having an affair with someone. Could it be with Brenda? Surely not. Her old friend was only too aware how devastated she'd been by Davina's betrayal. Brenda would never be so unkind or cruel. Then who might it be?

Cathie reminded herself that she should stop fussing as she greatly valued Steve's friendship, even if that's all it would ever be. Whether she wanted it to develop into anything more was a question she didn't feel ready to answer just yet, so he was perfectly entitled to have a proper girlfriend. They weren't a couple as such, only friends.

And maybe she was feeling a bit low because having been deserted by her father, and not receiving the proper love and care from her mother, this had created a sense of insecurity in her. Cathie felt no regrets over leaving Alex, although the way he had treated her hadn't helped. So perhaps she was just unable to ever trust a man again, despite a strong desire to find someone to love and care for her.

* * *

Cathie was beginning to worry about her mother. Was Alex taking advantage of Rona too? Feeling the need to know the answer to this question, she left her a note, suggesting Rona join her on Saturday afternoon in Peel Park for a walk. Now there she was, seated beside the statue of Queen Victoria in front of the Salford Museum and Art Gallery. They say that the old Queen suffered badly from loss and family problems too, Cathie thought as she strolled over, so maybe it was an aspect of life one had to accept.

'I'm so glad to hear you got the baby back.' Rona regarded her daughter with a rueful smile as Cathie lifted little Heather out of her pram to let her run free. 'If I'd ever imagined Alex capable of doing such a thing I would never have let him stay.'

'It was you who told him about that sum of money Heather's daddy left her,' Cathie reminded her, as she joined Rona on the bench. 'That's all he ever wanted, the only reason he wished to marry me, so poor little Heather would have been given away anyway, once he'd got his hands on that cash. Why on earth did you do that, Mam? It had nothing at all to do with Alex.'

'I thought if he was to be your husband and bring up that child as his own, he surely had the right to benefit from it. Why weren't you prepared to share it with the man you love?'

Cathie felt herself simmering with anger and resentment, as was so often the case when dealing with Rona. 'That money isn't mine to share. You really do need to keep your nose out of my business.'

'Mebbe you're right, and it was all my fault.'

Cathie looked upon the sadness in her mother's face, now looking quite worn and felt a deep sense of regret. Rona seemed to be ageing quite rapidly all of a sudden, anxiety clouding her eyes and marking her face with wrinkles she'd never noticed before. Perhaps her sense of loneliness had led her to make such a mistake. Cathie too had been equally fooled by Alex's charm.

'Not to worry, I was a bit of a fool to trust him too, Mam. Is he still around?'

'Oh, aye. He's nowhere else to live since his own parents have rejected him. Why don't you come home, love? I miss having you around.'

'You miss my cooking, more like,' Cathie scoffed.

Rona gave a wry smile. 'That too, but I also miss your company, and this little one, more than I might have expected.'

The toddler was running rings round them, giggling happily. Cathie played at chasing her for a moment or two, and then flopped back upon the bench giving a little sigh. 'So what about you and Alex, are you…?'

'Nay, don't even think such a thing. He's a mere lad, not my sort at all. But he regrets having been so stupid and is ready to apologise and start afresh.'

Cathie gave a snort of laughter. 'Well, I'm not. So far as I'm concerned, it's all over between us. That man's a selfish prig who never thinks of anyone but himself, and he certainly doesn't give tuppence for Heather. Don't let him bully you too, Mam. I've no idea where he gets his money from, but I'm quite sure he could afford a place of his own now. It's time you ordered him to leave and concentrated on living your own life, as I fully intend to do.' Putting her arms about Rona, she hugged her and, for once, her mother did not pull away but hugged her back.

Chapter Twenty-Four

It was early September and Cathie was out walking in Oldham Street. She could hear sounds of *The Messiah* emanating from Howards' Ltd, a famous music shop. Goodness, were they rehearsing for Christmas already? The sound reminded her of the concert she'd helped Steve to organise almost a year ago. So much had happened since but she felt a warm glow inside that he seemed to be back in her life, at least as a friend. It was as she was looking at shoes in Saxone's window, wishing she could afford to buy herself a new pair, when she spotted the old man whom she'd accidentally bumped into with the pram. He was standing by the hot potato cart buying himself some lunch. Picking up little Heather to sit the toddler astride her hips, she quickly hurried over.

'Hello, I hope you are well and your knee isn't giving you any gyp?' she said with a smile.

'By heck, what a surprise seeing you again, lass. I'm fine, thanks. How about you?' Glancing at her hand, his smile vanished. 'What's happened to your ring?'

'Ah, well, that's rather a long story, which I won't bore you with,' she said.

'I'm not easily bored. Let me buy you a hot spud, then you can tell me all about it. The name's Percy, by the way.'

They sat together like old friends on the same low wall, just off Oldham Street, where she'd previously tended to his bruised knee. Cathie quickly related a brief version of how her engagement had come to a catastrophic end. 'I handed him back the ring and chose my little niece here instead,' she said, indicating Heather, who was sitting on the wall beside them happily chewing on a small piece of baked potato.

Percy was silent for so long that Cathie began to wonder if she perhaps had bored him, after all. Then he began to speak. 'Normally, when a young lass loses the man of her dreams I'd offer heartfelt sympathy, but on this occasion I'd say you've done the right thing.'

'Oh, I think so too. If he doesn't care for children, and is a womaniser, he's not the man for me.'

'In addition, love, the chap's a thief.'

Cathie blinked. 'I beg your pardon, what did you say?'

'That ex-fiancé of yours stole that ring from my shop. Mebbe I was a bit too trusting fetching out so many trays just because he was an ex-servicemen, but after he'd gone I soon realised I'd been robbed. It was my good fortune to be knocked by this babby's pram that day, and had it been anyone else I would have reported seeing that ring. I instantly recognised it, as it's extremely valuable. But, as you were so kind, and so obviously innocent, I couldn't bring myself to do that. I did wonder afterwards if mebbe I'd made a mistake by not warning you. So, I'm glad to hear the engagement is off.'

Cathie found herself struck speechless, unable to quite take in what she was hearing. Eventually, she asked the all-important question. 'So are you going to report him?'

* * *

That evening she was still worrying over the old man's response when Steve arrived for supper, as agreed. He'd brought a bottle of wine for them to enjoy.

'This is to celebrate the start of my training as a teacher when so many ex-servicemen have not been so lucky. But it's also to remind you that I will still be around, so this is not goodbye.' As he said this, he gazed into Cathie's eyes with such intensity that she began to wonder if her earlier worries had been entirely wrong. Maybe Steve's caution signified he was simply leaving it up to her to decide the moment when she would feel ready for a change in their relationship. And from the relief she felt, Cathie began to wonder if she could possibly be falling in love with him.

She'd cooked steak and kidney pie as a treat, using up all of their weekly meat ration in order to do so, but it was worth it as his face lit up as he took the first bite.

'This is delicious.'

'Thank you.'

As they ate, they chatted for some time about movies

they'd seen, music they liked such as 'To Each His Own', the latest hit by the Ink Spots. Brenda and Steve did much of the talking, but when they reached the coffee stage, he turned to Cathie with a troubled frown. 'Is there something wrong? You seem rather quiet, not at all yourself.'

Taking a breath, Cathie finally owned up to what was devouring her thoughts as a result of her conversation with her Oldham Street acquaintance. 'Quite by chance, thanks to a silly accident with the pram, I met a jeweller called Percy Mullins. He's a lovely old man who has become something of a friend. But what he had to tell me today was really quite devastating.'

The pair of them listened in horror to what she'd learned.

'Heavens, Alex Ryman is a complete idiot,' Brenda retorted as the story of his theft unfolded.

'A dangerous one too, I'd say,' Steve added.

Cathie glumly nodded. 'I rather assumed it to be a cheap imitation diamond ring, not a real one. What possessed him to do such a thing?'

'Maybe because he's involved in black marketeering.'

'*What?*'

'I believe he may well be, which would explain how he happens to have so much money despite not being employed.'

Cathie blinked, suddenly remembering something. 'So that's why he had those extra ration books, and what looked like a few loose coupons. I saw those once when little Heather was playing with his gas mask pack. Oh, my goodness!' And perhaps how he had acquired those silver cigarette lighters that he gave to both Rona and Davina, she thought.

'It was also the reason he told that lie to the Co-op manager about me being involved in such crimes.'

'Are you saying that's why you were sacked?' Cathie asked in dismay.

He fell silent for a moment, a puckered frown marking his brow. 'It was indeed,' he said, as if gathering his thoughts. 'But I didn't know at the time that Alex had spoken to my boss and got me sacked, not until I returned. I managed to convince Mr Leeson that it was all a lie, and your assurance that the fight wasn't my fault certainly helped, Cathie. This old shopkeeper, does he intend to bring charges?'

Cathie flushed with embarrassment. 'I did ask him that question, but it seems not.'

'Why?' Brenda barked. 'That imbecile needs to be stopped from creating so much havoc.'

Stifling a sigh, Cathie agreed. 'I'm afraid that's my fault. Mr Mullins is very kind and understanding, and insists it could mess up my life were he to bring charges against my fiancé for a ring he presented to me. He has no wish to do that. He also said that Alex will no doubt have sold the ring by now, so there would be little hope of ever getting it back, therefore making my life a misery would achieve nothing.'

'It's definitely not your fault, Cathie,' Steve retorted, 'so don't even think such a thing.'

She gazed at him then with pleading in her eyes. 'Please don't ever challenge Alex over this issue, Steve. He's still living with my mother, remember, and I've no wish for him to take out any ill feeling on her that such an accusation might create. I think we just have to let things lie.'

The subject was dropped and they went back to talking about movies and music.

* * *

As Steve walked home he replayed this startling piece of news over and over in his head. It would seem that Ryman was not simply involved in black marketeering, as he'd come to suspect, but also in much worse crimes. What a dreadful bloke he was. Admitting his own suspicions to Cathie had given him pause for thought. What if it was Alex who was creating these new problems for him at the Co-op, possibly out of some sort of revenge?

If that were the case then what would be the best way to deal with it? Talking to the boss at the suppliers hadn't worked, but sitting back and allowing Ryman to create more mayhem wouldn't be wise either. Steve knew that if he was personally charged with the offence of dealing in the black market, he could well lose his teacher training place at the university. Such a situation would ruin his entire future.

First thing the next morning, Steve went to speak to

Mr Leeson, his manager. 'May I have a private word with you, sir?'

'Of course, Steve. Do sit down. I needed a word with you anyway. I'm aware you're leaving to start your course, and normally I'd be suggesting that you are welcome to work for us whenever you are on vacation. But I'm sorry to say that I'm not in a position to offer you a job again. And if you are seeking a reference I cannot provide you with one of those either.'

Steve blinked, somewhat startled by this remark. 'Why would you not?'

'As you are aware, lad, we've suffered numerous problems recently with deliveries and invoices. I'll admit that it's not exactly the kind of problem that occurred the last time you were employed by us, when you were accused of arranging the theft of goods from your delivery van. Nevertheless, it's so similar that it does make me question if you're at it again.'

Steve was horrified, realising he'd been right to be concerned. He took a breath, hoping to relieve the knot of fear clogging his throat. 'I rather thought you believed me, sir, when I assured you I hadn't done any such thing. I never left my cab door open, nor did I ever leave any stuff lying about on the passenger seat to be stolen. In actual fact it was this issue over deliveries that I wished to speak to you about. I believe that some of the workers down at the docks, and at the Co-op's main suppliers, could well be engaged in black market crimes. It certainly isn't me.'

Leeson frowned. 'If that's the case, I'm glad to hear it. But falsifying invoices or not delivering what has been paid for is a serious crime. Are you actually accusing the warehouse boss of planning this?'

'Of course not, but he needs to be warned. It may be a good idea were you to speak to him, rather than me, whom he clearly doesn't trust.'

'Then who do you think is responsible, or are you suggesting that the men are doing it off their own bat?'

Steve gave a little shrug, wondering how far he dare go to reveal his suspicions. 'They might well be, but I do have an idea who might be responsible. However, it could be dangerous to name names at this stage, without proof.'

'Ah!' Leeson sat back in his chair, arms folded. 'I'm beginning to read your mind, lad. Could you once have had an issue with this person, maybe even a fight?'

Steve gazed down at his artificial leg stuck out for comfort as he strived to think of an appropriate response. Revealing Ryman's name might be the right thing to do. On the other hand, were the fellow ever to get wind of the fact he was being investigated, he might take his revenge out on Cathie, particularly bearing in mind what she'd recently discovered about him. Steve looked up to meet his boss's enquiring gaze with open honesty in his own.

'I learned some rather troubling news about this person yesterday, which seems to indicate that he's not simply involved in the black market, but theft of a much worse kind. Unfortunately, the victim concerned has chosen not to bring charges, for personal reasons. But that doesn't make him innocent.'

'I see.' Mr Leeson got slowly to his feet. 'Leave it with me. I'll see if I can put an end to this devilish scheme without naming names. If what you suggest proves to be true and we can resolve it, Steve, then I'll review my decision about not employing you again, and with regard to your references.'

Since that seemed to be the best he could hope for, Steve thanked his manager and left. As his course started on Monday, he would then surely be free of Ryman's evil tricks. But would Cathie?

His life seemed to be in utter turmoil in so many directions at the moment, some of which he still needed to explain to Cathie, once he'd plucked up the necessary courage.

A few days later, Mr Leeson called Steve back to the office to announce that two employees had been found guilty and duly sacked.

'The warehouse manager sends his apologies for having assumed it to be you, lad,' Leeson told him, handing over his reference. 'So you're welcome to come back and work for us at any time.'

'Thanks, I'm most grateful for your support,' Steve said with gratitude, but deep down he still worried that Ryman might discover he was the one responsible for these side-kicks of his getting the sack. 'I trust you didn't name any names at this stage? There are other aspects to this person that need checking out before his identity can be revealed. It could prove dangerous for some friends of mine, were he ever to realise what we are up to.'

Leeson assured him that he had said nothing on that score. 'No names mentioned. I was asked, but explained the person concerned was still under investigation and that I'd keep the manager informed.'

'Thank you, that's a great relief.'

Steve knew that he really needed to get to the bottom of this other mystery too. How to go about it, that was the question. But it wasn't so much himself that he was concerned about, but Cathie. He hoped to God that she always remembered to lock her door.

* * *

When Steve called at the flat to tell them all about his first week on the course, Cathie welcomed him with a warm hug. 'How did it go?'

Giving a wry smile, he said, 'It will be a year of intensive training, both on an academic and a practical level with lots of hands-on teaching. Hard work but worth it if I get a good job at the end. I must say though that some of the blokes taking this course are a bit draconian, acting more like sergeant majors in charge of troops. Not at all how a teacher should behave with kids, in my opinion.'

'You're right there,' Cathie agreed. 'Having suffered at

the hands of a bully myself, I'd say that is definitely not the way to deal with children.'

He grimaced. 'Children aren't the only ones to suffer from such men, or you ladies. I too am now a victim.'

Cathie stared at him in dawning horror. 'Are you suggesting that Alex may have created the problem you have with the Co-op suppliers over orders?'

Steve nodded, and went on to reveal the tale of the attempt to prove him guilty of being involved in the black market, explaining the matter had thankfully now been resolved by the Co-op manager. 'And without naming names.' He still felt some concern over his caution not to name Ryman, as it could well achieve nothing, except to protect Cathie from any retaliation on his part. But it was perfectly clear that they knew who he was blaming.

'The man's turning into a real piece of crap,' Brenda snarled. 'I came across quite a few like him when I was in France; men who thought they could rule the world, and make a fortune for themselves while they sought to achieve it. *And* treated all women as if they were whores.'

Cathie patted her friend's hand, feeling the need to offer comfort as Brenda's face was wrought with anguish. 'You must have been so brave. I would like to hear your story in full one day, Brenda, when you feel ready to tell it.'

Her friend returned her gaze with that all too familiar stiffness in her own, the very truculence of her stance proving how capable she must have been at coping with the traumas she suffered. 'There are some things best not spoken of. Remember the saying, "be like Dad and keep mum". Right now, let's stick with your problems. What do we do about this blighter?'

Turning to Steve, Cathie's expression now turned rock hard, revealing the determined side to her own personality. 'All that I've learned about Alex recently does make me wonder about Davina, and why she vanished.'

Steve blinked, looking startled by this sudden change in the conversation. 'What are you saying? Vanished where?'

'That's a good question.' Brenda said. 'I wish we knew.'

Cathie went on to explain how they'd failed to find any sign of their missing friend, even at the Home for Unmarried Mothers where she'd apparently been lodged. 'Although I accept Davina may well have gone back to wherever she came from.'

'Those nuns were astonishingly unconcerned about where she might be,' Brenda put in, picking up the teapot to refill their cups.

'Don't they have her address?' Steve asked, frowning as he listened to this puzzling tale.

'Actually, I'm beginning to wonder if it's much more serious than that,' Cathie added. 'Following the walk we took by the canal that time when you slipped, Bren, I'm starting to put two and two together and maybe making five. But I'm wondering if the girl found under the bridge on the Rochdale Canal might well have been Davina, as it was around the time she went missing.'

The teapot dropped from Brenda's hand, smashing to the ground and spilling tea everywhere, while Steve went white with shock.

Chapter Twenty-Five

The three of them went together to the police station on Minshull Street to ask who the victim had been, only to be told the girl had never been identified. 'She carried no identity card, no bag, no ration book, nothing, and our inquiries got us nowhere.'

'So what had happened to her?' Steve enquired politely.

'We suspect she may have committed suicide, so the case is closed,' the desk sergeant said with a shrug.

'Shows how much you care about women,' Brenda retorted.

'The young lady was given a decent burial,' the police officer assured her with a certain degree of respect and apology in his tone of voice. 'Although not in a churchyard because of the circumstances of her death. The girl was pregnant, yet wore no wedding ring.'

Something resonated inside of Cathie at these words, as this must be Davina. 'Do you by any chance have a picture of her?'

'Only of her dead body, love. I very much doubt you'd wish to see it, particularly if you think you might know her.'

'We do need to check, as our friend is *missing*,' Brenda snapped.

Nodding sympathetically, the desk sergeant picked up the phone to speak to his commanding officer. Moments later, a young constable came out of the back office carrying a black and white snapshot, which he handed to Steve.

'Sorry, but I never met her,' he said, passing it over to the two girls despite a glower of disapproval from the sergeant who clearly didn't think women should be shown such things.

'Oh, Lord, that's definitely our friend, Davina,' Brenda sadly announced.

One glance at the grim picture was more than enough to bring tears flooding to Cathie's eyes. The next moment she was running out of the police station and they could hear her throwing up into the gutter, no doubt filled with terror that her worst fears had been confirmed. As Steve watched Brenda hurry after her friend, he asked the sergeant what the police intended to do about this tragedy.

'Nothing. As I say the case is closed. Unless you have evidence to the contrary to prove that it wasn't suicide or an accident,' came the calm response.

'Might I fill you in on a few details, which might help?'

Taking out his notebook, the desk sergeant licked his pencil and waited with a somewhat bored expression on his face. But even when Steve had told the entire story, or at least the outline of it as far as he knew, he was still bluntly informed that without further evidence there was little the police could do.

'You aren't even prepared to question Ryman?'

'Not without good reason.'

'So what kind of evidence would you need?'

The sergeant shook his head. 'Hard to say, a witness perhaps?'

Struggling to contain his anger, as he knew there was little hope of finding one of those, Steve stomped out of the station and went to put his arms about Cathie. 'I'm sure the police will do what they can,' he said, attempting to offer what comfort he could, against all odds.

'Not for one minute do I believe Davina would deliberately kill herself,' she cried, burying her face in his chest. 'She wasn't that kind of girl. She loved life far too much to give up on it.'

'Unfortunately, we need proof that she didn't.'

'How do we do that?' Cathie looked bewildered, as if her world were collapsing around her all over again, and she was desperately trying to block out fear. If her suspicions about Davina were proved to be correct, then there could be a serious risk of Ryman attempting to silence her too. The very thought filled Steve with a mix of fury and terror.

'Leave it to me, love. I'll see what I can find out from the nuns.'

'Good luck with that one,' Brenda caustically remarked, while Cathie hugged and thanked him for at least offering to try.

'I know she ruined our friendship, and my engagement by cheating with Alex, but I can't bear to think that this is the price Davina has paid for falling in love with the wrong man. It's too horrific to even contemplate.'

* * *

When Steve patiently explained to the young nun at the gate what he had learned from the police, she led him straight to the Mother Superior. As soon as that good lady was shown a copy of Davina's photograph, she put her hand to her chest as if it were pounding with shock.

'What a dreadful tragedy! We shall hold a special mass in honour of her memory,' she generously offered.

Moved by this, Steve nodded. 'May we, as her friends, also attend?'

'Are you saying that you're the father of her child?' the Mother Superior snapped.

Now it was Steve's turn to look shocked. 'No, I most certainly am not, although I do have an idea who that person might be. In fact, I never knew the girl personally but my friends did, so I would like to accompany them to any special service, as they are very upset by this tragedy. Right now, what I'm looking for is any information you might have about her. Davina Gibson hadn't lived for very long in Castlefield and, as is often the case with so many people these days, she didn't speak of the past. Do you by any chance have her home address?'

The Mother Superior shook her head; her grey-eyed

gaze now distant and cool, unconvinced by his declared innocence. 'You can ask Sister Teresa, who looks after the records in the office, but I am not aware of any. So who was the man responsible for getting her into this dreadful mess?'

'I don't think it's my place to reveal his name, but I may have cause to pass it on to the police, should that prove to be necessary. Did she make any friends while she was staying here?' He'd already passed on Ryman's name but had no wish for this to be widely known, particularly as the police didn't seem interested.

'Yes, she did make friends, and escaped with one, the silly girl. At least they weren't stupid enough to climb the wall and get themselves caught up in the spikes on top, as far too many have done in the past.' She tut-tutted. 'They must have stolen the key to the side door, as it was still sitting in the lock the next morning. It did them no good at all to run off like that, particularly considering how Davina has ended up. No doubt she had nowhere to go so the foolish girl threw herself into the canal. Goodness knows what happened to her friend.'

'And who might she be?'

The Mother Superior picked up the bell on her desk to call in Sister Teresa, the nun who kept the records. He was duly handed the address of one Barbara Cartwright.

'I suspect she may not have gone home either, as her father threw her out for falling pregnant with a Yank,' the young nun told him, as she was showing him out through the gate. 'But she does have a sister. Unfortunately, I don't have her address.'

'Thanks, I'll see what I can do,' Steve said, and walked away with a sad resentment growing inside him that these girls were so poorly treated they were prepared to take any risk in order to escape.

* * *

A Requiem Mass was duly held, which all three friends attended, together with the nuns. Psalm 23 was read, prayers were chanted, the organ played Mozart's Requiem in D minor, and communion was held. No other family members or friends of Davina's were present, which made Cathie feel even more sad. How dreadful to die and no one you once loved to even be aware of it. Who her parents were, or where they lived, was a complete mystery, assuming they were still alive.

'At least we, as her one-time friends, are here to pay honour to her,' Brenda said, lighting a candle in her memory.

'It's all we can do for her now,' Cathie agreed, as she did the same.

'I'm not so sure about that. It's our responsibility to discover how she died,' Steve said.

Cathie gazed at him in anguish. It was true that however foolishly Davina might have behaved, she did not deserve to lose her life. And not for one moment did Cathie believe she'd committed suicide. The blame for her death must surely lie elsewhere, a thought that brought a shiver of fear to ripple down her spine.

* * *

'She can't have been happy living there,' Steve said later, as he and Cathie sat together that evening on stools in the backyard, the moon glistening down on them from between the clouds. Brenda had gone out for the evening with a new boyfriend, and little Heather was fast asleep in her cot. Steve felt his heart clench with pain at the sight of Cathie's distress. She was sitting with her head in her hands, her lovely red-blonde hair falling over her face as if she wished to hide behind it. He ached to comfort her, to stroke and kiss her, but was afraid to do so in case she slapped him away, or even banished him from her life. It was bad enough to be convinced that she didn't feel the same way about him as he felt about her. But if he upset her by making a pass too soon, then he risked losing Cathie's friendship entirely, which really didn't bear thinking about.

The idea that she might be grieving for her one-time best friend, who had cheated on her, only proved what a sweet and kind person Cathie was. Although, for all he knew, it could really be Ryman she was missing, and she blamed Davina for having caused her to lose the man she loved. If only he could be certain.

'I thought I'd investigate this Barbara person, although I'm not optimistic that her father will be very helpful,' he said, explaining how she'd been thrown out when she fell pregnant. 'The war yet again taking a bite.'

'I'll come with you,' Cathie said, but Steve shook his head.

'Let me do it, you've had enough to deal with lately. I don't want you to become even more upset, and who knows how her father will react.'

A quiver of longing ran through him as she met his gaze with a warm glow of gratitude in her hazel eyes. Reaching up, Cathie gave him a little peck on his cheek and desire flared within him. How he loved her, with all his heart and soul. But all Steve felt he could do right now to prove how much he cared was to attempt to discover the answer to this mystery that was troubling her so much. And somehow protect her from that selfish bully.

'Enough of this, I'm going to pop out and fetch a beer and a glass of shandy from the pub, then we'll sit back and enjoy a drink on this lovely warm autumn evening, and not talk about this painful subject any more.'

Cathie laughed. 'Good idea.'

'I'll be no more than ten minutes,' he said, risking planting a kiss on her upturned nose before dashing off.

But, as he strode along Byrom Street, he heard the echo of footsteps behind him. Convinced he was being followed, he slipped quickly into a ginnel to hide in the shadows of a doorway. Moments later, who should stride past the entrance but Ryman himself. Drat the man! He must have been stalking him. Was he stalking Cathie too?

Steve shuddered at the thought, a beat of anger pummelling in his chest.

When Steve returned to the yard with a jug of beer and bottle of lemonade, he made no mention of having seen Alex, and set about making Cathie a shandy and pouring himself a beer. The pair of them spent a contented evening together, laughing over hilarious memories of the past.

'I remember Mam scolding me for playing by the barges on the canal, telling me how Jinny Greenteeth might get me,' she said with a chuckle. '"What will she do to me?" I would ask. "Eat thee all up," Mam would say. A total myth I never believed in.'

'I expect she was only pointing out the dangers of the waterways, and didn't want you to drown. Have you learned to swim yet?'

'Oh, I'm finding it so difficult, but Brenda is doing her best to help. Heather loves it. She's a real little water baby.'

They also shared dreams for the future. Steve, however, failed to summon up the courage to mention what his greatest hope for his own future was, that had nothing at all to do with a possible career as a teacher.

As they said goodnight he gave Cathie a tender peck of a kiss on each cheek, the sheer touch of her soft skin and the lovely scent of her creating a stir of longing within him that he found almost impossible to suppress. As she smiled up at him they exchanged a long, quite serious and thoughtful look, almost as if they were assessing and reviewing their emotions.

'Goodnight, love. Sleep well, and make sure you lock the door after me.'

The next day Barbara's father, who lived in a rather grand house out in Cheetham, refused to speak to him, denying that he even had a daughter. As the housekeeper showed him out, Steve asked if she knew where the girl was living now, but received no answer. He was getting nowhere. What a maelstrom of problems this war had created, he thought, as he walked slowly home to face more of his own.

* * *

Alex was savouring the charms of a pretty young wench he'd picked up at the Pack Horse, taking her round to an alley behind the pub. Her figure was a bit scrawny and childlike, but his needs were such that the lack of fleshy breasts didn't trouble him in the slightest. He revelled in the powerful pitch of excitement that brought him to a climax. Sadly, the coupling was over far too quickly, but then he had been in something of a desperate situation. Losing both Cathie and Davina had done him no good at all.

In addition, there'd been a fury cascading inside him as a result of two of his most useful associates having been sacked from the supply warehouse, their connections with his scheme against that Steve Allenby character having been found out. Someone must have been investigating those chaps. He would so like to know who it was, as they may well be aware of his own role in the enterprise. Alex's anger had been such that he'd pounded her hard against the wall. Still, the tart didn't seem too bothered. He handed her a shilling and sent her on her way, then, adjusting his clothes, returned to the pub.

As he ordered himself another pint of beer, together with a tot of whisky, a voice rang in his ear. 'Mr Ryman, may we have a word?'

Assuming this to be one of his black market colleagues, Alex swung round only to be shocked to find himself facing a tall gentleman in a somewhat shabby raincoat and trilby hat, standing between two uniformed policemen. For some moments he was struck dumb as his heart raced, then with a smirk of a smile he politely asked, 'What can I do for you?'

'What can I do for you, *sir*?'

'Sir,' Alex repeated with a snarl, recalling how his sergeant major used to address him in exactly the same tone of voice.

'I assume the young lady you were pleasuring has been paid and dispatched, and you are now free to accompany us down to the station?' the fellow airily enquired.

Alex swallowed as embarrassment skittered through him. 'Why would I wish to do that—*sir*?'

'We have a few questions that need answering regarding a former lady friend of yours.'

'And who might that be?'

When the officer said Davina's name, the desire to turn and run hit Alex like an exploding grenade. This was the last thing he'd expected, assuming he was about to be questioned about his black market activities. Unfortunately, there was no opportunity to escape as the two constables were now standing on either side of him. They clipped handcuffs on his wrists and, within seconds, Alex found himself being led outside and ushered into a police car.

Chapter Twenty-Six

The questioning went on for hours, taking so long that Alex found himself held in the cells overnight, only for the interview to start all over again the next morning. The interview was about Davina, and nothing to do with the black market, or even the stolen ring. They wished to know where and how he'd met her; why she'd followed him to Castlefield; and why he hadn't revealed his relationship with her to his fiancée.

'Do you know where she is now?' the sergeant asked.

Alex gave a sad shake of his head. 'Sorry, I've no idea. She just vanished.'

'With your child?'

Thoughts raced through his head as he wondered if he could deny any knowledge of her being pregnant, but then he remembered his conversation with the landlady. 'Sadly, yes. She wrote to tell me she was in a Home for Unmarried mothers. She must have moved in while I was away being interviewed for a job, perhaps because her landlady threw her out. When I returned, I replied and arranged to pick her up, but she never appeared.'

'Would this be her?' A snapshot was placed on the table before him, the sight of her dead body chilling him to the core.

'Oh, my God!' he murmured, hoping he sounded suitably shocked and distressed. 'What's happened to her?'

'Good question. The nuns believe the poor girl took her own life. What do you think? Did she show any signs of being suicidal, depressed or anxious?'

'Not at all. Why would she be when I had agreed to do the decent thing and marry her,' he blithely announced.

'Did you inform your fiancée of that fact?'

None of these were easy questions to answer, but Alex did his best to keep as close to the truth as possible, and not to trip himself up on his own lies. As a result of a fairly sleepless night, tiredness overcame him when the questions kept being constantly repeated, till finally he demanded permission to call the family lawyer. He was greatly relieved when instead he was released, thankfully without charge.

'You are still under investigation,' the officer tartly informed him, as he returned Alex's belongings and conducted him out of the station. 'Once we have more evidence, we'll call you back in for another little chat.' Leaning closer, he added with a wry smile, 'Don't attempt to leave town. We'll certainly know about it if you do.'

Alex's head was spinning as he marched smartly away as fast as he could go without appearing guilty. Something was very wrong here. Why had the police chosen to question him about Davina? Had someone used his name in relation to that stupid girl? If that was the case, he needed to find out who that might be and deal with them forthwith.

* * *

In view of her suspicions about Alex, Cathie was feeling such concern for her mother that she went to meet her at the mill at the first opportunity, hoping to fill her in on what was happening, or at least some of it. As she waited for Rona to come out at the end of her shift, Cathie glanced over at the barges tethered in the canal alongside. They brought coal every day, and she had a memory of her father trundling a loaded wheelbarrow across a plank, tipping it down the chute to the mill cellar, then hurrying back for more. She saw no sign of that activity today, but there were a few men standing smoking at the street corner who looked as if they might be in need of work. Were things really improving with the advent of peace, she wondered, or going worse? It was hard to tell.

The mill door opened and a host of women came clattering out in their clogs, laughing and gossiping, Rona amongst them. Seeing her daughter waiting she came bustling over, her beautifully made-up face puckering with concern. How could anyone look so lovely after a long day's work? Cathie thought with a sigh, feeling very much a shabby mess by comparison. But at least her mother was looking more herself.

'I suppose you're here because you've heard Alex was

arrested?' Rona said, the moment she reached her. 'Did you have summat to do with that?'

'Of course not!' Cathie retorted, a curl of fear unfolding inside her. 'I know nothing about any such arrest. I'm here because there's stuff I thought you should know.'

'Well, happen I know it already, chuck.'

'What was he arrested for?'

'He told me it was all to do with black market stuff.' Rona laughed. 'Nay, what a shock! Only half the population is involved in that.'

'I don't think that's quite true, Mam, and it is illegal. Certainly the way I believe Alex is doing it, making money he has no right to make.'

'Nonsense, there are too many flipping rules. I remember a woman being fined for feeding a few crusts of bread to the birds, and another for selling home-made sweets she'd made using her own sugar ration. Anyroad, the police issued no charges and he's a free man.'

A chill rippled down the back of her neck as Cathie wondered if he'd told her mother the truth. The police might have arrested him for some other crime entirely, which in the circumstances would be no surprise at all. She found herself glancing about her at the canal, across the bridge, and back along the road that ran between Ancoats and the city centre. There had been moments recently when she'd imagined she heard footsteps echoing behind her, as if she was being followed. But whenever Cathie turned around to look, she could see no one. Remembering Steve's careful instructions, she always made sure that she kept the door locked, and Heather in her sight. Today the little one was safely back at the flat with Brenda.

'Come on, I'll walk part of the way home with you, although I won't come in for a cuppa as I've no wish to see him again.'

'I reckon he'd be happy enough to see you, chuck. He never stops talking about thee.'

They walked down Blossom Street, then, crossing over to the Rochdale Canal towpath, took a leisurely walk home to Castlefield. Avoiding the main streets seemed like a good idea, as Rona would always check her appearance in every shop window they passed. This way she could only admire the barges, narrowboats and ducks. Besides which, it was a more pleasant walk.

Cathie was worrying about how much she should reveal of the information they'd learned. Dare she speak about their suspicions of what he might have done to Davina, even though they had no proof? Rona still seemed to be very much on Alex's side, so there was a danger she might reveal to him everything Cathie shared with her. But at the same time Cathie felt a responsibility to protect her mother, and make sure she was safe.

'Mam, what I have to tell you must be kept just between the two of us, all right?'

Rona gave a bark of laughter. 'Don't tell me you're about to share a secret wi' me? Can't recall you ever doing that before.'

Cathie flushed, not for the first time wishing they enjoyed a better relationship. 'This is not about me it's about Alex. Nor does it concern his involvement in the black market. I have learned, from someone who must remain nameless, that he didn't buy that engagement ring at all. He stole it.'

Rona stopped in her tracks, jerking Cathie to a halt beside her. 'What are you accusing him of now?'

'It isn't me making this accusation. I just need you to know all this so that you'll take care. The last thing we want is for Alex to start stealing from you. You've little enough left after what you've been through.'

Rona seemed to sober up a little at this thought, falling silent as they started walking again along the towpath. 'When I were a lass I realised my mother never had learned to read or write. She spent her life looking after me brothers and sisters, and I were expected to help her, which is the reason why I became sick of all that baby stuff from a very young age. But when she died, I discovered that Mam had saved all my wages, probably because she never had any of her own, as she wanted me to have a good start in life. I would never have been able to afford the rent on that house in Duke Street, let alone buy all the furniture and rugs we had, without her help. Then we lost it all when that bomb dropped.'

'Oh, Mam, I didn't know any of this. I do wish you'd told me before.' The more she heard of her mother's past, the more Cathie came to understand her. 'But it makes it all the more important for you to protect what you do have left, as well as yourself. And that I must protect the money Tony left for his own lovely daughter, Heather.'

Cathie made the difficult decision not to mention their suspicions about Alex's possible involvement in Davina's death. That might be one step too far, and incite Rona to rise again to his defence. Besides, they still had no evidence.

* * *

The next time Steve called, he asked Cathie if this time they could go out for an evening together. Thrilled to be invited out on a proper date, she happily agreed, and he explained that he'd bought tickets for them to see Vivienne Leigh in *The Skin of our Teeth* at the Opera House on New Quay Street.

'Oh, what shall I wear?' she asked Brenda, who readily agreed to babysit. The pair of them spent hours going through their respective wardrobes before deciding on a pink linen short-sleeved dress with a pleated skirt and bows on the neckline. Brenda lent her a navy blue beaded evening jacket to go with it, and a small embroidered purse, which made Cathie feel very classy. Could her old friend once have had more money than she'd perhaps appreciated? Despite always seeming to be short of cash she certainly possessed a marvellous wardrobe.

'I shall cook every meal next week to repay my debt for your kindness,' she told her, and Brenda chortled with laughter. 'This is about friendship, for which no debts are accrued.'

But then at the last moment, on the evening in question, Brenda suddenly announced that she had to back down on her offer. 'Sorry, darling, but my brother-in-law is creating absolute mayhem again, at which he is an expert, and demanding that I go over to deal with yet another family crisis. I dare say it's all to do with this legal dispute over land, which I won't bore you with. Fortunately, our kind forewoman at the factory has agreed to my taking a few days off work, since we didn't take a holiday during Wakes Week. So I'm afraid I can't babysit for you this evening, after all.'

'Oh!' Disappointment bit deep in her at having to cancel the date with Steve, which Cathie had been so looking forward to. In addition, a hollow feeling opened up inside at the prospect of being left alone. Brenda would be away at the family farm, or more likely an estate by the sound of it, and Steve far too busy working on his course to call in as often as he used to, even though he was still in Manchester.

'You'll be stuck in without a babysitter for a little while, I'm afraid.'

With the door locked, Cathie thought, remembering what Steve had told her. 'I accepted that fact of life when I decided to keep my lovely little niece, and I have absolutely no regrets. Don't worry, I'll let Steve know that it's all off,' she replied sadly.

'No, no, you won't. Your mother's on her way over. She'll be here any minute.'

'What? Are you seriously telling me that Mam has agreed to babysit?'

A knock came to the door at that very moment. 'Here she is, right on time. Enjoy yourself tonight, darling. Now I must go.'

'Oh, I will, thank you,' she said, as she ran to let her mother in. 'Since you've gone to so much trouble to help, let's hope Steve doesn't let me down by cancelling, as he has done on a few occasions recently.'

'I'm sure he won't. Have faith in him.'

Pulling open the door, Cathie sighed at the sight of her mother, gloriously dressed in a scarlet, drop waist floral dress, looking very much as if she was off to a night at the Opera House herself. 'Hello, Mam, what a pleasure to see you. Thank you so much for your generous offer to babysit.'

'Don't mention it. You just need to remind me how to change a nappy,' Rona said, marching in.

Little Heather came running over and flung herself at Rona. 'Nanna,' she squealed in excitement, giving her grandmother a beaming smile and a big hug.

'By heck, what a little sweetheart she is,' said Rona, her eyes suddenly awash with soft tears. 'Here, love, look what I've made you.' To Cathie's amazement, she handed the child a pink cardigan that she'd obviously knitted herself. She'd also bought her a spinning top and, within moments, the pair of them were playing together on the rug, her mother suddenly looking entirely captivated by the infant. Cathie smiled to herself in stunned disbelief.

Seconds later another knock came to the door, which meant that for once Steve had turned up early. He looked so wonderfully smart and handsome in a navy suit, white shirt and pale blue tie that Cathie's heart contracted at sight of him. Her mother gave a knowing smile as she held the child in her arms. 'Off you go the pair of you, and enjoy yourselves. This little one will be fine with her nanna, won't you, chuck?'

And putting her chubby arms about Rona's neck, the toddler happily nodded.

* * *

It proved to be a most wonderful evening. Cathie had always admired the Opera House's white façade with its sandstone pillars, but the interior stunned her even more by the size of its auditorium, the beautiful curtained boxes and the aura of its enormous two balconies. They had seats right at the top but the view was amazing as they were seated in the centre.

'This is wonderful,' she said, giving him a quick kiss. 'It was so kind of you to invite me.'

He astonished her then by putting his arms about her and kissing her far more thoroughly than any of the tender pecks on the cheek they had previously exchanged. 'You must realise by now how I feel about you, Cathie. I'm so glad that you're happy at last, after all you've been through. You deserve some fun.'

She stared into his blue-grey eyes in wonder at these

words. For so long she'd held back from giving any indication of her own feelings for him, worrying she could still be in love with Alex. But that was no longer the case, as she was far too fearful of her erstwhile fiancé. She did feel a certain nervousness over committing herself by appearing to expect Steve to take on her sister's child, just in case he too walked away, leaving her feeling hurt and rejected all over again. Even so, she couldn't resist telling him how she felt.

'I care for you too,' she said, responding to his next kiss with happiness soaring through her, so that she guessed he must be able to hear the rapid pounding of her heart.

He grinned at her, his eyes twinkling with delight. 'That's good to hear, and there's something else I need to tell you, but the show's about to start so we'll talk about it later.'

Sitting cradled in his arms, she enjoyed every moment of the show, marvelling at actually seeing this beautiful actress, made famous by her role in *Gone with the Wind*, performing here in Manchester in a play directed by her husband, Laurence Olivier. She daren't ask Steve how much he'd had to pay for the tickets, hopefully not too much as they were pretty well up in the gods.

As they walked home together, still with his arm around her, she said, 'So what was it you wanted to tell me?'

Steve met her questioning gaze with a slight frown, and then glanced around at the empty street. Giving a dismissive little shrug, he said, 'It can wait. Let's not spoil the evening by going over more depressing stuff right now.'

'I'm aware that Alex was arrested and later released, if that's what's worrying you, as Mam told me.'

'That was a bit of a blow, I will admit.'

'How can we possibly prove him guilty without any evidence?'

Steve was silent for a moment then gathering her hands in his,gave them a gentle kiss. 'Don't worry, if it's at all possible we'll find a way. I'll visit that Mr Cartwright again, as soon as I have time. The fact is I'm going off on teaching practice for the next two weeks, so I'll be working round the clock and won't be able to see you as much as I'd like, so do take care, love. I don't want anything to happen to you, or for you to forget me,' he softly added.

'I won't ever do that, Steve.'

'I'm delighted to hear it,' he said, drawing her into his arms for a goodbye kiss.

Letting herself back into the flat, Cathie was astonished to find her mother lying in bed with little Heather by her side, both of them happily wrapped up together and fast asleep. How amazing was that?

Chapter Twenty-Seven

Cathie had never felt so happy in her life before. A part of her did worry that Steve might still be keeping some secret from her, if only because of the number of times he'd let her down without an explanation. But it was certainly true that however much she might have imagined herself to be in love with Alex, her feelings for Steve were a thousand times greater. Their friendship had turned into something far more wonderful and exciting. So if she wasn't yet entirely convinced that he felt the same way about her that was no doubt as a result of the problems Alex had caused her. And both of them had felt equally cautious at first, but now they were together and she felt delighted about that. As always she went to see her Aunt Evie, keen to give her some happy news for a change.

'I think I've been in love with Steve for ages but didn't dare admit it, even to myself, let alone to him,' she laughed. 'Wasn't that silly of me?'

'Oh, I know all about such feelings, love,' her aunt said with a smile. 'Donald and I were like that once, childhood sweethearts who became absolutely inseparable over time.'

'Had I realised sooner how I truly felt about Steve, everything could have been so different. I might have spared myself all the distress I suffered with Alex.'

'That wasn't your fault, love, it was the war. Donald too is a changed man. He sleepwalks and suffers from dreadful nightmares, sadly no longer the gentle, quiet man I married. As for my girls, I can't seem to get back to the closeness we once enjoyed either, as they aren't prepared to share their personal problems with me. It's as if I've become a stranger to them.'

'Oh, Aunty, that's so sad. You were always such a good mother to them, and to me too in a way. Mam and I have always been a bit like strangers, although things are improving between us, at least I hope so.' Cathie told her how they sometimes met up to walk in the park, or by the canal. 'She's even showing some interest in little Heather, at last,' Cathie said, smiling down at the toddler who was trotting round after her aunt's tabby cat, pausing to give it a stroke as the pussy rubbed against her plump little legs.

'I saw Rona the other day and she couldn't stop talking about the child. She sounded entirely smitten. I'm sure your problems will resolve themselves in time.'

'I do hope so. It just worries me sometimes that if push comes to shove, she'll side with Alex, and not me.'

'It's a funny old world right now, every family in a bit of a muddle.' Returning to her own problems, Aunt Evie went on to describe how being evacuated had disrupted her two daughters' sense of belonging, as well as more practical issues such as their education. 'And young Danny has taken up with a gang of lads I really don't approve of at all.' She let out a heavy sigh. 'It's going to be difficult to wean them all back home, in more ways than one.'

'I'm sure you'll succeed in the end, Aunty. Meanwhile, I would love to find a home of my own. I'm very happy sharing a flat with Brenda, but it can't last forever. Have you any idea where I might find one?'

'Not offhand, but I'll keep my eyes and ears open in case I learn anything. I'm so glad you're happy at last. Steve sounds like a lovely man.'

They chatted for some time about various possibilities, including some prefabs being built locally, before returning yet again to Evie's family problems. And as her beloved aunt already seemed to have enough to cope with, Cathie couldn't quite find the courage to reveal her worst suspicions. Alex might, in any case, be perfectly innocent and Davina's death an accident, so she really had no right to make any accusations against him without proof. Besides, it was surely time to put all of that behind her, and just be happy and delighted that she and Steve were a couple at last.

* * *

Back at the flat Cathie found a bunch of red roses lying on the doorstep and her heart leaped with happiness. 'Oh, thank you, Steve darling,' she cried, picking them up. Cathie struggled with the key to let herself in, with a shopping bag hanging on her arm and as always Heather propped astride her hip. The toddler had long since grown bored of being stuck in the pram, although Cathie always kept her firmly attached to a harness or she tended to run off giggling. Having taken it off and settled Heather down in her cot for a nap, she went to find a vase and fill it with water. As Cathie set about arranging the flowers she found a small envelope attached. Smiling to herself, she pulled out the card.

'*Here is a small gift just to prove how much I miss you. Love, Alex.*'

Her heart almost stopped beating. She'd assumed these were from Steve. What on earth was Alex thinking of to be sending her flowers? Their relationship was over, had been for some weeks now. Cathie shivered as she glanced about her, then ran to the front door to make sure that she'd remembered to lock it after her.

Goodness, no, she hadn't, probably because she'd had her arms full of little Heather, as well as the flowers and shopping bag. It was as she turned around to go back to the kitchen that she heard the sound of crying coming from the bedroom across the hall. Running to the door, she was shocked to see he was actually there, leaning over the cot stroking the toddler's fluffy hair. 'Is she having more bad dreams, poor lamb?' he asked, beaming at her.

Cathie felt shock explode within her. 'Alex!'

He laughed. 'Surprise, surprise. You could at least say hello. Never mind, lovely to see you too, sweetie. '

'What on earth are you doing here? You and I split up some time ago, so you really have no right to just walk in uninvited.'

His smile now was patient and loving. 'Oh, dear, have I done the wrong thing? The door was open and I thought you'd be pleased to see me, since I'd sent you that lovely bouquet. You do like roses, don't you?'

'Of course, but not from you, not any longer.'

He looked somewhat crestfallen by this remark, then, giving a little sigh, said, 'I do understand your reluctance to welcome me, but I just popped in to apologise for what I did to this little one. And to let you know that it was your mother who insisted I write to the orphanage. It wasn't my idea at all.'

Could that be true? Rona freely admitted that she'd never been particularly maternal, but had given no indication she would ever do such a thing. Quite the opposite, in fact. And now she'd thankfully fallen under little Heather's spell and adored her almost as much as Cathie did. 'I don't believe you. Please leave.'

By this time Heather was screaming at the top of her lungs and Cathie felt desperate to run and gather the child in her arms, but fear prevented her from taking one step into the bedroom while Alex occupied it.

'I needed you to know that I'm quite happy for you to keep this little mite. I love you, sweetie, and I'm sure that you still love me.'

As he again stroked the toddler's head and Heather

shrieked, Cathie did at last take a step into the room. 'Please stop doing that. She's forgotten who you are and gets very upset by strangers, probably as a result of being taken away from me. I'd like you to leave *now*!'

He let out a heavy sigh, then came over to her and stroked her hair instead, his eyes glittering with desire. 'If you insist. I know we've experienced some problems in the past, sweetie, but can we perhaps talk about the future?'

'Not here. Not now!'

'Then perhaps at the Pack Horse, or the Market café some time, whichever you prefer.'

He appeared to be making every effort to win her back with his charm, trying to convince her it was all about love, and not money. But how could she ever trust him again? 'I'll think about it,' Cathie said, her heart beating like a drum as her nerves skittered.

'Good. Then we'll speak later.' And, placing a tender kiss on her cheek, he gave her the kind of smile that would once have melted her heart before walking out. Within seconds of him leaving, Cathie ran to the door, slammed it shut and locked it, before racing back to pick up little Heather to give her a loving cuddle.

The very next day, she found yet another letter lying on the mat, delivered by hand as it bore no stamp. This too was from Alex, once more declaring his love for her. '*I thought we could meet this evening at the Pack Horse. See you there at seven.*'

Never! Cathie thought, screwing the letter up and tossing it into the grate before she lit a fire.

The flat felt so empty and lonely without Brenda to talk to, and with little hope of Steve finding the time to call in any time soon. But she certainly had no intention of meeting up with Alex ever again. Even walking to work each morning with little Heather gave her a deep sense of unease in the pit of her stomach. She found herself constantly glancing back over her shoulder, quite certain she was being followed. Sometimes she would catch a glimpse of what might be the heel of his boot or flick of his raincoat vanishing up an alley, as if trying to hide from her. What had got into him? If it was indeed Alex who was following her, then he was behaving most oddly, which was certainly not the result of some supposed trauma suffered during the war. Not according to Steve, anyway, as Alex's war might well have been boring but generally safe.

She found more flowers waiting on the doorstep on her return home, and yet more cards and letters lying on the mat over the days following, even the odd box of chocolates, all of which she threw in the dustbin. Far from feeling flattered by his attention, Cathie felt as if she was being mentally assaulted.

And she never forgot to lock the door ever again.

* * *

It was with great relief that she welcomed Brenda back home a few days later. Her friend listened with great sympathy to the tale she had to tell. 'Wish I'd been here, I'd have socked him one for daring to invade my flat,' she spat. 'Thank goodness you weren't foolish enough to agree to meet him.'

'I would never do that, although I could have kicked myself for being so stupid as not to make sure I'd locked the darned door. Won't ever make that mistake again.'

They soon settled back into their normal routine, but it troubled Cathie that she still had the feeling she was being watched, and the letters, cards, chocolates or flowers continued to arrive almost daily. Brenda stuffed them all in a rusty old bucket by the front door.

'At least then he can see that you want nothing to do with him.'

It was an even greater joy when Steve's teaching practice was finally over, and the pair of them were able to sit enjoying a supper of corned beef hash together by the fire. Little Heather was fast asleep in her cot, and Brenda out with her new boyfriend, a young ex-serviceman she'd met at a dance.

Cathie loved listening to Steve's amusing stories of how the young children in his class had behaved. 'They are so lively and curious, interested in everything and constantly asking questions. One young boy asked: "How can the moon be made of green cheese if a man lives there?"'

Cathie burst out laughing. 'What fun. It sounds as if you've enjoyed yourself.'

'Oh, I have, Cathie. It was hard work planning all the

lessons and doing all the preparation and definitely a bit nerve-wracking when my tutor came in to check on my progress. But I loved every minute of it, as I'm very fond of kids. I'm quite sure I made the right decision to take up this teacher training. How about you? Has anything interesting happened while I've been away?'

Setting aside her empty plate, Cathie quickly related her own, far less amusing story. 'Thankfully, I haven't heard from Alex for a few days now. Nor has he sent anything recently, so hopefully he's finally got the message. Brenda leaving all those supposed gifts stuffed in that bucket might well have done the trick.'

He was frowning, looking somewhat distressed. 'We must do something about this. Now that my teaching practice is over I'll have a bit more time to pay this Mr Cartwright another visit.'

* * *

As promised, Steve went once more to see Barbara Cartwright's father, but was refused admittance by the housekeeper.

'Didn't he make it clear the first time that he has no wish to discuss his daughter's problems. Please do not call again,' she tartly informed him.

Steve put his foot in the door to prevent her from closing it. 'I accept that Mr Cartwright may be angry or disappointed in his daughter, but the reason I need to speak to her is because she knew our friend Davina, who sadly vanished from the Home. In fact Barbara may well be the last person to see her alive.'

The housekeeper appeared shocked by this, even more so when she heard the full story, carefully related with no names attached. Glancing over her shoulder to make sure she would not be overheard, she hastily whispered the sister's address to him. 'That's probably where Barbara is living, but please don't ever let Mr Cartwright know that you got this information from me.'

'I won't. Thank you so much.'

It proved to be an address in Ancoats, quite close to Castlefield, and Steve made it his next stop. What he learned from Barbara shook him rigid. First, that Davina had been evicted by her landlady and had written day after day to Alex and even his father while being kept in solitary by the nuns.

'When finally he responded, it was then that we planned our escape. It turned out to be remarkably easy. But the minute we'd said our farewells and Davina dashed off towards the canal, I saw this piece of card blowing away in the wind. Realising it was the bit I'd torn off the packet of Persil washing powder, on which I'd written my sister's address, I ran to grab it. By the time I managed to catch the darned thing and chase after her, she was already wrapped in the arms of her boyfriend, just by the bridge. I held back, hiding in the bushes, waiting for an appropriate moment to reveal myself, but then…'

Here she paused, sucking in her breath, her eyes

clouding over with a sickening horror before going on to describe how he had tossed the poor girl into the canal. 'Just as if she were a rag doll he no longer wanted to play with.'

Steve uttered a silent curse under his breath.

'I must have gasped or cried out because he spun around, his furious gaze scouring the towpath and banking. I'm afraid I ran away at that point, hell for leather. A cowardly thing to do, I know, but I was afraid that if I hung around, I might be next.'

'Did you tell the police what you saw?'

The girl gave a sad shake of her head. 'Sorry, no. I didn't have the courage to do that either.'

'Wouldn't that have been the right thing to do?'

'Barbara has enough problems of her own to deal with right now,' said her sister. 'Not least the loss of her child, as well as the man she loved.'

'She has my sympathy on that score. The war has done enormous damage to many, but this blighter can't be allowed to create more mayhem. He needs to be arrested. Would you come with me now to tell the police what you witnessed?'

'Ooh, I don't know. I'd need to think about that,' Barbara said in tremulous tones.

'Please do, but don't take too long over it. He's proving to be a dangerous man. If he remains free he could do the same thing to another woman, or to my friend.' Turning to her sister, he added, 'He could even attack Barbara herself if he spotted her as she ran away, or ever finds out who she is. I found her easily enough, so why couldn't he?'

This gave the two sisters pause for thought as they stared at each other in dawning dismay. 'But even if she did tell, he might well take his revenge out on her,' her sister responded, sounding deeply anxious. 'So talking to the police could be very risky.'

Since Ryman had chosen to take his revenge upon him too, Steve found it difficult to dispute this argument. 'Please think about, that's all I ask.'

Promising they would give him an answer soon, Steve found himself ushered out of the house and the door slammed shut. Drawing in a heavy sigh of despair, he walked away. He could but hope that the girl would come round in the end. Then if the police took her witness statement seriously, Ryman could be dealt with, and Cathie would be safe at last. In the meantime, until he was certain that this friend of Davina's was prepared to act as witness, he didn't feel it would be wise for him to reveal to Cathie the full horror of what Alex had done. Fortunately, she was already taking much safer precautions against him, so there was no rush.

Chapter Twenty-Eight

The weeks passed by in a blur of happiness, and despite Steve being busy on his teaching course he always managed to find time to call in at the flat for a chat or cup of tea at least two or three evenings each week. Sometimes he would take Cathie to the Hippodrome, the Palace, or to the flicks. On a Saturday afternoon, they would enjoy a walk in Peel Park or take a bus across to Philip's Park through which the River Medlock ran. Sitting holding hands on a sunny autumn day while little Heather played was a joy to her heart. They never went anywhere near the canal and carefully avoided any conversation on Davina's fate, the subject of Alex being very firmly blocked out. Their friendship had blossomed into something really rather wonderful.

Fortunately, there was never any problem now in finding a babysitter, as Rona was always happy to oblige. Alex still rented a room at her mother's house, but she assured Cathie that their relationship was strictly businesslike.

One evening, Steve arranged to meet Cathie at the Gaumont cinema on Oxford Road to see *It's a Wonderful*

Life. Christmas was approaching and stamping her feet in freezing temperatures she felt a little concerned that he was yet again late, as so often seemed to be the case. As she waited for him to arrive, Cathie found herself reliving the grief she'd felt at hearing of the death of her beloved sister after she'd visited this same cinema. So much had changed since that day early in 1945 when the bus bringing Sally home had crashed, and Cathie's loss felt as raw as ever. Sal would ever be in her heart, and hopefully in little Heather's too one day, when she learned more about her real mum. Right now, Cathie was the only mummy the child knew and loved, which felt like some kind of consolation for them both.

Realising the rest of the queue had entered the cinema and she was left standing alone, she glanced at her watch and then down the street. Where was Steve? The film would be starting soon, and it was far too cold to stand about too long outside. Deciding to go in and take their usual seats near the back where he'd be sure to find her, Cathie paid for a ticket and sat listening to the cinema organ playing 'Every Time We Say Goodbye' by Cole Porter. It brought back the anguish she used to feel whenever Alex had returned to war following a short leave, as if she really would die a little. But then he'd returned a changed man and, unknown to her, had engaged in an affair. How foolish she'd been to agree to marry him so soon after he'd returned home before they'd even got to know each other again.

The film had been running for at least half an hour when

finally she heard a shuffle of feet and Steve sank with a sigh on to the seat beside her. 'Sorry I'm so late, love,' he said, taking her hand and giving it a tender kiss. 'I'll explain later.'

Thoroughly engrossed in the heart-warming story where James Stewart suffers all manner of traumas but is saved by a guardian angel, Cathie just wished her lovely sister had been so fortunate. But then this was a magical Christmas yarn, not real life.

As they walked to the tram stop, arm in arm, Steve repeated his apology, begging her forgiveness.

'I assumed you must be working hard,' Cathie said, not wishing to make a fuss.

'It's true, I have been working hard, but there's something I need to tell you.'

Smiling up him, heart thumping, she asked, 'Oh, and what might that be?' Was he about to tell her that he loved her, just as she knew in her heart that she loved him? A tram pulled up and they got on-board, thankful to be out of the cold. Cuddled up close on a wooden seat, nothing more was said as there were far too many people around to engage in a private conversation.

They disembarked at the stop just off Deansgate near to Liverpool Road, but it was not until they were approaching the flat that, taking a breath, he said, 'The reason I'm sometimes late, or find myself obliged to call off our evening out, is because of a family problem.'

'We all seem to be suffering from those,' Cathie said

with a sigh, thinking that perhaps his mother had been fussing over him too much, as she tended to do at times.

'The fact is I recently discovered that Maggie, my late wife, who was killed in a bombing raid, had given birth to a child without telling me.'

Cathie stopped in her tracks to stare at him, utterly stunned. This was the last thing she'd expected to hear. 'Goodness, why would she do that?' Then remembering how reluctant she too had been to reveal little Heather's existence to Alex, gently asked, 'Was there a problem she didn't wish to trouble you with, on top of all that you were already suffering from in the war?'

'Possibly.' Rubbing his jaw, he gave a resigned sigh. 'My mother-in-law, who was looking after the boy, eventually told me the tale and informed me that he wasn't mine. He was the result of a fling my wife had with a sailor.'

'Oh, Steve! No wonder you gave me that little lecture on the temptation of affairs during war-time.'

He gave a pragmatic shrug. 'I should have admitted that I was speaking from personal experience, then you might have taken onboard what I had to say. I did love Maggie, and grieved for her, but sadly it seems our marriage was probably over even before I lost her. I'm sorry I failed to tell you the whole story, Cathie, but I didn't feel able to talk about it just then. Now I've discovered that the child's actual father is married and has no wish to claim his son. My mother-in-law is prepared to keep the boy rather than see him end up in an orphanage.'

'I agree with her there. That's exactly how I feel about little Heather.'

'She is, however, getting on a bit so I've suggested that I could perhaps share the responsibility of bringing him up. James, or Jamie as he likes to be called, is Maggie's child, after all.'

Cathie met his troubled gaze with amazement then put her arms about him and hugged him tight. 'How kind and loving you are.'

'Thank you. I think of him now as my stepson.'

'That's very generous of you. Most husbands would not view the child in those terms.'

He sighed. 'Well, there was a war on. I would have forgiven her, had she lived. Whether or not our marriage might have survived I'll never know, but I can at least take care of her child.'

'I'm glad for the little boy's sake that you're prepared to do that. Sadly, orphanages are now packed with children who should be living with a loving family, even if it isn't their own. It will do them no good at all to be brought up in an institution.'

'Having been adopted myself, Cathie, I know that to be true.'

'Really? I didn't know that either.' Why had he kept all of these secrets from her?

'I was fortunate to be picked out of a crowd of homeless kids when I was about seven years old. It was quite brave of the Allenbys to take me on, as I was a bit of a mischief-maker and rabble-rouser.'

'Oh, I do remember that,' she said, and he laughed.

'But they have proved to be kind and loving parents, and saved my life from eternal misery. This young lad is three years old, so I feel the need to be as generous and loving with him as my adopted parents were with me.'

Moved by his story, Cathie felt emotion block her throat. 'Oh, Steve, that's wonderful. But why didn't you tell me any of this before?'

'I thought you had enough problems of your own to deal with, and even if they aren't entirely resolved yet, at least Alex is no longer creating havoc in your life.'

It was only after he'd gone that the thought popped into Cathie's head that this decision of his might affect her too, and her sense of caution and insecurity flared. Could the real reason Steve hadn't mentioned the boy earlier possibly be because he wanted her to fall in love with him first? Alex's desire for her had been motivated by the stash of money left for little Heather by her own father. What if Steve's motivation for his initial caution, and for now finally confessing the reason, was because this child was in desperate need of a mother? Depression washed over her at the thought.

Cathie had secretly hoped that Steve was about to tell her he loved her, yet so far he had done no such thing. Dare she allow herself to fall yet again into the trap of believing a man's feelings for her were genuine? At first she'd been too trusting, now she didn't feel able to trust anyone.

* * *

Cathie had never expressed any desire to go again to the Ritz ballroom, or back to Joe Taylor's Dance Hall at Belle Vue where Alex had proposed to her, so it came as something of a surprise when Steve suggested they go to the Palais de Danse on Rochdale Road.

'I don't think I want to go,' she told Brenda.

'Whyever not? With Christmas almost upon us, it would be a lovely evening out.'

'I'm no longer interested in going dancing.' A part of her thought it might have been the magic of the dance that had led to her falling for Alex in the first place. If so, then it was not a mistake she wished to repeat.

'It's not as if he's taking you to the Ritz.'

'But why didn't Steve tell me the truth about this child, and his own adoption?'

'I thought he'd explained all of that, and you know full well that some things are hard to talk about right now. But what does it matter, when you're happy together? As for that little boy, if Steve proves willing to accept little Heather, why would you not accept Jamie?'

'My worries are not about the child, but whether I can ever trust a man again.'

'Steve is not Alex, and it's time, darling, to put the past behind you and be happy.'

'Oh, you talk such sense, Bren. What would I do without you?' Smiling, Cathie hugged her friend.

'I'll make sure I keep that night free so that I can babysit for you.'

'There's no need to sacrifice your own night out with this new sweetheart of yours,' she said with a grin. 'Mam will be happy to do her bit. She's come to parenting rather late in life, but really loves little Heather. Now I'm going to ask the same old question, what on earth should I wear? Since I can't think of anything I own being quite classy enough, maybe a trip to Campfield market to buy some suitable fabric is called for.'

* * *

When Rona arrived on the night of the Christmas dance, she stared at her daughter in amazement. 'By heck, thee looks beautiful, lass.' A compliment Cathie had never heard before in her entire life. But it was rather a lovely long evening dress in pale gold silk with a scooped neck, draped sleeves and rhinestones stitched into the bodice. Cathie felt rather flattered by her mother's approval, having made the dress herself. Rona even offered to help pin up her hair in a stylish fashion, and put rouge and lipstick on for her.

'Now you look a real bobby-dazzler,' Rona said with a satisfied smile. Then just as Cathie was kissing little Heather goodnight, she whispered, 'Did you hear that the police called by to question Alex again?'

Startled, Cathie met her mother's bland gaze in shock. 'Have they arrested him?'

Giving a little frown, Rona shook her head. 'He wasn't in at the time, so they said they'd call again. Anyroad, why would they?'

Cathie really had no wish to even think about Alex tonight, let alone discuss her suspicions with Rona, so without another word she walked away.

* * *

The benefits of being a grandmother, as opposed to a mother, Rona thought, as she cuddled little Heather on her lap, is that you can walk away when you feel tired and leave the responsibility to someone else. There'd never been any opportunity for a moment's rest when she'd been young, or anyone with whom to share the job of child-rearing. Her own parents had been long dead, her husband brutalised by the First World War, and she the only breadwinner with two daughters to bring up pretty much alone. It had been heart-breaking and yet a relief in a way, when eventually he'd put himself on a ship and gone off. At least she'd been free then of all the beatings she'd been forced to endure, even if her heart still ached for the love they'd once enjoyed.

But maybe as a result of her loss she hadn't been the best mother in the world. Far too exhausted and impatient, run ragged with all the work and responsibility of raising a family alone. Going out and enjoying herself had felt like a form of escape, something she deserved, but maybe that hadn't gone down too well with her two daughters.

How she admired Cathie for her strength and determination. Rona now deeply regretted being so unhelpful, largely due to the grief and anger she felt over the death of Sally. No one could ever understand how the loss of a beloved daughter affected one. It changes your entire view of life. Nothing seems important any more. You just don't care about anything or anyone else. The disappearance of someone who fully occupied your thoughts and love leaves a big black pit into which you keep falling.

How fortunate she was now, though, to have this little one to remind her of Sally. She'd grow into a perfect replica of her mum. 'Nanna loves you, chuck,' she told the toddler, as she tucked her into her cot. Giving her a kiss, Rona sang a lullaby she used to sing to her daughters. '*Hush, little baby, don't say a word, Momma's gonna buy you a mocking bird*.'

It was then that she heard a hammering on the door. 'Now who can that be?'

* * *

From the moment it began, Cathie was convinced this would be a magical evening. The dance hall wasn't as crowded as it used to be during the war, and with not a single uniform in sight. But Steve looked so handsome in a navy pinstriped suit that she didn't mind at all if he wasn't up to dancing anything too lively because of his artificial leg. He certainly was not able to join in the jiving some folk were doing, but then neither was she. But the band played with such style and fun, Cathie was content to sit and listen, and he did treat her to a dish of ice cream.

It felt wonderful just to be held close in his arms as they smooched to the music 'Dancing in the Dark' with the lights suitably dimmed, apart from one overhead lamp that moved about, making the men's white shirts and the girls' dresses glow. A singer came strolling elegantly across the stage, her wonderful voice adding to the glory of the music. Then balloons began to fall from the ceiling, and the next instant everyone was laughing as they tried to catch one.

It was as they were happily shuffling along to 'Don't Sit Under the Apple Tree' that Cathie mentioned what her mother had told her about the police calling to speak to Alex.

'Really? Let's hope they question him soon. Actually, I think there's something you need to know, love,' he said.

'Not another secret?'

'I've put off revealing this information so as not to unduly upset you.'

'I'm stronger than you might imagine, Steve. I would have thought you realised that by now.'

Looking a little guilty, he abandoned the dance and led her back to their table where he explained as briefly and kindly as possible what Barbara had witnessed that night. As shock resonated on her lovely face, he kissed her gently by way of comfort. 'I offered to accompany her to the police station but Barbara said she needed to consider the matter carefully as it would demand considerable courage. If the police are again about to question Ryman, then it may be because she's finally spoken out and they now have the necessary evidence. They will need to check his version of the story, and his alibi. Hopefully, it will result in an arrest.'

She gazed up at him, transfixed with horror. 'Oh, I do hope so. The thought of what he did to Davina is unbearable.'

As always when Alex's name came up it was quickly dispatched. 'Right, that's enough about that stupid blighter. Now I think we deserve a glass of wine, don't you? It's almost Christmas, after all. Back in a moment.'

Cathie smiled as he walked away, thinking how strong and fit he looked now, not at all the thin weedy man he'd been when first he came back from the war. And he was so much happier, as was she. How lucky they were to have found each other. Closing her eyes, she conjured up an image of Steve holding her in his arms as he proposed to her.

'You are no longer alone, my love,' a voice whispered in her ear. 'I'm here for you, at last.' Cathie eyes flew open in startled disbelief.

Chapter Twenty-Nine

'Alex!' Cathie could feel shock reverberating through her as she met the coldness of his expression. His mouth was twisted into a caustic smirk of triumph, while his narrowed eyes glinted with lust.

'You look lovely,' he said and, taking her arm, he began to lead her towards the door. His grip was unyielding, but, gathering her strength, Cathie made a valiant attempt to break his hold. Struggling to shake her arm free, she slapped and pushed him, even made an attempt to stamp on his foot, but he soon put a stop to that. 'I've already collected the little brat from Rona, so if you wish to ever see her again I would advise that you don't make any more fuss.'

A trembling weakness now replaced that brief flash of defiance. 'Where is she? What have you done with little Heather?' Cathie tried to turn and look behind her, desperate for a glimpse of Steve, but, grasping her by the shoulders, Alex shoved her around and propelled her out the door. Once outside, his grip on her tightened even further as he marched her rapidly along a path.

'Don't worry, the child is perfectly safe. For now. And will remain so if you do as you're told.'

'I hope to God she is. If you hurt her, I'll *kill* you!' she hissed, which for some reason made him chuckle.

'I'd like to see you try.'

'And where's Mam?'

'Why would you care? You and Rona never did get on very well.'

'We've had our problems but we get along fine these days. Is she with Heather?'

'Stop fretting about those two and start thinking of us. You and I need to talk. We belong together, and since *you* wouldn't come to me, *I* have come to you.'

Cathie suddenly realised that they were heading for the canal and fear escalated within her. 'Stop this at once,' she yelled, again frantically attempting to free herself from his punishing grip. 'I'm fully aware of what you did to Davina, and that you should be charged with her murder.'

He roared with laughter, as if she'd made some sort of joke. 'That's what the police seem to think.' And, pulling her into his arms so that his mouth was close enough for her to smell the whisky he'd been drinking, he sneered at her. 'Sadly for them, they can't quite find sufficient evidence to make such a charge stick, or even arrest me. Now stop fussing, girl.'

'They do indeed have evidence,' Cathie protested. 'A friend of Davina's was witness to what you did, so don't for a moment think you'll get away with it.'

'Who is she?' he barked.

'None of your business, but she's genuine.' Not for a moment would she reveal how Steve had found Barbara, let alone give the girl's name, which could be dangerous. Striving to remain calm and keep her wits about her, she said, 'I happen to know a great deal more than you might think. Such as your theft of that ring.'

He jerked, releasing his hold upon her. 'What the hell are you talking about?'

Relieved to be free of him, Cathie flicked back her hair, which had come unpinned in the tussle, and smoothed down her beautiful new dress. 'You know full well. You didn't *buy* that engagement ring; you *stole* it from a shop close to Oldham Street. I found out quite by chance and sadly the person concerned was not prepared to bring charges because he feared involving me. But he certainly will once I have told him what you are doing to me now, and whatever you've done to poor little Heather. The police too will be very interested as they are already looking to question you again. They might also ask about your black market activities.'

'Huh, me and the rest of the nation,' he laughed.

'Involving yourself in the black market is still illegal and punishable with time in jail.'

'You've no proof of that either. In any case, how would you know what I've been up to?'

'Because I'm no fool, Alex, even if you take me for one. I saw all those unknown coupons when little Heather was playing with your gas mask pack that time. And I'm quite convinced that the silver cigarette lighters you gave to Mam and Davina were stolen too. Where would you get the money to buy them otherwise? You never did find yourself a proper job, so far as I'm aware. You're far too lazy and self-obsessed to work for anyone other than yourself. I doubt you've ever done an honest day's work in your life. So if the police wish to question me, there's a great deal I can tell them.'

He slapped her face, so hard that she fell to the ground, sprawled on the towpath. 'You'll say nothing.'

'I certainly will!' Cathie shouted, despite the ringing in her head from the blow. 'You can't be allowed to get away with this. *Tell me what you've done with my lovely little niece*.'

'None of your bloody business! You do as I say because you belong to me.'

Staggering back on her feet to face him with every ounce of courage she possessed, Cathie yelled at him. 'No, I don't! I hate you, Alex Ryman. Nothing would ever make me wish to return to you. *Not ever!*'

'Then I can at least enjoy your body,' he said, and, pushing her up against the wall, his hand reached down to tug up the long skirt of her evening gown. 'I've waited a long time for this,' he said, as his hands roamed over her. Then he was devouring her with a kiss, forcing his tongue into her mouth. As she fought to free herself, Cathie felt as if she was about to throw up. Within seconds, his fingers were fumbling with her underwear, as he'd used to do in the past. She could remember not particularly enjoying his lovemaking once she'd learned of his betrayal and he'd moved into her home, but this was even worse. Bringing up her knee, she drove it into the most tender part of him. Letting out a yell, he swept her up in his arms and threw her into the canal.

Cathie found herself sinking fast into the muddy water, as if she was falling down into a giant basin rather like the one at Potato Wharf. Weeds tangled about her legs, cans of rubbish and dead rodents battered against her helpless body. She could taste oil and filth, and, knowing she couldn't swim, her head buzzed with terror. Was this how poor Davina had died? It was then that all Brenda's careful lessons from their weekly attendance at the Corporation Baths on New Quay Street finally kicked in, and it came to her that she could indeed swim.

Forcing her legs and arms into action she began to move slowly upwards. Her lungs felt as if they were bursting as she manoeuvred her way through the blackness in what she hoped was the right direction towards the towpath. The minute her hands touched the earth of the bank she lifted her head gently out of the water to snatch some air. A dark silhouette hovered above, just a few feet away. Realising Alex was looking for her, Cathie grabbed hold of a clump of weeds to keep herself low in the water, out of his sight.

'Where are you, sweetie?' he called. 'Oh dear, are you in trouble?'

She edged closer, moving slowly so that she made no ripples in the water. Once she was beneath him, Cathie shot up a hand and grabbed his ankle. Just then she heard a whistle. Could it be the police? But it was too late as she'd already yanked at his leg, watching with pleasure as he fell, feet first, into the canal, yelling with fury.

* * *

'You were so very brave,' Steve said, pulling her into his arms as he wrapped a blanket around her soaking body. 'And don't worry, Heather is perfectly safe. Rona took great care of the little one. He locked them both in his shed on the allotment, tying your mother up with garden twine. Fortunately, she managed to break herself free and hammered on the window until someone heard and let them out, then rang the local police station. The police tell me that the pair of them are back at the flat, and just fine. Thank God you are too. I love you so much. What would I do without you? Please say you'll marry me.'

Happiness soared through her at these words. 'Oh, yes, I will. I love you too, Steve. But how did you find me?'

'I wish I could have got here sooner, but I was queuing for drinks and unaware of what had happened. By the time I returned, I was a little concerned when I realised you'd disappeared, hoping at first that you'd just gone to the powder room. But a few questions among folk who saw you leaving with Ryman sent me into a complete state of panic. Remembering what had happened to Davina, I feared he might do the same to you. Fortunately, there were already police on the premises, as there generally is on busy nights like this, so I quickly called them into action. Amazingly, you seem to have coped pretty well on your own. Well done, love.'

Steve kissed her, and her heart sang. Then, holding her close in his arms, they watched in silence as the police clicked handcuffs on to Alex's wrists and led him away, leaving a trail of mud in his wake.

'What will happen to him now?'

'He'll be charged with assaulting you and, more importantly, with Davina's murder as Barbara has revealed to them what she saw. He'll no doubt be found guilty and hanged.'

Cathie shivered, feeling little satisfaction in this, yet relieved at last to be rid of him, and all the problems Alex Ryman had brought into her life.

Later, after a joyful reunion with little Heather and Rona, they sat by the fire in the flat. The police had driven Rona home, and the toddler was now fast asleep in her cot, no doubt exhausted by the night's trauma, but very content to be safely back home with her mummy.

All seemed to be well with her world at last, Cathie thought, with relief and joy in her heart.

Chapter Thirty

Snow was falling as her wedding day dawned, but so far as Cathie was concerned that only added to the glory of this special occasion. This was the day she would marry the man she truly loved, the man she'd probably loved all her life but hadn't realised that fact until almost too late. Had she done so, she would have spared herself a great deal of anguish and trauma. But every cloud has a silver lining, as the saying goes, and even the snow felt magical.

She and Steve had enjoyed a most wonderful Christmas together, the best ever with little Heather and his stepson Jamie, and Brenda too. Cathie had hung a stocking at the bottom of Heather's cot, which Father Christmas had filled with fruit and sweets, coloured pencils, a magic painting book, *Little Grey Rabbit's Christmas* by Alison Uttley, and a pair of mittens knitted by Rona. The twenty-three-month sold had opened her gifts with great excitement the minute she woke at six in the morning.

A tall Christmas tree stood rather grandly in the front parlour adorned with all the much-loved decorations that she and Sal had once made. As always, Cathie had spent hours making paper chains, not only with Heather's help, but Jamie's too. He was a very lively little boy with a cheerful smile and brown spiky hair, and Cathie knew she would soon love him as her own.

Everyone had arrived to join in the fun at Rona's house in good time for a Christmas dinner of goose with all the trimmings, this time without any risk of her mother giving it away. Christmas crackers were pulled and jokes read. They'd listened to carols being sung by the King's College choir on the wireless, and played lots of games, including Snap, Ludo and Monopoly. It was a wonderful day filled with fun and laughter, love and friendship and the magic of Christmas. Neither Cathie nor Steve had much money to spend on the celebrations, but that wasn't important. All that mattered was they were together as a family.

On Christmas Eve, they'd all gone to church, not only to celebrate the start of Christmas, but also to pray for Sally, for Jamie's mummy, Brenda's late husband, Davina, and all other friends, loved ones, and brave young men lost in the war. They would never be forgotten.

And now it was her wedding day.

For this most special occasion, Cathie had made herself a new gown, unable to bear the thought of wearing the one she'd stitched for the wedding with Alex. Thank goodness she'd insisted on postponing that day, despite Alex's efforts to bring it forward.

Now, as she stood at Steve's side happily answering 'I will' to the questions asked by the vicar, happiness engulfed her. Little Heather stood patiently holding her train, no doubt the youngest bridesmaid ever. Jamie was acting as page boy, and Brenda taking the roll of matron-of-honour. It was the most perfect day of her life. Smiling into Steve's blue-grey eyes shimmering with happiness, Cathie knew that he loved her as much as she loved him. They would soon be moving into a house he'd found for them to rent and begin to build a new life together. How wonderful was that?

'Home is most definitely where the heart is,' he told her, giving her a kiss as the vicar pronounced them man and wife.